BLACK MARIAH

Book design by HeatherLeeShaw.businesscatalyst.com

For information about reviews or forthcoming books, contact Maple City Books at bobmartel@hotmail.com

Printed in the United States of America.

BLACK MARIAH

BOB MARTEL

MAPLE CITY BOOKS

This book is about me. I started it twenty-plus years ago when two friends of mine were injured in a car bombing late of a Thursday morning on the edge of the Free Democratic Republic of Berkeley, California.

In times of secrecy it is uncomfortable to tell a story about the most vulnerable ones of us, so I offer myself as the subject, not for fame or exposure—neither of which is on my list of needs—but because the choice was the only one I could make. The story wants to be told.

The Black Mariah is my name for this book. I picked the name one day as I was walking down the hallway through the Humboldt County Jail. I was released to go wherever one goes at 5:30 a.m. on a rainy winter's day. The judge would later apologize in between fits of laughter. We had become friends, but that wasn't why she laughed. I had been arrested in the early morning by two deputy sheriffs as a "practical joke" following a "bloody battle" over which was more corrupt, the Eureka Police Department or the Eureka County Sheriff's office. The Sheriff won on the strength of my reporting, and as he and I passed in the hallway that morning he explained to me how short my life was going to be if I did not find a good hiding place. That was the first time I left Humboldt County for the safety of Mexico. When the law man was safely behind State prison bars, I wandered back for more.

This book has to be called The Black Mariah. If you play the poker game enough, you get accustomed to seeing the queen of spades staring into your disbelieving eyes, and then you get it. You may not like it, either as a card game or the name for a book, when you know the rules that may change.

My name is Robert Devine. I will not address you again after this bit of an intro. I prefer my disguises and the writer is my best one.

THE DARK FOREST

OCTOBER 23, 1989

From Highway 101—the Redwood Highway—the problem is invisible. But lurking behind the panorama of green is a disturbing secret: the green is just a narrow corridor of trees.

The human eye sees and the brain interprets. The uninformed brain accepts this sea of color to mean lush forests, but too often, all that is left of the forest *is* this corridor. To the uninformed passerby the view will be as good as a real forest would have been. But where natural ecology allows, destroyed forests are replaced by industrialized fiber farms, and the chaotic burgeoning of the under-story beyond the redwood curtain is very unlike the old forest it replaced.

Redwood and Douglas fir have been cut constantly since the arrival of the first logger to this North Country less than 150 years ago. In that short period almost all the natural forests have been destroyed, as they have been destroyed all over the world where humans have learned to live.

Some people want to save the very last ancient forests from the chain-saws. The wisest amongst them want the old growth to remain for its place in the future of the steelhead trout and salmon, two species among many formed in symbiosis with the forests themselves. As the ancient forests disappear, so do the fish that depend upon the clear running, cool streams that flow only from the old forests themselves.

But the last virgin forests—the Dark Forests—are also gold mines for corporate raiders like Charles Hurwitz from Houston, Texas. Hurwitz used his power to turn the forests into money. Saved or cut, Hurwitz will make a bundle of money.

Legend has it that Robert Devine and Charles Hurwitz became interested in the Dark Forests of Humboldt County on the same day, in the spring of 1989. Robert had seen an article in the business section of the *San Francisco Chronicle* about the fact that Pacific Lumber still had virgin forests which were under-valued and available at bargain-basement prices.

Here were these ancient forests, thousands of acres in size, which had so far survived the onslaught of modern technology's recent invention of the chainsaw and the insatiable desire of big business to turn resources into money. Robert and Hannah's initial interest was concern for the workers involved in this enterprise.

Robert Devine and Hannah Caine were partners in the *Country Activist*, a small regional newspaper dedicated to an evolution of consciousness and a humane social reality. They published the *Activist* monthly from their offices in Arcata and Garberville. Contributions from loyal readers and the advertising of the counterculture's successful entrepreneurial businesses enabled the *Activist* to disperse 5,000 copies to local citizens each month: Not the *Wall Street Journal* in either size or editorial position, but Robert called it "radical." "'Progressive' sounds like an incurable disease," he explained.

About the same time as the *Activist* was being read in Northern California, Charles Hurwitz became a stockholder of Pacific Lumber Company. And then on October 22, 1985, Hurwitz succeeded in wresting control of Pacific Lumber and its Dark Forests away from its other shareholders in a Michael Milken "junk-bond" funded, hostile corporate take-over.

Robert and Hannah were in their office within the labyrinthine quarters of the Action Center, on the third floor of the only three-story building in Garberville—the top of their world. They were on telephone extensions, getting the news first-hand from Bill Bertain, the Eureka attorney for the old stockholders who had been forced to sell out to Hurwitz.

"We are going to fight him. Murphy wants a fight. I want a fight. We sued this morning and expect to be in the courtroom soon to prove Hurwitz and Milken are crooks. They stole PL. It's ours; we want it back," Bertain fumed, sometimes breaking down into a resounding string of expletives. Robert uh-huh-ed him, growing bored with the tirade, but giving Bill an electronic shoulder to cry on for the moment. He couldn't help but smile, thinking of the graphic impossibility of Bill's choice of swear words overburdened with sexual innuendos.

Hannah listened intently too, nodding about the "rights of the employees to the jobs in the woods and mills" part of Bertain's rant.

She looked up to see Robert end the conference call to tend to someone in the outer office. He was a wiry, feral-looking creature she'd never seen before. "Just another day in Paradise," she thought, as she turned her attention back to the heart-broken attorney.

Robert, following what was generally his urge to help those in distress, approached. "Hi, can I help you?"

"I need a phone. Now! The guy at the bookstore said you had one I could use. Where is it?" Out of breath, the electrically vibrating person hesitated, pulled on his ear and started again, "My name is Isaac Winwood and I'm from New York. I just arrived. I brought an Indian brother who was hitching down from Oregon. Look I need to use the phone to get him a lawyer. Any ideas?"

Robert was never at a loss for ideas. "Yeah, go get something to eat and come back when you are calm. Here's ten bucks…food before lawyers."

Isaac looked as if he'd argue, but quickly changed his mind, grabbed the ten dollar bill and trotted out the door.

"God, where did he come from?" Robert asked no one in particular. And things just went on from there.

HARVEST TIME

The streets of Garberville run in squares for about a dozen blocks. Then the roads snake off into all directions, up through the hills and low mountains to the many subdivisions of logged-over forests regenerating into tanoak, madrone and "brush."

The subdivisions were sold in the 60s and 70s to the back-to-the-landers who, now in their 40s and 50s, looked like the rising middle class. Trouble was, not many of them made a clean living. They had continued through the half-dozen years of police surveillance, known as the Campaign Against Marijuana Production, to make a living growing and selling agricultural products, most notably pot.

Garberville was once a wide-open community where the rednecks and the hippies mixed their economies harmoniously enough so that everyone seemed to own a new pickup truck. The talk was loose, and often enough one would see a tie-dyed free-thinker smoking a joint outside the ice cream parlor.

A decade later, the new generation had melded the cultures into a third form called the hip-necks: dope growing rednecks or the children of hippies who roamed the hills hunting for deer or worked in the logging operations that still were on-going in the area.

These days everyone was less obvious, yet everyone guessed which of the right-wing redneck parents sported successful pot-growing children: the unemployed father driving an beater while the son drove a new Nissan 4x4. The opulence was taken as a sign the son had struck green last year.

The unexplained wealth of the community had drawn the attention of law enforcement. First it was helicopter raids on the most obvious of the pot plantations. Then the merchants who sold the basics for pot growing—fertilizer, grow lights, water line—were raided for lists of their customers. The fear level grew and more growers moved inside, away from the line of sight of pilots who crisscrossed the hills in search of a hippie's patch—this they did for a bounty offered by the State.

Times had changed. The years of free growing had left some with piles of one hundred dollar bills buried in their back yards in what was called the Bank of the Woods. Some changed what was invisible into a new means of support, opening legit businesses alongside the traditional redneck shop owners from the past.

Some of the hippies had been different from the first and never grew pot at all. The saying was that only the rich or the stupid didn't grow pot. Robert and Hannah lived in one of the 40-acre subdivisions, and for ten years they hadn't sprouted even one illegal plant. They had seen the face of greed on their neighbors and noted how the unexpected wealth had changed their friends from vegetarian homesteaders into coke-heads whose level of paranoia had risen to the point that nearly everyone was armed in their homes for fear of being robbed. Many had been, and continued to be, the victims of local ruffians or thieves from "the City" who came north to try to get rich by finding the hidden gardens the cops missed.

On any given day, stories could be heard about the plight of the hill people. In the summer months and into the fall, one could encounter knots of nervous women and children in front of the market in Redway, chattering about a CAMP raid on their homes. At times the bars were filled with newly busted pot farmers, dressed in the camouflage so popular in the woods, drinking themselves into a stupor and lamenting the loss of their "ladies"—as the potent female marijuana plants were affectionately known. The loss amounted to the end of that year's dream to avoid a return to the city, or the loss of the new truck everyone so badly craved.

Robert returned home one afternoon to discover the long dirt road into his area blocked with a dozen vehicles. Surrounded the vehicles were his neighbors, each as tense as refugees on the road from Hue, watching the horizon for the sight of a helicopter. Every time the whirling blades were heard or sighted the crowd burst into speculation.

"Damn they're over my place. Shit there goes the crop."

"Oh, I hope they miss me. Have you any word about what they plan to do?"

Robert passed through the roadblock and drove along the gravel lane over the ridge to his cabin, knowing what he would find when he got there. Parking, he set out on foot back to the top of the ridge in time to see the helicopter rise with a bag of newly cut pot plants dangling below.

Well, there goes the Dome's crop. Robert knew all of his neighbors by their homes. The Dome. The Hovel. The Roundhouse. The Octagon.

Another morning he had risen to find his Hell's Angel neighbor patrolling their common road with a large-bore rifle, searching for the rip-offs who had stolen his drying plants right out of his living room. The poor man had cranked himself up on meth and was as frightened by the invasion of his home as he was frightening in his anger.

Just another day in Paradise, Robert lamented, as he reached the road above his house and coincidentally the place the helicopter had off-loaded its compliment of LAPD officers to seek and destroy pot gardens. Robert knew there was no pot on his land—he regularly patrolled his perimeter in search of any signs of renegade growers using his land or water for cultivation. But it never matters whether you are innocent or guilty. The feeling one gets from encountering armed men—cops or otherwise—is the same. He quickly ducked under the tall oaks by the side of the road to hide from the choppers. In minutes, the helicopter landed on his road and was quickly filled again with the now exhausted CAMP crew. He watched the aircraft lift off in a whirl of dust to fly across the canyon to another drop spot.

Once the dust settled, Robert emerged from the brush and onto the road. He found the marks the copter had made in the loose dirt and there, by the side of the road, he found a message from the crew: "Have a nice day—CAMP 89."

"What clowns." Roberts words fell upon a deaf forest. Today wasn't going to be much fun out here.

So, without even going into his house, Robert returned to his office in Garberville. *I'll give this place a few days to shake off the karma of those thieves,* he thought. *Maybe work is the only life I want anyway.*

THE HOOP

THANKSGIVING

Carl Running Deer sat inside the lodge on a small mat, his knees almost touching Robert's knees. They'd built the sweat lodge together, near Bear Harbor, to share a ceremony of parting.

Robert had found him in a cabin ten miles up China Creek. All his beer was gone. He looked very sick with a broad extended belly. Robert took him to the health clinic where an hour later the doctor told Carl he would only live a few more days if he did not stop drinking.

"Doctor, your medicine is not my medicine," Carl spoke for the first time. "I follow the Red Road. My body is afflicted with alcohol."

Robert knew his friend in ways he had learned in sweats and peyote circles. They had shared many tepees and more than a few beers.

"Where do you want to go?" Robert asked, as they climbed back into the old red and rusting '73 Datsun pickup he'd borrowed from a neighbor.

"To Bear Harbor, to be with the Wiyots and the Sinkyone. We need medicine."

Robert and Carl drove to a house off Whitethorn Road. They had been there often. The Road Men who carried the medicine along the Pacific Coast left a stash of peyote for those who followed the Red Road. Men like Carl who lived in and around the Mattole River Valley had built it for times like these.

Carl spoke many times about the Hoop, the Four Directions and all the Relations. Robert felt the tug of Carl's cosmology. He'd sat in the circles and shared the visions of a white eagle who he saw as a spirit greater than himself, not a source of fear, but a reminder of his common relations with Carl.

Now they sat face to face. The sun had set. A modest fire burned between them. Carl sang the songs and Robert fed the fire. Some of the songs he sang Robert knew from other times. He knew the AIM song he had drummed to for the first time fifteen years earlier.

Carl passed the medicine to Robert, then Carl built a fire to heat a pan of water into which he carefully poured the medicine. It would be easier for Carl to digest as a tea rather than whole. He had not eaten in several days. Chewing wasn't possible for Carl. No teeth, he would explain.

"Robert, the Hoop is broken. My body is broken. You are here to help release me. Keep the fire. I will sing my dying song. You will watch my spirit rise. Take my body to my wife and children."

"The Hoop is broken?"

"We are all one people when the Hoop is whole."

Robert had no response. His experience with sitting up with Grandfather, staying awake all night with dozens of people following the Red Road, had been that talking did not work. He agreed with Carl. The Hoop was broken.

Carl's arms were weak. His drum beats were slow. His voice was near silence. The hours passed as Carl led them through his ceremony.

The firewood Robert had brought into the lodge was gone. He rose to bring more from the pile outside. When the doorway was opened, Robert saw that dawn was near. The sun would rise above Usal Ridge, but not find them until nearly noon.

It was time to eat. Carl and Robert had sometimes fished in the surf. They had not brought a fishing net. Carl was beyond fishing anyway. Carl ate a small bite of fruit. Robert stared at the surf. He saw no fish. They watched the sun rise as the ocean caught the rays first as far as they could see, then in the surf and then the sun itself.

By the time the sun's rays struck Carl's legs he was asleep. Robert covered him and kept a fire going downwind, near him, not so much for heat but as a reminder of who they were and where they were going.

Carl was restless as the sun warmed him. He sat up, recognized where he was and laid back down. Robert sat next to him keeping some sage smoking up wind from Carl.

"Brother," he said. "Do not feel sorry for me. We all begin. We all end. It is beautiful here on the beach. The sounds are soothing."

"Ah Ho."

"I was alone in Oklahoma. No family members were left. My clan was scattered. I sat up and dreamed about a place and started moving west, one town at a time, until I got here."

Robert knew Carl's history; the parts he wanted to tell. When he drank too many beers he would start talking. His stories always began in the middle.

"That's when my cousin, Sheldon was his name, decided we should both join the Army," was how he would begin. The story would circle around until he told the part about some petty crime the tribal police were after them for. Robert had questions about this and that but if he asked one Carl would laugh and chide him for being a white man with all the white man questions.

"Stories are gifts," he would say. "The teller knows the story he is giving. Receive the gift, or not, but do not question it."

They laid on the blanket Robert had taken from the sweat lodge. It was big enough to cover Carl.

"How do I look?" Carl had asked.

"Like a taco."

"Am I the chicken?"

"Nope. Ground beef."

Carl laughed. "Maybe I need a beer."

"Are you going to die here today?"

"No," he said. "Maybe tomorrow."

"I'm hungry. Let's go to my place."

"Let's stop at the Whitethorn Store."

"Are you hungry?"

"Thirsty."

"We have no water or beer."

"Now I'm in a hurry."

Robert did not want Carl to stand and walk to the truck. He did not want his friend to die.

Carl knew Robert as well as he knew anyone. He had good eyes and saw the thoughts cross his friend's face.

"What does that crazy lawyer friend of yours say? He quotes a play. Something about this is a good day to die."

"Bertain quotes Henry V," Robert said. "The king wonders how the men who did not join him would feel when they found out they missed a chance to be the king's brother by not dying for his dream of conquering Europe."

"What am I thinking?"

"Maybe Crazy Horse," Robert said. "I think you are joking me. No way you missed it."

"Where were you on St Crispin's Day."

"Brother, I think we have all gone crazy." Robert stood and offered his friend his hand. They took their stuff back to the lodge and left it there for another day.

The road to Whitethorn was long and dusty. They found a parking spot in front of the store. Whitethorn has no sidewalks or curbs. It barely had pavement. The county had paved a quarter mile through town "to keep the dust out of the beer."

"Hey, Robert." The shout came from the doorway of the post office across from the Whitethorn Store.

"Hey, Audrey. What's up?" Robert answered.

"Two phone calls from people looking for you. Some kind of emergency. Call Hannah at Gil's farm."

"Damn." People in the hills had many ways to find someone. The last thing you did was drive around looking. The first thing you did was call around looking for someone who'd seen them or who had information. Robert and Hannah had no phone at their cabin. The phone line was three miles away. The nearest pay phone was nearly ten miles away in Whitethorn. When things were busy he slept in his office in Garberville.

Robert went back into the store after handing Carl the beer he wanted through the truck door.

"You have an opener?"

"Those are twist offs. I gotta make a call."

He came out and backed the truck up to the gas pump.

"We are in the wind, bro," he told Carl. "Need gas."

The day was at its peak temperature. There was no breeze. Robert finished screwing on the gas cap and went back into the store, came out with two more six-packs of generic beer which he placed in the bed rather than risk it to Carl's thirst.

It would take them almost an hour to get to the farm where the meeting was going to happen. Hannah had been explicit, they would wait for him to get there.

"Who is going to be at this meeting?" Carl asked when he was told about the change in their itinerary.

"You've been hanging out with me too long," Robert said. "It's a meeting we have been working on for some time. You know everyone. Hannah, Vera, Isaac, Tarzan, and two lawyers—Harris and Mike."

"What is it about?"

"Plan is to divide up the work so that we do not argue so much or conflict in a way that weakens us."

"That's how they do it, how they win."

"What are you saying?"

"They make us do things their way, the way that breaks the Hoop." Carl said. "Tepees, igloos, powwows are circles. Towns are squares."

"Oh."

"The Hoop includes everyone. The square divides us, sets us looking at each other as sides. A circle has no sides. We don't sit across from the other side. We sit across from someone just like us."

Robert drove on, Carl's words working on him, blocking thoughts of strategy, substituting mystical considerations for what the others felt important.

The road followed a ridgetop that traveled north above the Upper Mattole River, then dropped down to a bridge across the river. Just before the bridge, a wide gravel road continued north. Many twists and turns later they arrived at their destination; an old farmhouse with barns and a yard under a towering apple tree with a long picnic table and preschool toy litter.

It was almost dinner time. Some people were preparing food while others tended the various children brought by the attendees. There were three times as many people as Robert had anticipated. Hannah saw him get out of their neighbor's truck. He headed straight to her with Carl slowly moving after him. They met alone halfway between.

"What's with all the people? What happened to a small quiet conspiracy for good?"

"That was your idea. It's the first sunny day in a while. It's a holiday. People have families. One thing leads to another. Voila! The good news is that we have a plan. Some will meet while others eat. We will keep our own counsel in private."

"Do you have the agenda we proposed?"

"Yes."

"Let's start asap. Carl and I are a little stretched for time."

"I see."

"No. You will, but not this moment."

"Mystery?"

"Mystics."

"Grandfather?"

Robert did not respond. Hannah nodded. They arrived at the picnic table. The table was clear of everything except paperwork. A pile of agendas plus maps, maps and more maps.

Isaac and Tarzan were talking and pointing wildly at maps they had just picked up from a printer. These were blowups of topo maps, some of them accompanied with Timber Harvest Plan (THP) applications. It made an impressive mess.

Robert walked to the end of the table. Everyone sat down. Robert handed the agendas to Hannah at his left and the diminishing pile continued around until none was left. Carl walked up and stood at the other end.

Carl picked up a pile of THPs lifting them over his head, then put them back down on the table.

"The Hoop is broken," he said. "Do not do this their way."

Robert waited for someone else to speak. He spoke into the silence.

"I hesitate to interpret the words of my friend, but he is asking us to sit in a circle and maybe not use so much paper to make our point. Thank you for the reminder."

No one grumbled. They happily moved from the table, encouraging each other to find good places to sit in a circle, knee to knee. Someone asked to hold hands, someone else began a short chant. Silence won for a few seconds. Then a small redwood seedling was passed around the circle. If you had it in your hands it was your turn to talk. No one said this, it was understood.

"Isaac and I are committed to direct action in the woods," Tarzan said, when the seedling resting in his hand.

Vera said she was with them, and that media attention was their point.

Hannah spoke about legislation and lobbying.

The lawyers talked about the THP appeal process, and litigation to force the State to enforce the law.

Robert spoke about organizing local communities. He finished by asking how they could do all these things without hurting each other's work.

"Robert," Hannah said. "It's the circle that will keep us together."

"Ah Ho," said Carl.

Somebody yelled "food" from the house. The redwood made its way completely around the circle in silence.

Robert stood and helped Carl up with Hannah's help. They walked back towards the truck.

"You guys are leaving without food."

"Yeah," Robert said. "Carl and I are headed south." He turned to Carl. "More beer?"

"Two more."

Robert grabbed the now hot beers from the pickup bed, handed two to Carl and the rest to Hannah.

"See you at home in a few days. Carl has something to do and I am the fireman."

"You know what it is and you won't tell me?"

"Ask Carl."

Hannah tried a kiss and backed away. "You need a shower."

The ride back to the sweat lodge was quiet. Robert thought Carl was sleeping until they reached Bear Harbor when Robert could not awaken him. Robert thought about the options. He thought about the parting ceremony and felt no need for more than that. He thought about what the doctor said and saw no need to take Carl back there.

The sun was setting.

They sat together in the truck for one last sunset. Carl had not opened the two beers. Robert opened them both. Set one in Carl's lap and took a sip of the other.

"Carl, I am going to miss you." He raised the bottle in a salute, drank a sip. "I have so many questions."

BRAINSTORMS

THE NEXT DAY, FRIDAY

Trees are America's renewable resource.

"Jobs are renewable, you cretins," Robert snarled at the bumper-sticker in front of him. Driving through the persistent rain didn't do much to improve his already bad attitude. He lit up another cigarette and grabbed a sopping rag to wipe the condensation off the windshield.

"Not if you're a cretin," Hannah flung out. She sat cross-legged on the front seat of the old pick-up truck, reading through piles of papers. She grumbled and swore as she wielded her pen with the precision of a dissecting tool.

The truck in front of them was carrying a single log; it came from a redwood tree so large and so old that only one enormous log—just a portion of the entire tree—would fit on the huge flatbed.

They continued down the highway, exchanging little of what could be called conversation, as the windshield wipers swished against the glass. The rain was relentless. Here on the Northcoast, the redwoods demanded the moisture and some of them had been luxuriating in it for over a thousand years. Not many living things were older than that, though water itself is as old as the planet: four billion years, at least. The very same water molecules which had circulated through the bodies of extinct dinosaurs now flowed through the veins of ancient redwoods, only to be transpired as mist into the night.

Hannah shuffled the papers, stuffed them into a folder and turned to face Robert. "How much longer are we going to slave away at this damn paper?" Her voice was permeated with frustration and Robert didn't even have to look at her to know that her lips were tightly pressed.

"You look older when you frown, you know," Robert chuckled slightly to himself as he jammed his cigarette into the ashtray.

"You bastard; stop avoiding the issue. You know damn well this newspaper exists so your friends can see their opinions in print. Unfortunately, most of these idiots can't form a coherent paragraph." Hannah brushed the hair off her brow and abruptly dropped her pen in her lap. "You know what? I think I've finally reached my limit editing this crap. It's no longer amusing."

"What's going on? Are you low blood sugar? I should have made you eat that bagel this morning." Robert's gaze stayed focused on the road.

Hannah glared at him, mustering all her self-control to keep from strangling him as he drove. "No; I'm not LBS, or PMS, or too much caffeine, or not enough sex." She looked over at him to see if he was listening and when she saw his face light up upon hearing her last word, she knew she had him. She continued, "Listen you arrogant son of a bitch, our entire lives are absorbed by producing that paper."

Robert flinched slightly, but continued staring straight ahead. He knew there was more to come. Hannah's exasperated sigh filled the cab of the truck.

"You just can't stop, can you? You're so damned determined to keep in the center of the conflict. Sometimes I think you're like a shark; you have to keep swimming, in order to survive."

Robert just smiled.

As the rain pelted the old truck, they drove on in silence for several more miles. Finally, they reached the crossroad and Robert pulled onto the gravel road which led up to Isaac Winwood's home. He down-shifted noisily and cast a furtive glance in Hannah's direction, hoping that the requisite cool-off time had passed. She could be so flaming passionate; unfortunately, not always at an opportune time. He knew when to keep his mouth shut, though. She'd work it out eventually. He peered out through the rain and saw Isaac waving from the deck.

"Okay, I guess we'd better make a run for it."

Robert pulled the hood of his rain parka over his head, grabbed a bundle and jumped down from the old truck into a mud puddle. This was the Northcoast; mud puddles were standard from November through May. If there wasn't mud, then there was dust. Nobody worth knowing lived on a paved road.

Hannah followed, tightly clutching an armload of papers, purposefully walking behind Robert, keeping the gap intact.

Isaac was in fine form for a rainy day. He gave both Robert and Hannah a big hug as he led them towards the wood-burning stove.

"Guess what you guys?" Before anyone could begin to conjecture he launched into an account of a news item. "Get this: The president of Pacific Lumber says that Earth First!ers are preventing honest men from doing their jobs. Isn't that just too ironic?"

Robert smirked, "The honest part is a bit of a stretch."

"Yeah, well listen to this: 'It's time for people to live by the law of the land.' Like that jerk has any understanding of how the land lives."

"Well Isaac, much to my amazement, you have again succeeded in irritating someone." Robert gave his friend a playful punch.

Isaac smiled proudly back. To Isaac, irritation was synonymous with recognition.

Vera, who was in the kitchen grinding coffee, shouted out to the others, "Yeah, isn't it great to see our names in the paper?"

Hannah responded reluctantly, "Well actually, Vera, I'd rather see some positive stories about political activism than all this conflict stuff."

Vera sighed behind the kitchen door and then called out again, "I know what you're saying, but Earth First! needs this. We need more volatile exposure —front page stuff."

Robert wandered into the kitchen to help Vera bring the coffee out, hoping to cool the rising tide of tempers. There was a perceptible air of tension in the already dreary day. What was with everyone? Maybe it was the full moon. Or maybe it was the five straight hours of rain.

Robert and Vera returned to the living room with the freshly brewed coffee and they all stood huddled around the wood stove, warming their hands on the steaming mugs. They chatted about Isaac's cat's latest batch of kittens; they chatted about their mutual friends.

Vera, impatient with frivolity, spoke again. "Look, I'm not into crazy stunts like they did in Arizona. We need to work within the system. I'm just not sure how."

"Are you talking about that fake crack that the enviros draped over the Glen Canyon Dam? That was hilarious! I love it! Why can't we think of things like that?" Isaac was clearly inspired.

Robert laughed. Hannah found herself chuckling, too. It was true; no one was injured and a great deal of press coverage resulted from a simple act of civil disobedience. But Hannah was still disturbed and brought her concerns up to the others.

"I agree that exposure of the issues is crucial, but furtive midnight pranks—hmm—well, they sap a lot of energy and don't necessarily create the kind of change we need." She shook her head, "We can't keep going on fundraisers and donations. It's getting really old."

Vera continued Hannah's train of thought. "Okay then, let's work within the system. Let's change the rules by playing by the rules."

"And that would be…?"

"An initiative. We create a ballot initiative."

They sipped their drinks in silence. Even Isaac looked seriously thoughtful.

It was Hannah who first spoke. "I suppose you had Robert and me in mind for the development of this initiative?"

"Okay, yeah. I mean, c'mon, you two have the experience and, of course, the expertise. Just look at your newspaper. It draws in the right kind of supporters and you know that Alice and Lou and Gus—all of us at Earth First!'ll be in on this." Vera flashed a tentative smile at Hannah, who was by now looking at Robert.

Isaac jumped in. "Of course! An initiative is exactly what the people can relate to. Besides, that gives us over a year to qualify, right?"

"Let's see…yeah," mused Vera. "We'd have to gather signatures by next spring for the November ballot."

Robert nodded affirmatively. "You're right. It's do-able. Besides, who could argue with preserving a national landmark?"

"Try Pacific Lumber, or Louisiana Pacific, or the thousands of employees of the timber industry, that's who." Hannah responded testily. "Get real. Do you think the timber corporations are just going to sit back and just watch us hack away at their livelihoods?" She was always the one to puncture their bubble of idealism.

No one replied. They weren't young enough to be fearless, or old enough to be worn out.

Hannah looked at each of her friends and saw the resolution on their faces. *Why couldn't someone else call the bullshit?* She shrugged her shoulders and spoke more softly this time. "Do you all really think we could pull this off?"

"I know we can do it," Vera exclaimed. "Isaac and I can pull together all the demos. If you just keep on top of all the filing details we'll keep the publicity going." Vera sat up excitedly, looking at Robert and Hannah for confirmation.

Robert stood up and paced across the room. He paused in front of the big window and gazed out at the mist drifting heavily through the trees. He noticed the orange and fluorescent green mosses clinging to the ancient trunks. He looked over at his old pick-up truck, appearing remarkably small amongst the towering trees surrounding it. The redwoods were an incredible creation.

Vera, persuasive as always, broke his reverie. "The people want this protection for the redwoods. Earth First! can instigate it. All we need is exposure." Her friends looked at her curiously. She proceeded, "Look, picture this—a chained hippie on a huge redwood; an aggressive bulldozer lurking in the background…"

"Of course, that's sensational. Perfect," Isaac interrupted the scenario. "When the cameras arrive, we'll be there." He raised his mug in a gesture of a toast. "Let the show begin; Earth First!'s on the front page of every paper in California!"

Hannah laughed at his exuberance. "Isaac, with the kind of tactics you dream up, the front page may not be such a great place for your face to be!"

"Oh yeah? I want to be a household name!"

'What, like Clorox?"

Isaac cocked his head in consideration. "Hmm, actually I had something a little less toxic in mind."

Vera laughed as she reached over to hug him. He was several years younger than she and sheer delight to work with. He never missed a beat, he never stood still. That she had quickly grown to love him was really no surprise to her; he was one of the few men who could keep up with her.

Robert looked longingly at Hannah as the other two were embracing. She felt his gaze and returned it with a sly smile. No point in dragging on an endless debate now when they could easily pick it up later. She reached out to stroke his knee and he gratefully placed his hand on top of hers.

Isaac suddenly jumped up and scurried down the hall towards the back of the house. He quickly returned with a guitar and a gleam in his eye.

"Okay you guys, check out this ballad."

Spike a tree for Jesus, now is the time
He'd like you to help him save our forests from dyin'
Stop all those loggers from cuttin' 'em down
We gotta save the oldgrowth …

Vera joined in with the singing, easily ad-libbing lyrics to Isaac's composition. The others chuckled approvingly and occasionally shouted out their own contributions to the melody. The verses became more ridiculous until they all succumbed to laughter. As they broke into fits of hysteria, Vera reached over to the desktop and extracted a joint from an ornately carved wooden box.

Soon the air was filled with the cloying scent of Humboldt's most famous export. The mood relaxed as the tension went up in smoke. Even Isaac was rendered speechless. Hannah smiled to herself as she observed all the energy in the room consumed by THC. She sat back against the cushions and gazed out through the mist and rain into the forest. These forests were worth the effort. Indeed, Isaac, let the show begin.

FUN AND GAMES

THAT NIGHT

"Whose deal is it? Robert's?" Lou gathered up the cards and tossed the loose pile to Robert to his right. "Let's take a break first—I need some fresh air."

Grunts of approval followed Lou as he rose from the kitchen table. *Middle age,* he thought, as he stretched the kinks out of his back. He grabbed some matches and his pack of cigarettes as he let out a deep cough. *Whew—I suppose it's about time to give this crap up.*

Walking out through the side door, Lou exited onto the deck overlooking the Mad River. The full moon was gleaming as it crested the mountain tops, casting a luminous sheen to the slowly moving water.

"Nice view," he said into the night air, firing up the end of his hand-rolled cig.

"Great on a moonlit night like this," came the unexpected reply from Hannah. "I get hypnotized just watching the shadows; it's great when the bats go darting by." Stretched out in a lounge chair, she sat up and turned to face her old friend, "How's the game going?"

"Hey Hannah, I didn't see you there," Lou responded. "Well, I'm about breaking even, but Robert's sure looking good tonight. He's lucky enough for all of us." He took a drag off his cigarette and slumped in the chair across from her. "Why aren't you playing? We could use some female energy."

Hannah laughed derisively, "'Female fortune is more like it! With my kind of a poker face the rest of you don't even need luck!"

"Good point, I seem to recall going home a few six-packs richer when you've been in the game." Lou patted his surplus belly and sighed, "Ah yes; gambling and six-packs—I guess I've got a few bad habits." He reached over for his beer. "Been thinking about doing sit-ups one of these days." He took another swig.

Hannah looked over at him. He had a little more flesh and a little less muscle than he did twenty years ago, but he also had more spirit. She smiled to herself as she glanced through the window at the guys leaning against the kitchen counter; they were laughing, chatting, as the familiar refrains of Van Morrison poured out the open door.

"You know," she said, looking back at Lou, "where have you ever seen a more interesting group of people? Adventurers, inventors, instigators… You guys really know how to live."

Lou looked at her curiously, "Are you kidding? I was just feeling like such a loser. You know the divorce and all…" His voice trailed off with the smoke of his cigarette. The tranquility of the river only heightened the discomfort they both felt about this subject. He finally stood up and peered off into the distance before resuming.

"Hannah, what's going to become of us? Careers are upside down, relationships are inside out, bank accounts empty—is this really the life we planned?"

"Hmm, well as Lennon said, 'Life is what happens to you while you're busy making other plans.'"

"Then judging by my life, I've been putting a little too much energy into the planning part."

Hannah stood up, touching Lou on the arm as she spoke, "It takes strength to follow your heart; you've had to make a lot of rough decisions lately. Don't be so hard on yourself."

He smiled at her, momentarily comforted by her words.

She looked back at him with melancholy in her eyes. "I know how it feels. Some days I gotta wonder about some of my own decisions…you know…going into my own business. I'm never really certain that giving up a steady paycheck was a wise move. Then again, playing bureaucratic games never sat well with me either."

"Yeah, well speaking of games, I better get back in this one if I'm gonna take home any lunch money." He flicked his cigarette into the night air. "Sorry to be so blue; it's been a heavy week. Mortgage is due, divorce's coming final, winter's almost here—makes me miss the kids already."

Hannah nodded, noticing that men always got up to leave when the conversation turned to real issues.

When Lou entered the kitchen, the others were seated, fresh beers had been opened, and the table cleaned for the next round.

"Have a seat, let's go," Isaac said impatiently. Lou sniffed at the cloud of pot smoke which had easily filled the tiny kitchen. Gus's house was one of the few remaining small cabins on this stretch of riverfront. He had been able to secure its purchase just before the developers and retirees bought up all the best places. Now he possessed a little piece of paradise and the dubious honor of hosting the monthly poker game.

As Lou slid into his chair Robert ordered everyone to ante up. "Five card draw."

Robert was a traditionalist. He never called a wild game or a wild card on any of his deals. Raised, as he was, by a mother who enjoyed her parlor poker games more than her children, Robert grew up respecting the odds in life. Educated as a mathematician, he played the game to win. And to win, one had to play a game without surprises—keep it simple, keep it clean.

The hand was uneventful. Lou's two small pairs beat Will's aces. Robert folded after the draw and felt lucky to have a clear-cut choice.

The deal then went to Will who often had a wild idea of what a poker game was about—ever the rebel.

"How about some seven card stud? High spade splits the pot with the high hand. Hey, I'm feeling a bit crazed tonight; let's make it the Black Mariah Option."

"Okay…split the pot…. But what's this option thing?" Gus took another hit off the pipe and apparently needed time to process this new information.

"The Black Mariah is the queen of spades, right? No matter what hand you've got, if the queen of spades is dealt face up to any player that hand's over without a winner. See? Then we ante up again and re-deal—adds a little spice to sweeten the pot." Will smiled sardonically; he loved the drama of the hidden Mariah.

"Let's do it, I'm in," Robert said as he threw in his quarter followed by the grunts of the other players as they, too, tossed their twenty-five cents into the middle of the kitchen table.

The dealer pulled cards from the top of the deck, one at a time, dealing twice around the table. The first two rounds were dealt face down. The third round of cards was then dealt face up.

"Robert's got an ace; it's your bet."

Robert looked his cards over methodically while he twisted his quarter over and over, using all the fingers in his left hand. "Two bits," he proclaimed, throwing the coin in the center.

The others studied their hands, and in turn saw the bet by pitching in their money. No one raised. *Got it,* Robert thought. Two aces with the ace of spades hidden. *I've got it all.*

The next cards were also dealt face up, and the hands showed the usual sprinkling of pairs and possible straights or flushes. Bets were made and still no raises. Robert's hand still looked pretty good.

Why are these guys still in the hand, he wondered? Some players held on hoping for a three of a kind, some for a high spade on the last down card. Regardless, they all made the bets just to stay in the game. *Nothing like a fool or two to make the pot bigger. What was it his mother used to say? "If you look around the table and can't figure out who the sucker is— then it's probably you."*

The fifth card was face up. Robert got another ace. He held three of a kind; aces—two showing and an ace "in the hole." As often as he played he never became accustomed to holding the best hand and usually overplayed it, betting too much and scaring away the poor bastards who had nothing but hope to bet on.

"Robert's pair of aces bets again."

Robert tossed a quarter into the center barely able to contain his eagerness, feeling all the confidence of the sure winner.

"I'll see you and raise a quarter. Your aces don't scare me." Isaac chimed in as he brazenly flung his two quarters into the substantial pile of coins.

"Damn, that means it's fifty to me, but I'm staying," Lou complained as he picked through his dwindling collection of nickels and dimes.

Gus threw in his quarters, swearing at the cards. Will saw the bet without discussion. Robert felt his arm pits moisten with a nervous sweat he hoped would not betray his excitement.

"And I'll raise it twenty-five again," Robert snorted, unable to hide his glee. *I've got them now, he* thought, *right where I want them.*

The clatter of coins filled the air as the players followed Robert's lead. "The pot's looking sweet and here's your next card," Will intoned like a Las Vegas dealer. "And it's an ace for Gus."

"Lot of good that'll do me." Gus's pile of coins was decidedly more copper than silver.

Will continued dealing the sixth card face-up with an exaggerated flourish. "A heart for Lou—don't thank me now, Lou—and a possible flush." Will paused for a hearty hack while Dylan's nasal voice twanged from the speakers in the background.

"No help for Isaac," he said as he swiftly dealt him an unimpressive eight of diamonds. Isaac mumbled as Will continued, "A Jack for Robert. Hmmm; got a straight, Robert?" Will was enjoying his fleeting status as the dealer of fates. His eyes squinted as he took a sip of his beer, and he masterfully flung the next card onto the table in front of Gus.

A round of gasps and a fair sprinkling of unoriginal epithets were heard throughout the room.

"And there she is boys: The Black Mariah. This hand is officially over. Throw in your cards." The queen of spades glared up at the players, as Will smirked with a perverse pleasure.

"Damn. I was so sure. Damn it; I know I had the best hand." Robert shook his head incredulously, feeling dejected and incompetent. Those were emotions he seldom experienced. He wasn't accustomed to losing.

"A round of bong tokes," Isaac ordered, pushing his chair back. The entire table burst with energy as the players welcomed a change of attitude.

Robert glanced over at Isaac who was packing the bong surrounded by the smiling group. Raising his beer bottle in a toast, he said, "To the Black Mariah, may I never cross her path again." He drained the remaining third of his beer and collapsed back onto the couch.

THE SAW BLADE

THAT SAME DAY

In a saw mill there are many very dangerous jobs, but none like those of the off-bearers, the men who stand at the head-rig where the first cut on a whole log is made. The blade that pierces the wood turns ferociously—so fast it seems to disappear altogether, becoming a 12-inch-wide blur. The head-rig carves off slabs of wood into cants for the re-saw operation that will make 2 x 4s. Of all the millworkers, the off-bearers stand nearest to the blade. Not hard to do if you have a face mask and ear protection and if you are without fear for your life.

Trees have a history of being used as fence posts. Huge nails and spikes have been driven into so many of them that before logs are brought into the mill for sawing, company inspectors use metal detectors to find and remove large metal objects. The reason is that when a blade hits one of these spikes, or other metal debris, the blade sometimes break or come loose. Old men talk about blades lying in a tight coil on the floor after having escaped. These, they say, are so dangerous that all that can be done is build a brick wall around it and leave it alone. Other tactics have proved fatal.

In any given year, one hundred men working as off-bearers are severely injured in California alone. Their wounds are usually on the face, neck and chest. Often the blade, upon shattering, runs across the top of the partially cut log and into the upper half of the off-bearer's body—all in an instant. The instrument that carved their youthful bodies into bleeding hunks of hamburger was the saw blade that burst from its pulleys.

This morning, payday morning, George Alexander moved to his position by the blade. He was worried about the blade. He'd complained about it for the last two shifts, trying to talk the boss into changing it. Yesterday the boss just got pissed. George saw him later on, he was on the catwalk above the saw with a grinning Division President Joe Wheeler and they were pointing at him, kind of telling him to work or get out. There were always more men like George—ready for any job—so the threat was real.

The night before George had talked with his wife about quitting before he ended up like his uncle, who'd been caught up in a de-barker with two other men.

"Linda, I hate working for this company. They don't care about me or you or anyone. The word is they're closing this mill and moving the machines to Mexico. Imagine that. They say the environmentalists are locking up the woods, but we'll lose our jobs and the logs will go to Baja for milling. Environmentalists didn't cause that."

"Honey, we need the money, but do what's best. Maybe I can find a job and if you find another one somewhere then we can still make it." Linda was in love with George. He kept her and their children first in his mind—not a smart man but a good one, one to stay with.

"I'll look for something else, but you stay home with the kids. We can pray for guidance on Sunday. The minister said we need to trust in God's will, whether we know what it is or not." George resigned himself to his fate and was content that he had, at least, Linda and the boys to care for him. They were blessings he prayed a thanks to God for every night.

That same night Joe Wheeler had walked onto the cold deck to talk to the foreman. "DeWitt, last night the metal detector broke down so we have no clean logs to run today. Give 'em a visual once-over, then send them through."

"Gotcha." DeWitt enjoyed the production bonuses as much as anyone, so keeping the line moving with new logs fit his idea of the right thing to do.

The next morning George drove to work with his brother-in-law, Joe Junior, who worked up the line from him. Joe listened to George complain about the blade, the boss and the lies about the Mexico mill LP was building. "George, I hear you but we aren't anything. We can't make anything different. So why whine about it? Like the foremen say all the time to the whiners, 'Work or get out.'"

Oh, well, George thought as he stood before the rig, waiting for the first log, *maybe I can get out of here soon.* Then, as the first log hit the blade the usual scream of the saw drowned out thought and talk. George yelled out his anger, "Shitty boss, shitty job, shitty company!" In midcurse the blade splintered into his face. Blood spurted from the severed veins in his neck. His jaw hung to the right side of his face, his upper teeth were exposed to the last molar.

Many things can shut down the whole production line and when a kill switch is tripped, alarm horns will sound. Most of the time the switch is thrown to halt some part of the line to keep the production sequence from becoming clogged or chaotic. Today, as the line shut down, the scream of the saw blade was replaced first by the horn, then by a dying echo, then the rising screams from men moving swiftly to the head-rig.

The sawyer, George's cousin Josh, had turned from his station at the sound of the head-rig launching its blade. There was no mistaking the sound and, as always, a icy stab of fear hit his chest. In seconds he realized that George was down and that the blade had snaked out past him onto the cement floor.

"First-aid kit!" he yelled as he hit another kill switch. The horn drowned out his words. "Someone get the kit!" he yelled again and began running. George's face and neck were spurting wounds and without a hesitation Josh grabbed them with both hands to shut the flow. He closed his eyes and prayed he would not pass out or barf. Later, he would be recognized by the family as having saved George's life—the company never did thank him.

A city block from the mill, at corporate headquarters, the morning quiet was broken by a buzz on the management intercom. "Mr. Wheeler?" It was the line foreman on the phone. "The head-rig blade blew. We've got someone down."

"Send everyone to the lunch room. I'll be there soon. Make sure nothing is moved." Wheeler was Division President and had been at Cloverdale on a three-day visit to prepare the executive staff for the move to Mexico, which was still a secret. He would handle this accident quickly before things went haywire. He straightened his shirt and hair and went down the hall to the walkway to the mill. On his way past the Sales and Community Relations offices he stuck his head in and asked the secretary if Jean Moran was in.

"Yes, sir. Shall I announce you?"

"No I'll do it," he replied as he entered the office marked Public Relations.

"Mr. Wheeler."

"Jean. How are you today? Want you to take the next five days off. I'll handle press relations while you are gone. You need a rest and now is as good a time as any. Care to argue?"

"Joe Wheeler, sometimes you are a pleasant surprise. Of course I want time to ski. This year has been hell so far and the future looks just as grim. A few days now will make a big difference. Thanks. Can I leave now?" Jean was on her feet and almost past him before she had finished speaking.

"Wouldn't dream of stopping you. Have a good rest and see you Wednesday. Deal?"

"Deal."

Good, he thought. She went without a hint of suspicion. Wheeler wanted no one talking to the media for awhile. As he walked hurriedly to the lunch room he turned his attention to the men.

An ambulance was just departing from the mill building, hitting its sirens as it cleared the fence onto the public road.

MEET THE LAWYER

MONDAY MORNING

Harris Collins called Robert Devine's office in the Action Center in the middle of the morning.

"Harris. Good morning! Or should I ask, 'Good morning?'"

"Not for you," the lawyer replied.

"Ouch. What's up?"

"Coffee at the Woodrose in five. Okay?"

"Yikes. I'll be there."

When Harris wanted to meet, it was usually in the kitchen of some local restaurant. It was his style. This morning was no different. The few minutes it took to meet up gave Robert little time to speculate as to the cause.

"Robert." The long-haired attorney stood leaning against the kitchen galley sipping some of Woodrose's fine coffee and looking anxiously around for any ears that might hear. "LP has set EF! up big-time. A mill worker at Cloverdale was nearly killed in a mill accident on Friday. LP claims a bandsaw hit an EF! spike, shattered and severely wounded the man. Joe Wheeler refused to let the county law enforcement come anywhere near the site and now, of course, it's been completely scrubbed of evidence. LP has set the narrative for the accident."

"So we only know what LP wants to tell us. Is that right?'

"Yup. The sheriff said he didn't need to investigate since LP had conducted its own investigation."

"Harris, I've had info lately about a second growth forest LP's been logging that was heavily spiked. Not by EF!, though. It's some right-wing nut that objected to his view being reduced to rubble. He sent a threatening letter to LP telling them they were wasting their time and money. He warned them that the trees were spiked and dangerous. Apparently, he was hoping that LP cared about such things. I've been waiting for news since the trees were felled, but heard nothing."

"Well, now you've heard it. And you've heard LP's story." Harris said.

"EF! isn't focused on fiber farms, they would never spike those trees."

"You know that and I know that, Robert. What we'll never know is if Wheeler created this incident to make a handy reason to call EF! 'terrorist.' Definitely has the earmarks of a setup. All I can tell you now is that LP's accusations will be the page one headline tomorrow morning. Expect press calls today."

"Harris, call me sometime with good news."

"Why? You don't pay me for that service. See you on TV."

THE END OF THE BEGINNING

DECEMBER 1

Robert groaned as the blaring of a phone assaulted his sleep. He pulled the covers over his head in a vain attempt to re-enter slumber. *Where am I,* he thought. *Oh, yeah, this old couch.* The early mists in his head were not receding gracefully at all. He rotated his neck slowly from side to side, wincing with each creak of his miserable muscles. He pried open his eyes just wide enough to see the phones, the copy machine on the counter, the stacked boxes of recycled paper. *Oh yeah...the office.*

Robert sat up laboriously and rubbed his swollen eyes as he dropped his feet onto the cold floor. With deliberate steps, he made his way toward the kitchen, groping the wall for support. He glanced at the empty cardboard six-pack next to the empty bottles and managed a half-smirk. *Good brew,* he recalled. *I like that "Redneck Lager."* Indeed, he had enjoyed every exuberant swig, as rapidly as he could swallow, for as long as he remained conscious. Ah, nothing like a good beer or two to drown out the frustration of trying to understand a woman. Beer didn't really make any better sense of them; it just made making sense less sensible.

He refocused his attention to last night and how Hannah had erupted in jealousy over some attention he had paid to another woman. He seemed to recall a young student-type with holes in her Levis, a headful of curls and astounding brown eyes. Had he really suggested that he show her how to play pool at the tavern down the street? No? Well, not really. He probably just meant that some of the crowd was heading that way for billiards and libations.

Robert was uncomfortable justifying his natural way of being to any other human being. Hannah decided her behavior never needed justifying, so he'd slunk out the door against a flurry of accusations. It was easier to be miserable on an old couch than it was to be castigated, vilified, accused and abused on a queen-sized bed. He had felt quite smug about his noble retreat and celebrated accordingly.

Just as he started the coffeepot and headed bleary-eyed for the bathroom, Hannah came in the door, looking rather contrite. "Hey…did you sleep all right here?"

Robert exhaled a slow, deep sigh and menacingly glared through his crusty eyes. It was easy to look mean when he felt that ugly. It was difficult to stay mad; he found her so beautiful. Her somber gray-blue eyes smoldered under her dark lashes. Her long hair was pinned up, furnishing a glimpse of the pale, soft flesh on her neck. Ah, skin be damned; he was pissed. In response to her query, he cracked his neck with an irreverent "screech."

"Okay, I was a bitch," she said. "I ate too much chocolate, I didn't have enough coffee, I couldn't zip my favorite jeans. Okay?" She writhed in self-loathing as she cast her eyes to the floor. Robert slumped against the wall trying to absorb this turn of events. "Sometimes…. Well, sometimes I just don't know how to control my passions…you know…sometimes that's what you like in me." She looked at him imploringly, slightly dropping her chin, biting on her lower lip.

"Hannah. You can really push my buttons. I just don't have the energy for chaos in my personal life. Damn it, we have to work together here." He shrugged his shoulders with exasperation and managed a smile. His face hurt with the effort.

She was about to respond sarcastically with, "What personal life?" but gathered her composure. "I'm sorry," she said simply and walked over to him, throwing her arms around his neck. She stroked the back of his head with her long, knowing fingers. She nibbled on his earlobe to really deliver the message. Suddenly shock waves of arousal coursed through his entire body. He felt himself awakening quite rapidly for one whose brain was enshrouded with the mists of barley.

He reached down, grabbed her rear end with both hands and kissed her forcefully on the mouth. She languidly collapsed into his arms, then returned his affection, now stroking his hips and thighs. Robert's alcohol ravaged body responded with the intensity of a well-trained dog. He definitely wanted to please.

"Come," she commanded.

Slyly smiling, he grabbed her dress in back, edging them both towards the counter. "Oooh, have you ever done it on a photocopy machine?" Robert asked. "No? Perhaps we should just push the 'enlarge' button and see what happens?"

"Hmm interesting. However, I think we should engage the 'multiple copies' button."

"As long as it doesn't buzz when something gets stuck, it could be great."

But just as Robert picked Hannah up and placed her on the machine with her dress up to her waist, the door burst open and Vera entered, carrying a bulging box of papers. She looked sideways toward the copy machine and threw her head back, laughing. "Oops…bad timing. Sorry to disrupt your conference, but do you think I could use the machine first? I have several fliers to print up before we can leave for the demo."

The lovers grinned sheepishly. Hannah's face was flushed and Robert's hair was bordering on involuntary dreadlocks, but at least they were fully clothed. Hannah jumped up, snickering and wandered into the kitchen to find some coffee. Robert, now partially revived, surveyed the office and realized he needed to straighten up his mess from the previous night's one-man party.

Vera talked enthusiastically about the upcoming abortion rally as the machine hummed rhythmically and spit out copies. A strong crowd of pro-choice activists was expected. This would be a good time for Vera and Isaac to make new connections and elicit more support for Earth

First!' actions. *"No compromise in the defense of Mother Earth!"* could easily be extrapolated to include the defense of unwilling mothers. Civil rights took on many forms in the keen political eyes of Vera.

Actually, Vera's rally was a pro-choice stand against an anti-choice demonstration planned for the Planned Parenthood clinic in Willits, a three-hour drive down Highway 101. It had been organized by a right-wing preacher determined to keep the devil out of Mendocino County by attacking distraught, nauseated women. Only the devil would want a woman to have control of her very own uterus.

"So, Hannah, you still coming with me?" Vera asked as she collated and stacked the copies spewing from the machine.

Usually everything Vera and Isaac did together was explosive and Hannah wasn't sure she wanted to take part in another of their guerrilla theater performances. But reproductive rights was an important issue to her and she wanted to support social justice. Besides, it was Saturday and Robert had a hangover. And she enjoyed Vera's company.

Hannah yawned and gave Robert a hearty pat on the backside, "Well since I'm obviously not coming with him, I guess I should do something worthwhile and go with you. But I need a ride back home; will that work out?"

"Yeah, sure. Someone should be heading up this way, though I think Isaac and I will be staying down south. We'll figure it out."

Robert continued with his original plan of coffee, shower and infinite research—he was tenacious in his quest to unravel every move that Charles Hurwitz had made in the takeover of Pacific Lumber. He knew the information existed to implicate Hurwitz as a criminal and he knew he could find it. When he did, Hurwitz would pay. Robert had a winning hand; he could feel it. It was amazing that this trail of deceit was so obvious. Hurwitz must have some really low friends in really high places. Robert smirked to himself as he considered the irony of his own situation, as in high friends in low places. He wasn't discouraged in the least. In fact, he was stimulated by the challenge. A lot could be accomplished when you studied the methods of the best.

MEETING EARL

LATER

The highway between Eureka and Willits is more of an adventure than a rapid transit method of traveling. The road winds through miles of forest, punctuated occasionally by a forgettable roadside vendor. Along a steep, precipitous road-cut, barely clinging to the sheer rock face of the canyon walls, this road parallels the Eel River. The abrupt descent to the turquoise waters of the Eel below invokes both awe and terror.

The Eel River is named for the lampreys which reside there; extremely primitive fish which attach themselves to their victims—generally other fish—by using their mouths to rasp holes through which they can drink blood and other body fluids. While negotiating the narrow, second-gear turns 150 vertical feet above the canyon, many a traveler is reminded of their own bodily fluids.

Sitting in the back seat, Hannah was definitely feeling the urge to release her bladder. Vera pulled over onto a turnout and Hannah headed into the bushes. Rest stops never seemed to be strategically placed.

Isaac's voice in the background was excitedly chirping away, followed by the occasional "um" or "uh huh" from Vera. Hannah listened to him rave and smiled inwardly. Isaac was an artist, a musician; his world was composed of possibilities and potentials. He often ignored the facts, which are found on the outside, in order to seek the truth, found on the inside. Hannah loved him and accepted him, as all of his friends did and gave him the emotional support to contribute in his unique and tireless way.

Isaac was at war. He wore "camo" pants with a T-shirt which shouted some pledge to dance, sing and shake a fist at everything he found offensive. He swore the names of his enemies and sang the names of his friends. He loved his friends unconditionally and he loved the ancient forests passionately; especially the ones on Pacific Lumber land.

With Vera at the wheel and Isaac providing a running monologue framed in a backdrop of Neil Young's insistent whining, Hannah was able to leisurely observe. Isaac, with his head full of generous curls, bobbing and twitching as he spoke, only highlighted Vera's sedate demeanor.

Vera had been a fighter for so long that she almost seemed to lose her sense of self. Certainly she obscured her more feminine side, even while being an ardent crusader for feminism. Her hair, worn long and parted in the middle, was harnessed in an efficient braid, further testimony to her personal rebellion. She invariably dressed in jeans, a T-shirt displaying her "political message of the day," an oversized jacket for her petite frame and comfortable sandals or hiking boots. No "cruel shoes" for Vera; she was all business all the time.

The carload arrived at the health clinic just before noon. As always, Willits was basking in full sun, with clean sidewalks and cheerful townsfolk. "Willits: a nice place to raise a family—bad place to get an abortion." The pro-choice people were lined up on the shady side of the clinic, while the anti-choice folks took the sunlit side. They squinted fiercely as they proudly marched back and forth, invoking the name of God and the sacredness of life as they saw it.

Vera waved at her good friend, Alice, who had arrived from the south. They had been quite close for years and always enjoyed talking business—which wasn't their shared trade as carpenters, but their shared passion as political activists. Both women had endured discrimination in predominately male fields—politics and carpentry—and were adamant about supporting women's rights.

The recent flurry of protests at abortion clinics throughout the United States inspired them even more. The rhetoric against abortion was as stale as it was worrisome: these people claimed to have a god on their side—similar claims had been made to cover every heinous crime in history. Vera thought about this often, as if it was the subject of a Ph.D. thesis: *Even Hitler had a chaplain in his inner core.*

"Great to see so many people here!" Vera was pleased with the opportunity for exposure. As she and Isaac unloaded the musical instruments, she flashed a sardonic smile, "But, we can't let those fanatics dictate the program. We've been working on some songs which ought to heat things up here."

Alice helped them set up the stage, "Yeah, I was concerned when I saw how nice the weather was; it's hard to devote time to protesting when the short weekend arrives." She glanced over her shoulder at the man walking towards them. "Oh, I'd like you to meet my newest housemate, Earl. Interesting guy. You may recall meeting him when we were all involved in the El Salvador campaign?"

A large, heavyset man with a beard and glasses stepped up. He appeared to be in his mid-40s and judging by the breadth of his belly, he was well fed and little exercised. Though he smiled warmly as he extended his giant paw of a hand, Vera detected something odd. She might have paid attention to this gut feeling had Isaac not been simultaneously handing her music notes as he hurriedly bounced by. Her fleeting sense fled as she shook Earl's hand and grasped the loose papers.

"Pleased to meet you, Earl." She looked him over carefully. "Actually, I do recall seeing you a few years ago. Glad to see you're still active in human rights."

"I hear you. I know there are a lot of supporters out there who don't have the guts to act. Not me. I'm not going to sit back while this government interferes with my freedom." Earl's size alone would render him a formidable opponent once angered. "I hear you're drafting legislation for the ancient forest protection. Right on! We need more defenders." He extended his fist in the air and grinned in solidarity.

Vera smiled back and said, "True, if more people would stand up for their beliefs, the rest of us wouldn't have to work so hard." She appeared wistful as she unpacked more boxes. "But, we gotta understand the social intimidation that these professional people are under. When your income suffers because of your convictions…"

"Well hell, I'm not intimidated by much of anything. I know what our government's up to and I'm gonna fight them all the way," Earl proudly proclaimed.

Vera mumbled, "See you later," wondering if he was a Vietnam veteran. He looked about the right age and certainly had that eerie, disjointed sense of bravado so common to survivors of war trauma.

She headed over to the smiling group assembled around Isaac and his guitar. She glanced at the opposition marching angrily in the bright sunlight. *Why were those people always so unhappy looking? Was it because their husbands insisted on "eminent domain" of their bodies? Was it because they carried so much tonnage that they were forced to wear voluminous shiny-fabric blouses over their skin-tight polyester stretch pants? I'd be unhappy, too,* Vera thought, *if I was wearing synthetics in the noonday sun.*

As Isaac gathered the group with humorous chants and slogans, Vera joined him with her fiddle. He picked up his guitar and together they performed a set of original protest and freedom songs. *They're pretty good,* Hannah thought, as she watched the crowd clap their hands. Isaac was an accomplished guitarist, even if his voice wasn't much more melodic than Neil Young's. Anyway, Isaac had a broader range than Neil's and when accompanied by Vera and her fiddle, his voice needed to be less impressive than his lyrics.

Will the fetus,
be unborn now;
by and by, Lord,
by and by…

Sung to the melody of "Will the circle, be unbroken…," the song was definitely irreverent; in fact, downright tacky. Hannah was embarrassed; *couldn't they find a less offensive way to express their views? They're so intense about defending…don't they realize how insensitive they are?*

Just then, a marching, male anti-choicer, walked menacingly towards the musical performance and shouted: "Murderers. May the Lord strike you down for your blasphemy!"

Someone retorted with, "Get the U.S. out of my uterus!"

"You're pagans, doing the work of the devil!"

A volley of angry cries was fired from both directions, which only inspired Isaac to hop around more excitedly as he changed chords. He watched Vera as she deftly moved the bow across the strings of her fiddle. He was more in love with her at these moments than ever. How perfect to bond with another tireless warrior; someone who felt his fears and pain and who shared his joys and triumphs. He shared everything with her. He couldn't imagine being closer to another human being.

The performers seemed unimpressed with the fusillade of ugliness directed at them as the television cameras captured it all. The rally proceeded with more music, more shouting, more references to women's rights vs. devil worshiping—a predictable scene for an abortion demo. They got what they wanted: media attention. And there was no physical violence. Vera was an experienced organizer with a reputation for non-violent confrontation, with an emphasis on confrontation.

After the demo broke up, Earl was walking back to the cars with Isaac, describing his experiences as a political organizer in the Bay Area. Isaac seemed to warm up to Earl, enjoying his fearless approach to third party electoral campaigns. Isaac, himself, was contemplating a run for Congress opposing a political carpet-bagger from the Democratic Party.

"Yeah, Vera and I were just talking about Congressman Bosco's endorsement of offshore oil drilling. What a slime—he sells out the resources of the Northcoast even when the citizens voted to preserve them. We thought it would be hilarious to stage a protest in Doug Bosco's own backyard…you know, a nice little oil slick in his family's swimming pool!" Isaac and Earl were still chortling over the image as Vera caught up to them.

"Let's get together tonight. You guys are filled with great stories." Earl said he hadn't met such interesting folks in ages; he looked as though he was thoroughly enjoying himself.

Isaac was always up for new encounters. "Sure, Earl, why don't you follow us back to my place and hang out for a while?"

Earl shrugged affirmatively, "Sounds good. I've been meaning to get up into the redwoods anyway. Looks like a plan." The large man's eyes crinkled as he smiled, creating deep furrows on his cheeks. He walked purposefully to his car, opened the trunk briefly and then locked it. Earl was eager for this trip.

After leaving Willits, there was continued discussion of future actions, of potential logging atrocities to monitor. Isaac had heard that Louisiana Pacific was closing their Potter Valley mill and moving production to Mexico. Speculation was high that the environmentalists would be fingered as the cause.

He and Vera were already planning strategies to counter such allegations. Isaac favored a theatrical approach, "Let's dress up like logs wearing sombreros—we could even play mariachi music!" He licked his lips as his mind raced over the possibilities. "Yeah. Maybe we could get a few disgruntled employees to join us in the demo. We could serve everyone old-growth burritos!" He smiled wickedly as he envisioned the colorful media event.

Vera favored a press conference speech. Of course, a new song would be needed to commemorate the whole occasion. Talk continued; in fact, talk never ceased with Isaac and Vera around.

Shortly after Isaac's carload arrived at his home on the Eel River, Earl pulled up to the house in his trashed-out American sedan—a classic narc car, which caused everyone to chuckle. Earl and Alice walked up as Earl held out a six-pack of "good beer." Everyone enjoyed a nice cold one after the drive, sitting on the deck, chatting in the mid-afternoon sun.

They reminisced about the demo and how the abortion issue always seems to attract Bible-toting fanatics. Hannah mused, "Funny how society gives so much credence to the Bible as a source of authority."

Vera replied acidly, "Yeah, right, so I protested the Contras in Nicaragua—totally legally, right?—and I get arrested. But no problem harassing legal protests, as long as you carry a Bible. Makes good sense."

Isaac guffawed, "Hey, Earth First! is still facing trespassing charges for blockading that illegal logging road in the Enchanted Meadows. It kills me; those loggers were in direct violation of the timber harvest plan. I guess we forgot to mention that Jesus sent us!"

Everyone had a laugh about the hypocrisy of justice in the name of a god. Hannah listened to her friends and reflected on her own beliefs about the meaning of god and reverence.

"How can they claim to love and honor the creator, but not the creation?"

Vera, pragmatic as always, replied, "Because to honor the creation takes creativity and work. To honor the creator just takes lip-service and maybe an hour on Sunday."

Earl broke the silent tension. "Maybe we can lighten things up here with a fat doobie—it usually helps me!"

Hannah went into the house to search for matches. She wished Vera wasn't so negative about everything. *"Can't we just have a pleasant philosophical discussion without it becoming part of her battle?"* She returned with a lighter and handed it to Earl.

"Hey Vera, I heard you might know where I can score some more weed?" Earl asked as he dropped the herb onto the rolling paper. "You know, just a few ounces; maybe even a quarter pound if it's really good."

Isaac hurriedly interjected, "We never buy or sell that stuff. Where did you hear that?"

Vera glared at Isaac, then cautiously responded, "Uh, yeah, I really don't know about that. I hear it's around but I'm not into it."

Vera was a little disturbed by Earl's request, but quickly rationalized that since he was with Alice, he had to be okay.

People in Humboldt and Mendocino counties often receive requests for varied amounts of pot. Everyone knew that tens of millions of dollars' worth of high-grade marijuana was grown in this part of northern California, "The Emerald Triangle." Some consider it to be the finest in the world. It was only natural for outsiders to assume that if you lived there you must be growing it alongside your primroses and daffodils.

Alice lit up Earl's freshly rolled joint. Hannah lay on the grass, inspecting the wildflowers. Isaac sprawled on the porch steps tuning his guitar. Even Vera, serious and thoughtful, sat back in a state of mellow repose. They all seemed calm and comfortable after hours of discussion and action. Alice got up slowly and took a leather satchel out of the car. She unzipped the bag and extracted a camera. Stepping back, she took a couple of shots of the smiling group on the deck, as if memorializing the day for posterity.

"I have a great idea for all you tireless warriors," Earl suddenly exclaimed. He fished in his pocket for his keys as he lumbered over to the trunk of his car. He then extricated a large, bulky bag and returned to the steps.

With a great display of mystery, he grabbed Vera's hand and pulled her to her feet. She giggled a bit as he positioned her in the sun, with trees for a backdrop and called out to Alice to ready her camera.

"C'mon, Earl, what are you doing?" Vera laughed, as Earl made a big show of arranging her stance and even positioning Isaac's Earth First! baseball cap on her head.

Earl brought the still burning joint over to Vera, put his arm around her shoulder and said, "See, this is one way we can defend the earth; enjoy the resources!" He then asked Alice to take a photo of them while Vera and the rest cackled.

As Vera leaned against a large madrone, still smiling, Earl walked over to his bag and proudly pulled out a formidable looking semi-automatic rifle.

"Whoa, that thing isn't loaded is it?"

"Ha! No, but we are—that's the important thing, right? Here Vera, hold this rifle. It will make a great picture with your T-shirt and hat; there's no doubt that you won't compromise!" Earl seemed tremendously excited by this idea. "This is going to be a classic photo, kind of like the Patty Hearst one as 'Tanya.'"

Alice took several shots of Vera with the AK-47, as Vera affected various militant postures and aggressive stares. She actually enjoyed the theatrics while everyone was laughing it up and cheering the display on.

Isaac was itching to be in on the action; he wasn't about to be left out of this kind of fun. He ran into the house and returned, sporting his own "No Compromise" t-shirt. "Shoot me, too," he yelled, as he grabbed the rifle from her arms with all the fervor of a three-year-old snatching an ice-cream cone from his little brother's hand.

"No rush, there's lots of film and there are plenty of rifles, enough to go around." *Skinny poet with the big gun,* Earl laughed to himself. *This will be worth it.*

The camera clicked on and on with Vera, then Isaac, then both, posing like Huey Newton and the Black Panthers. "It's a damn good thing *60 Minutes* isn't watching this. We'd be 'dead media meat' in the first minute," declared Isaac as he experienced some vague realization that these photos could actually be damaging if taken out of context.

"You want a copy of these? Great for the scrapbook."

"Sure Earl. A copy for each of us and, uh…you will destroy the negatives?" Vera asked, still giggling as she aimed the rifle at a picture of Charles Hurwitz, which adorned the dart board hanging from Isaac's front door.

THE BOARD MEETING

MEANWHILE

The 36th floor of 100 California Street looks down on Coit Tower and across San Francisco Bay to Alcatraz and Angel Island. To reach the law offices of Morrison and Forester and its three hundred attorneys from the street, requires a journey through fifty-foot high golden bronze doors and a stroll across the Italian marble and granite lined lobby to the richly adorned elevator doors.

Thirty-five floors later the elevator empties out into Mo Fo's lobby. Mo Fo is one of the mega-firms with corporate clients reading like the Fortune 500 industrial giant list.

The first thing you notice when disembarking is the view past the receptionist's desk—itself a thing of beauty—through a large meeting room and beyond. The glass walls of the room and then the external walls, allow the City to be brought up close. The startling panorama evokes the feeling of flight. Clerks, visible through the walls, come and go from the meeting room bringing coffee and juices to the six men who were about to meet. Well-dressed paralegals and staff attorneys buzzed up and down the wide, intersecting corridors. Finished, the clerks withdrew, sealing the meeting doors from intruders.

"Gentlemen, does everyone know one another? Perhaps not, let's introduce ourselves. I am William Castle, senior vice-president of Hill and Knowlton. My responsibilities include supervising special operations requiring the coordination of a crisis response team." Clad like the others in gray pinstripes, Castle spoke with an obvious military command. The others sat at attention, not anxious, but alert.

To Castle's left was a younger man, with a slick, severe haircut and an aura of self-importance, a tempered arrogance. "Donald Wink, vice president for media relations with Hill and Knowlton, based here in the San Francisco office for this campaign. My responsibility is to manage local and regional media in northern California. We will merge our efforts with the larger national campaigns of the organizations forming the so-called Wise Use Movement." Wink smiled and moved his left hand away from his body, palm up, to the bulky man to his left.

"My name is Herbert Gordon, with Ketchum Communications. We have been engaged by the Louisiana Pacific Corporation and the California Forest Products Association to provide services worldwide. We work in every country hosting an LP operation. I am president of Ketchum's subsidiary, the Special Operations Division, boasting highly-trained experts in programs with high visibility. Our responsibility is to perform counter-operations. Generally, our projects form local opposition to terrorist groups." Bald, well-dressed, looking every bit the executive but with features and gestures suggesting benign violence, Gordon was a spook in every sense of the word. He'd once served his country in the CIA. Now he served the clients who sought Ketchum's services. These clients tended to be owners of his country, as well as a number of foreign countries.

Across the table from Gordon sat Joe Wheeler, president of Louisiana Pacific's Western Operations. Short and stout, Wheeler spoke with a voice free of emotions. "Joe Wheeler; LP. We provide the organizing of local citizen groups, including those engaged in political action favoring our point of view. We maintain two separate in-house public relations staffs in Mendocino and Humboldt counties. We are prepared to operate within our overall campaign in any way that serves our common goal."

Wheeler turned to his left, looking directly at the younger, thinner man who waited gracefully for Wheeler to signify that he had completed his speech.

With a nod of recognition the younger man gestured his readiness to begin. "I am Jacques Lazard, in-house counsel for Maxxam Inc. I am assigned to assist a coordinated response to the political threat to Pacific Lumber's timber operations in nCalifornia. We, too, have local in-house PR within our larger corporate system."

Lazard had more. "Please let me remind all of the participants in this room of the need for utmost confidentiality. We assume Mr. Gordon will be empowered to act as a result of this meeting. It is our position that he must be given our complete confidence and support—secrecy being a major component.

"Further we insist that each of us make the most of Mr. Gordon's efforts by supervising our respective public relations staff effectively. Any concerns which may later arise should be placed with Mr. Castle who is empowered by both Maxxam and Louisiana Pacific to coordinate our various chores." Lazard was every bit a lawyer, cool to the colder Wheeler, speaking from a deeply ingrained belief in his right to dominate.

The last man, sitting to Castle's right, listened quietly to Lazard's longer speech. He turned his attention from Lazard to Gordon as he began to speak. "Julius Steinberg, with Paul Butterfield Associates. Our role, on behalf of Mr. Lazard's firm, is to provide specific intelligence as to the whereabouts and itinerary of various persons engaged in terrorist activity, or in support of this activity, as well as identifying their political and financial supporters, wherever they may be. We will work closely with Mr. Gordon in this respect and provide services from the Bay Area to Humboldt and Mendocino counties."

Abruptly Steinberg squared his broad shoulders and nodded to Castle.

"Thank you, gentlemen." Castle rose slowly from his chair, turned toward the nearby display of charts. Gesturing, he said, "We each have adequately described what will be our working roles for the next year through the November '90 election. Focus groups have brought our attention to what must be our prime objective if we are to defeat the environmentalists in the coming elections. Namely, we must develop a plausible case that environmentalists support terrorism, want to destroy the American family and are willing to force radical ideas upon all of us—especially the poorly educated working men—harming regional and national economies.

"Hill and Knowlton has developed a larger game plan. There are six stated areas of concern in the written plan, but we here today need only to address ourselves to the seventh unstated concern. This group, meeting here, is for Special Operations and functions, as Mr. Lazard suggested, providing thoughtful, coordinated action—but discretely, as required by the circumstances.

"Mr. Gordon's firm will act outside of our individual knowledge with the assistance of Mr. Steinberg's firm to ensure events occur in the opposition's camp that will ultimately defeat them. Mr. Gordon is experienced in our nation's intelligence organizations. He has the network of the Center for Strategic Information Services to draw upon.

"Mr. Steinberg can rely upon his contacts with the FBI—his former employer. We should not doubt our capability to succeed if we develop a sense of the desired timing by which Mr. Gordon and Mr. Steinberg will guide their operations. So let's roll up our sleeves and get to work."

For anyone who walked through the lobby, the meeting was a small event in the bustle of important affairs occurring throughout the building. Six men in a glass cage, seemingly surrounded by the gray-blue sky of a typical November day. Clouds sped past in what must have been a blustery wind on the streets below, but there, sheltered from nature, the view could have been nothing more than a version of Koyaanisqatsi thrown up behind them on a screen.

MEET CHUCK CUSHMAN

The meeting ended with a bit of confusion and acrimony. LP's people were not happy sharing the stage with others. As they left, their leader informed everyone that they would do as they pleased, without the need for consultation.

Castle had tried to calm the nerves but failed. With LP gone, he assured everyone it was a "plausible deniability play. They want to say they were out of the room, if they have to."

Within minutes everyone was moving toward the door.

Herbert Gordon stayed in the boardroom until everyone had left, then carefully collected all the papers the participants had left behind. He was trained to see the value in trash, and he knew that others, like competitors to his client, may someday find these scribbled notes and cryptic agendas valuable.

As he finished, his cell phone nagged him.

"Julius," Gordon answered.

"Herb," Steinberg said. "Good to see you today. Wonder if you have time to meet someone who will come to our aid."

"I have a few minutes before I must leave for SFO. A drink at the bar downstairs would work for me. Five minutes."

"Done."

Gordon was getting tired. East Coast time was demanding sleep while the West was still working. He took the elevator to the ground, carrying two large valises. When he walked in the door to the bar he was escorted to a table with Steinberg and a rough-looking fellow dressed in Levis and a collarless shirt. As Gordon approached he stood and offered his hand.

"Chuck Cushman, National Inholders Association."

"Ah, yes. Your name was mentioned to me earlier today. Julius spoke of you."

'Herb, Chuck only has two minutes."

"Thanks, Julius. Mr Gordon, Julius and I have been working together for a year or so, building a grassroots organization that will train local citizens to resist the leftists who are trying to take our resources from us."

"Skip the rhetoric," Gordon cut in. "From time to time I will ask Mr. Steinberg to deliver a suggestion to you. He consults me for some of the finer points of strategy. Glad to meet you."

Gordon stood and waited for Cushman to rise, shake hands and leave. He did. Gordon sat down.

"Herb, so we're back together again. It's been a decade or more."

"Italy. 1965."

"How is private enterprise suiting you?"

"I am just riding a desk and getting fat. You?"

"Very well, thank you. Same tasks as always."

"Getting wet?"

"No more of that. Letting the young deal for now."

"This job feels like it will go in that direction."

"If so, we'll tap Cushman's contacts."

"I have others in mind, but that's for later. My plane is twenty minutes from loading. Must go."

"Have a good flight. My best to the wife."

Steinberg watched Gordon leave. The waitress paid attention to him. He ordered a scotch. He thought about a vacation in Hawaii. His wife had left him a year ago and he considered stepping out again to see what was what in the dating world. Hawaii made that easier in his estimation. Maybe next year, he thought, when this job is over.

ARGUS

I t was just a typical winter day in Ukiah. Even with the status of the county seat of Mendocino, this small town was generally quiet and law-abiding. The townsfolk were good citizens: farmers, ranchers, loggers and business owners serving the needs of their community. Willits and Laytonville to the north, as well as the city of Mendocino on the coast to the west, harbored a consistent population of hippies, but even those folks seemed more interested in legitimate coffee houses, micro-breweries, bookstores and a host of cottage industries than illegal activities. Sure, there were pockets of marijuana cultivation, just as in Humboldt County to the north, but the growers were generally peaceful; the government raids often confiscated the pot but left the people. Only so much can fit in a helicopter.

Ukiah Chief of Police Fred Clinger slouched back in his chair as he opened the daily mail. He recognized the usual sprinkling of official announcements and policy revisions. Glancing at each missive, he tossed them laconically into the appropriate pile. Some of this would have to be filed—leave it for the night clerk. Not much night action in the winter, anyway. The summer tourists would soon enough bring their own form of headache for law enforcement.

Reaching for an envelope addressed as "personal & confidential," Clinger suddenly sat up in his chair. He immediately noticed that there was no return address and that the postmark was from the North Bay—

that covered a huge area. Carefully opening up the envelope, he pulled out a photo of a woman in an aggressive stance pointing an Uzi-type rifle. She was wearing a hat and a T-shirt, both emblazoned with: "Earth First! No Compromise in the Defense of Our Earth!" Now, the Chief had met some of these folks—environmentalists—but he'd never thought of them as causing much trouble. He adjusted his reading glasses as he extracted the type-written letter accompanying the photo. He read the letter quickly through once and then a second time more carefully.

Dear Chief Clinger:

I joined Earth First! to be able to report illegal activities of that organization. Now I want to establish a contact to provide information to the authorities. The leader and main force of Earth First! in Ukiah is Vera Greene. She is facing a trespassing charge in connection with the Earth First! sabotage of a logging road in the Mendocino area. She did jail time in Sonoma County for blocking the federal building to support the Communist government in Nicaragua.

Greene and the Ukiah Earth First! are planning vandalism directed at Congressman Doug Bosco to protest offshore oil drilling. Earth First! recently began automatic weapons training. Greene sells marijuana to finance Earth First! activities. She sometimes receives and sends marijuana by U.S. mail. On December 23 she mailed a box of marijuana at the Ukiah post office. There is no point in pursuing local charges. But the use of the U.S. mail means serious federal charges. If you would like to receive confidential information on short notice to make possible an arrest on federal charges at a U.S. post office next time she mails dope, please do the following: Place an advertisement in the "Notices" section of the classified ad section of the Ukiah Daily Journal. It should be addressed to "Dear A" and give the name and telephone number(s), preferably 24-hour, of a detective who should be called to receive

this information. When a call is made, I will identify myself as
"Argus."

Clinger put the letter down and took another look at the photo. The woman looked serious enough. But then, again, his ex-wife had looked seriously in love in their wedding portrait.

He thought about some of the memos he'd seen lately about those environmentalists. Humboldt County was enmeshed in a pile of lawsuits between timber interests and those tree-hugging types and more legal action was anticipated here in Mendocino County. Louisiana Pacific had warned of suspected tree spiking, but no one had ever mentioned any use of firearms.

The Chief, perplexed, but not disturbed, thought about all this awhile longer before discussing the letter with his deputy. "Well, Peterson, what do you make of it?"

The deputy looked it over thoroughly for about the tenth time while nodding his head. "Gee Chief, I'd say this woman looks like she means business."

"Yeah, that's true. But what about the letter? Notice anything in particular about the letter?"

Peterson looked blankly at the letter and then the Chief, waiting for some clues to jump out at him. He saw nothing unusual other than that it was typed on an old typewriter, or a well-used one.

"Most letters these days seemed to come from home computers," Clinger said, then paused to wipe the corner of his glasses. "The writer says that he wants to establish a local contact with authorities…that he's already obtained membership in this group…ah…Earth First!."

"Hey, then that means this guy is planted by some agency, right?"

"Correct. So, if this…Argus…is already an informant, who is he working for? It's not us, or I sure as hell would know about it! No; it's got to be FBI. It's got to be some secret operation. But," Clinger paused again to reconsider his idea, "but if it were the FBI they would have briefed me."

Peterson jumped in excitedly: "But what if the FBI needed all this secrecy because they were closing in…ah…they almost had their suspect…ah…they…were setting up a sting! Yeah—*Miami Vice!*"

Chief Clinger nodded his head thoughtfully, then picked up the photo again. He scratched his neck a few times and scrutinized the photo. "Well, I'd say this letter is pretty slick. Maybe this guy has watched too much TV—like you Peterson!"

Clinger scratched his neck again. The Chief had lived and worked alongside pot growers and pot smokers enough to know that they were not fearsome or unusually difficult folks. It was those speed drugs he was seeing so much of these days that seemed to really rile people up.

Peterson squinted his eyes as he spoke: "You think maybe this Argus is an ex-boyfriend or lover or some angry guy she knows? Maybe wants to set up his ex so that she pays for dumping him?"

"Hmmm. Could be, could be. I just think it's mighty unusual to be setting up someone for dealing pot." Clinger liked his Ukiah post because it was all so simple. They didn't get much violence or even much mystery in this county. He wasn't looking forward to some big city FBI agent waltzing into his office and ordering his men around for some classified big government purpose. He made the decisions around here and he was in charge.

Peterson spoke out, "Well, Chief, do you think the FBI is operating this guy? Who else could he be informing for?"

"Let's just place a response for our Mr. Argus and take it from there."

A few days later, in the *Ukiah Daily Journal*, a small inconspicuous ad appeared in the personals:

Dear A

Please call Mark at 463-1708

The ad ran for two weeks. Chief Clinger and his deputy waited for further contact. No response was received. The photo and letter were filed in the "Suspicious Activities" folder under "Drugs."

"60 MINUTES"

The well-groomed reporter towered over Isaac, even when they were sitting. Isaac, to his credit, had sported his best attire: clean Levis and a wrinkled, but unstained, Guatemalan print shirt topped by a handsome wool vest, a nice contrast with the reporter's own three-piece suit. His infamous shoulder-length, kinky black curls bobbed with every fidget he made, creating an uncanny resemblance to those spring-mounted cutsie dolls placed in the back of certain individuals' cars.

The backstage director barked orders over the microphone and the attending crew responded immediately. He coughed to clear his throat and then spoke, "Okay; we have a take for *60 Minutes*, episode 27. Mr. Bradley, you can begin."

The reporter smiled benignly and began speaking, giving a history of environmentalism and a synopsis of the recent Northcoast events, especially those of Earth First!. He turned to Isaac, "So what exactly is this 'Redwood Summer'?"

Isaac smiled and took a deep breath. "We are planning a series of mass protests and acts of civil disobedience to call attention to the plight of the last remaining old growth redwood. We hope that by staging these events we can garner national attention on the current logging practices which threaten the health and vitality of our lands."

"So you will be trespassing on private property—timber property—as well as demonstrating on public lands to make your point?"

"Yes, sir. We believe that by focusing attention on destructive timber practices we can slow the corporations down to a sustained yield before there is nothing to save."

The reporter looked at his notes and spoke: "How many protesters are you expecting and who are these people?"

"We are reaching out to college campuses across California and the United States. We also have affiliates in other environmental groups. We are anticipating at least one thousand, and probably several thousands to attend our various rallies and demonstrations throughout northern California."

"And what sort of training can you provide these roaming bands of protesters?"

Isaac sat up straight in his chair and smiled warmly at the skeptical, but good-natured dig. "We are calling only for nonviolent protests this summer. We will be providing nonviolence training and strict nonviolence guidelines. We have held hundreds of protests and, although violence has been directed against us, we have never initiated violence against others. We will be working in conjunction with the county sheriffs and local police departments. We intend to inform our law enforcement contacts of all of our plans—and of course we will keep the media well informed, too." He beamed his most engaging smile. "After all, without constant media exposure, we can't accomplish our purpose."

The reporter smiled back. "Well, Mr. Winwood, you have said that these planned demonstrations are patterned after the civil rights protests of the sixties. What do you think will come from these Redwood Summer protests? Do you really expect thousands of protesters and the thousands of timber workers to maintain an atmosphere of respect and nonviolence?"

Isaac responded quickly, thankful that he had made notes in advance of arriving at the TV station. "In the 1960s, civil rights workers were arrested and injured while maintaining their nonviolence approach. The same will surely happen here and, as a result, there will be a heightened local and national consciousness as to the right the forest has to exist for its own sake. We will further the civil rights of the earth."

"This brings up some interesting questions about civil rights and the issue of environmentalism intruding on civil rights. Some people would say that the rights of human beings must always come before the rights of other species." The reporter picked up his glass of water as he eagerly watched Isaac answer this delicate question.

Isaac cleared his throat. "I'm not an environmentalist, I'm an earth warrior. I am earth defending itself. I'm trying to feralize myself." The reporter eyes widened as he looked at his guest. Isaac persisted, "You see, once you start thinking biocentrically you start to see everything in a new light." He picked up his glass of water and grabbed the napkin underneath. "This is not a napkin, it's a tree. The language is different but the thing's still the same. If you want to call someone something 'bad,' call him a human."

After regaining his composure, the reporter asked, "Just how far would you go, Mr. Winwood, to call attention to your cause of saving the last of the old growth?" Inwardly he was praying for something sensational with such a baiting question; Isaac was ripe for the picking.

"Well," Isaac mused, settling back comfortably in his chair, "if I contracted some fatal disease I would definitely do something like strap dynamite on myself and take out the Glen Canyon Dam. Or maybe the Maxxam building in Los Angeles after it's closed up for the night."

Even the stage hands were wide-eyed after that statement and the director fortuitously called for a break. The reporter responded quickly with, "Well, the redwoods certainly have a defender in you, or should we say, an eco-warrior? We'll be back after these messages from our proud sponsors."

The interview was concluded on a less sensational note and Isaac left the studio shaking hands. Before leaving the station he immediately sought out a phone and dialed Vera. "Whaddya think? C'mon wasn't it just outrageous that we made it to *60 Minutes?* I'm so stoked I can hardly stand still—this was such a blast." He was panting, breathless with excitement.

There was a weighty pause when Isaac finished speaking. Vera tightened up her mouth and then almost hissed into the phone, "You fucking idiot…you are truly incredible."

"Whaaat? Uh…ah…what do you mean?"

"Isaac—go away. Just go away somewhere where no one knows you. I can't believe that I'm associated with you." She exhaled forcefully. "I'm serious. You didn't make any points with that bravado crap—I'm still stunned."

"But Vera—look at the passion and power I showed. Look at how I described the redwoods and how I explained how dedicated we are. Wasn't that the point?"

"I think the only point was for you to get your face on national TV. I gotta go now. Don't call me for awhile." He felt the slamming of the receiver in his head.

Isaac stood there, dangling the dead phone in his hand, mystified at her reaction. She sure was hard to please these days.

FORESTS FOREVER

Isaac still had his fan-base. Hannah, Alice and some of the others, who had spent a month to write the initiative they called "Forests Forever," stood at the podium admiring Isaac's ability to gather the representatives of the media to an event.

A warm buzz filled the air. The Lady Bird Johnson Redwood Grove held the ocean breeze above its canopy, leaving the sound of rushing wind at a distance, its ebb and flow reminiscent of foaming surf. The few insects, having survived the first cold weather of winter, spun around theirs ears like messengers from nature's heart singing about the web of life.

From her place on the platform Hannah could feel the forest looming above her head. Even here, in a parking lot, the ecstatic experience of an ancient forest affected her. Her imagination conjured scenes of fern filled creeks and the powerful spiritual lessons she had learned from the wilderness. She felt every bit a defender of her legacy. *Glorious*, Hannah thought, *a moment to remember. I hope I can recall this day for my journal. I wonder if giving birth feels this way.*

As her thoughts returned to the news conference, suddenly animated again, she tossed her hair out of her face and took the step forward to bring her to the microphone. The two dozen reporters with pens, recorders and video cameras ready, raised their eyes to take her in. A human silence grew, raising the volume of the grove's constant reminders of the living earth.

The "Forests Forever" emblazoned banner, behind the small group on stage, was rustled by a whirling stream of cold air moving up the canyon in front of her. Taking it as some signal of readiness Hannah placed her mouth to the edge of the microphone.

"Thank you all for coming here today to hear the announcement of Forests Forever's historic attempt to alter what appears to be the inevitable destruction of the last ancient forests in private hands and to turn back the tide of resource exploitation threatening countless species, including the birds that fill the grove around us and the salmon which for an eon have fed the people who have inhabited this region." Hannah spun her words like fibers for fine cloth. She spoke with a determined slowness, each word carrying a kiss for every mind and heart she hoped would hear her.

Robert, who stood amongst the reporters, felt the wetness on his cheek he had come to expect from Hannah's mouth. His mind joined the breeze as it fled past him. He thought of her and their beloved Mattole River as one and the same. Her words ran over his face—a strong current rushing to the sea.

He turned slowly, bringing his mind back to the scene around him. The nearness of so much electronic equipment made him nervous and he felt out of place. "They steal our souls," he was fond of saying, but now he added, *And probably a good thing to have happen here today if it would help get the story straight.* A momentary fear caught him as he recalled the media's recent tendency to turn everything about the struggle for the forests on its head. Black became white in the evening news. *I hope they get it right this time.*

"….we hope we will complete the process of qualifying our initiative in time to make the November 1990 election ballot. If we are correct in our assessment, we will begin gathering signatures in the spring of '90, culminating in early May when the Secretary of State, March Fong Yu, announces that the signatures we will file with her are sufficient to bring Forests Forever to a vote next fall." Hannah's voice became more mechanical when she abandoned her poet's tone for the efficient organizer's certitude and conjecture. She was bolstered by contingencies. Her announcement of the plan to make new law was absent doubts about the small group's ability to deliver on her promises. She broke out in beads of perspiration, worrying her eyes with a salty sting while her mind cast stones at the smooth surface water of her heart. *I hope we can do this*, she silently prayed.

Questions rang out from the crowd at the end of her speech, but nothing out of the ordinary. Details were contained in the handouts Alice and Isaac had passed out to the reporters as they arrived. No reporter asked a question not included in the summaries.

As the reporters left to return to town and their offices, Hannah joined Robert for the ride to the Eureka TV studios for sit-down interviews for the six o'clock news. It had been Isaac's idea to hold a conference in the grove followed by a special interview at each station. He had been certain Forests Forever would get a better report if Hannah went the extra mile for such potent news outlets.

One good thing about Eureka was that parking was easier than in San Francisco. They pulled up to the front door of the station, disembarked and entered the lobby of the studio. Smaller than most TV headquarters, Robert and Hannah quickly found the taping studio. Hannah was rapidly absorbed by the crew to prepare her for the lights, finding a drinking glass, fixing her microphone, readying her for a sound check. In a minute the news director called for camera and they began.

"We have the footage from the news conference to run behind this interview, but we will tape this just in case." Jim Reynard, the local newscaster reported to Hannah.

"I'm ready when you are."

"Okay. This is Forests Forever spokeswoman Hannah Caine for voice over." Reynard paused, then continued as he turned his head to look at Hannah." My first question is about Earth First! and its advocacy of spiking. Do you know anyone who has spiked a tree? Are there any Earth First!ers in your group?"

"Jim, that's off the subject I've come here to discuss." Hannah rose in her seat shoving her shoulders forward aggressively.

Robert, standing against a wall out of camera range, let out his breath in a sigh so loud that Reynard turned to him and asked him to move farther into the outer studio. Robert didn't move an inch.

"Reynard, we are here regarding our press release, at your invitation. Can we stick to the subject?" Robert spoke slowly, hoping a kind voice would deflect Reynard's fervor for spoiling Forests Forever's debut. As he spoke Robert had wandered closer to the interview set.

Reynard stood up as Robert began talking and with every step Robert took forward, Reynard took one step backwards, moving as if he feared being assaulted. "Stay back," he ordered, "We are not here to suit your needs, Devine. We never restrict our questions to those questions you want. It's news if this is Earth First!'s initiative. Besides Isaac set this interview up and Isaac is Earth First! around here."

Robert had stopped moving forward because he could see Reynard's reaction. "Don't get me wrong Jim. I feel a set up. I wonder where your concern comes from? PL? LP?"

"You're being paranoid."

"I'm paranoid? Jim do you understand who it is who brought this initiative to the Secretary of State? No? So why don't you ask that first?"

Reynard removed his microphone, declared the interview over and left the room. Robert turned to Hannah, "Do you get this?"

"Yes, we're being branded as terrorists. Nothing we do is seen for what it is. Everything is being taken as a threat. Why? Remember Cassandra— Kill the messenger." Hannah rose, grabbed Robert's hand to lead him back to the car. "There are two more stations. Let's go."

The local evening news was a disaster. "Radical Environmentalists introduce a new initiative opponents describe as draconian." "Spokeswoman, Hannah Caine, refused to deny Earth First!'s alleged connection to Forests Forever." The only visuals were of mill workers leaving work with their pails. A timber industry spokesman, who could not possibly have read the initiative text since no one but the Secretary of State had a copy, declared the industry's "commitment to fight the environmentalists to keep jobs on the Northcoast." Not one frame of Hannah, nothing from the news conference. Disaster. A set up.

The morning paper was worse. The *Times Standard* ignored the announcement altogether. That was a disappointment, but the editorial was a character assassination. "Eco-terrorism is on the rise!" blared the headline. The text offered no evidence, but reported that the paper had received a hand-written anonymous note with a large nail claiming that these would be put in trees to hurt workers. It was signed by someone calling him or herself "The Avenger." The editor believed that the letter was a fake since it showed no signs of authenticity—but no matter, this letter still indicated a rise in "eco-terrorism."

Hannah had a flamer. "Bastards. You can just see them at the Ingomar Club pinching butts, drinking scotch and trying to come up with this outrageous shit." She walked back and forth across the office floor picking up the dictionary then slamming it down each time she completed a lap.

"Princess, we are not in a fair game. We are fair game. The problem we suffer from is that we act without power when we act within the electoral system. This may be a democracy, but we better not use it or we'll lose it." Robert felt like chugging a beer or two, but had too much work to do to indulge his tendency to flee from reality before the banks closed. "Someone is acting behind the scenes to slander us. We were set up big time. I can feel that bitch, Mariah, in the cards but there is no doubt we have our Ace in the hole. We have got to raise the bet, not fold."

Hannah broke into tears, sat at her desk and sobbed, "Robert, I had visions of the beauty we are trying to preserve from selfish people. Vera, Alice and I hoped we were giving birth to something for the generations. The media gave us an abortion." Her voice broke into tremors of weeping.

Poor dear, Robert thought. "Let's head to the Sinkyone Wilderness, maybe to Bear Harbor, watch the tide come in. Up for it?"

"I love you, Robert. Give me ten minutes. I could use a rest. The others can handle the phones for a day. Tell me it's all worth it."

"It's worth it." *But the price is still going up*, he added to himself as he walked to Hannah to hug her weeping form.

THE ALBION NAVY

FIRST OF FEBRUARY

The four-wheel-drive pick-up easily negotiated the rough forest road. Here in the watershed of the Albion River, the forest was luxuriant, healthy and rich in all forms of life except human. Several endangered species had been documented there, including spotted owls and tailed frogs.

The two men in the pick-up truck arrived at the proposed helicopter site just as the sun crested the ridge. In this terrain, big rigs and heavy equipment couldn't make it into the logging site; only a helicopter could pull the logs out. The site was an intact stand old growth redwood and Douglas fir, comprising several hundred acres, though it probably only existed because of its inaccessible location. Much of Mendocino's forests had been clear cut, so that by the late '80s there was little remaining worth saving or harvesting.

In the fresh morning air, they disembarked from the truck and slowly removed their thermoses, each pouring another cup of coffee. They spoke very little. They both appeared to be inspecting the lay of the land, the feel of the forest. Though they both loved the smell of the outdoors and were comfortable with the ways of the wilderness, they would be offended if referred to as "nature lovers."

"Chilly here in this morning," said Bob as he buttoned his denim jacket over his flannel shirt and suspenders. His neatly trimmed beard and freshly washed jeans suggested a man well cared for.

In contrast, his partner, Darryl wore jeans which could have stood up by themselves and his wrinkled flannel shirt was untucked and missing a few buttons. Darryl's wife had left him a few months ago and evidently he was in no mood to attend to his laundry. Darryl was a hard worker and a good man; Bob liked his approach to completing a job with pride.

"Yeah, I noticed the dog's water had a layer of ice on it this morning. Good sign though, it should be a sunny day."

The two men busied themselves in silence, uncovering equipment and measuring the potential helicopter pad. The sun continued to crest over the last tall trees until it illuminated the river in glittering sparkles of dancing light. Bob looked over at the water and stopped in his tracks.

"Hel-lo; what the heck...?"

"I'll be damned," said Darryl, as he, too, caught sight of a brightly colored caravan of canoes and kayaks paddling steadily up the river towards them.

There were turquoise and yellow boats and there were orange and fuchsia ones; there were boats with two people in them, boats with one; there were boats with dogs, there were boats with flags and banners. A two-man kayak appeared with a fellow sitting in front playing guitar, while the guy in back played a harmonica with a small wiener dog perched in his lap.

Gus put down his harmonica, adjusted the dog's position and paddled more vigorously. "C'mon, Isaac; give me a hand here. This current's stronger than it looks."

"What a great day for action!" Isaac cheerfully responded, laying his guitar down and reaching for his paddle. The sun was beginning to warm up the entire river valley. Isaac looked across the banks to the proposed logging site, then turned to signal to the rest of the boaters to advance. Gus continued steering the boat.

"According to my map this is the spot. What a gorgeous place. I can see why LP hasn't raped it yet—they can't carry the logs off in a kayak!"

"They aren't going to carry them off in a helicopter either; we've got enough protesters to cause them a nice little delay." Gus's response between quick breaths of exertion.

The "Albion Navy," as the activists liked to refer to themselves, advanced up the river to converge with Isaac and Gus on the wide shore opposite the site. There were close to thirty activists who'd come by water and they were expecting thirty more by land. The local landowners who were also unhappy with the prospect of this old growth being logged would arrive on foot.

In sheer amazement, Bob and Darryl watched this spectacle from the forest. They'd heard about these environmentalists doing some crazy things, but never this. Though neither man expressed it at the time, each was impressed with the parade of boats and the aura of adventure surrounding this flotilla on the little Albion River.

Bob and Darryl were joined by several more private contractors' pick-up trucks loaded with men and equipment for a heavy day of logging. They knew this would be a rough job, due to the helicopter yarding, but they had no anticipation of running into protesters.

All the loggers just stood there, leaning against their trucks, surveying the scene. Most of them were bewildered; the drive in took close to two hours and no one had figured on any other access—especially by water. They'd been warned by other crews that these enviros had been showing up on job sites lately, preventing them from getting their work done. If they didn't log, they didn't get paid and the drive in had already cost them precious time.

Bob and Darryl chatted with the other men, trying to make sense of this turn of events. These were simple men; they'd grown up in their fathers' footsteps and hadn't had much chance to dream of any other kind of life. They knew the forest, they knew the trees. They knew their equipment. They more than likely didn't know each other because all that mattered in the woods was that you could trust a man to do his job. They didn't really know why these long-haired hippies were getting in their way. They just wanted to work. Employees and contractors all liked working for Louisiana Pacific because that company paid well and treated its woods workers fairly.

Static from a CB began to chatter and Bob went into his truck to respond. He slid out of the seat and walked back to the others. "Well," he cleared his throat, "that was Joe with the logging truck. He says that the deputy is following him out here. Those longhairs actually called the newspaper to do a story on them."

The boats had by now paddled over to the loggers' side of the river and the "enviros" had unfurled a large banner which stated, "Earth First! Profits last!" There were several signs which proclaimed Louisiana Pacific to be careless, even lawless, in harvesting its property.

The enviros walked over to where the loggers were clustered around their pick-up trucks. A few shoulders were hoisted up with the suspenders and some general pawing of the dirt occurred, but both groups remained quite civilized.

"Good morning, gentlemen," Isaac sunnily called out as he approached them. "We regret any inconvenience our little navy is causing, but we feel that LP has illegally begun its logging here today and we've filed for a court order to stop it."

"Listen here, buddy. We contracted to do this work and I'll be damned if I let some long-haired dope-smoker tell me I can't." Darryl was not of a mind to be told what to do by anyone these days. He'd already put up with a woman who'd told him what to do for five years straight…and look where that got him.

Isaac had anticipated some resistance and used his most persuasive voice. "I hear you. We all want to put in an honest day's work and that's why we're so upset with Louisiana Pacific for their dishonest operations. We think that there are other, easier forests to log which aren't in folks' backyards and which aren't precious old growth."

Bob spoke up, "I agree that there are other easier forests, but that's not our choice. All we can do is bid on a job and hope we get it. We leave that legal stuff up to the timber holders."

Gus walked up to the group and cut in, "See, that's the problem. We shouldn't be trusting these timber companies—not now that they're owned by big business back East. This is a local forest and it belongs to those of us who live and work here."

"Work? So what do you do for a living, buddy? How do you earn your keep with your long hair and earrings? Who pays you for messing up our work site? You welfare bums make me sick." Darryl spat into the dirt for emphasis.

Gus turned towards the bigger man and outstretched his hands in a gesture of acceptance. "Sir, I happen to be a mechanic *and* I work to protect the environment. I believe this planet belongs to all of us, not just the filthy rich."

"You little shit. I wouldn't let you near any machines I had," Darryl snarled. "I don't need shits like you telling me how to do my job. Get your sorry ass outta here." He started walking towards Gus.

"C'mon man, let's discuss this reasonably. We both want healthy jobs. We both want healthy forests."

Darryl continued to advance menacingly towards Gus as the others nervously fidgeted. Gus remained steadfast in his position, indicating no intention of retreating. The logger walked up to him and gave him a hard shove. Gus bounced back and returned the shove.

Isaac came running over, yelling, "Hold it guys, we aren't here to fight. We can talk about…" Before he could finish Darryl swung with a hard right and clipped Gus on the jaw sending him sprawling to the ground. Everyone jumped up. Bob, with the help of two other loggers, held the fuming Darryl back.

The Albion Navy gathered around Gus to see if he was hurt while the loggers walked with Darryl back to their trucks. Just then, the first of the logging trucks arrived, followed by a deputy's vehicle. Right behind the deputy was the newspaper crew with a camera.

Though they had missed the confrontation, the contrast of the somberly clad loggers in their cork-soled boots next to the brightly dressed enviros in their Tevas was more than enough for a great shot. As if on cue, the forest limbs were parted to reveal an astounding parade of about 25 people: men, women and children, with a fair sprinkling of dogs. These were the local neighbors of the logging site, who were understandably displeased with plans to log it.

The news crew was in heaven. They began interviewing anyone who could talk. The deputy asked the two men involved in the fight and some of the witnesses to retell the incident, as he took notes. While Isaac spoke with the deputy, another musically-inclined fellow had taken up his guitar and was playing a protest song from his kayak. The media loved this.

The scene began to take on a festival atmosphere with people milling about and talking. There was actually a picnic blanket spread out in the sunny clearing with bread, cheese, fruit and other food. One woman, dressed in a long skirt and sandals with wool socks, struck up a sensitive discussion with Bob as he drank from his thermos and shared fruit and cheese with her. She later referred to him as "enlightened."

A few enviros had since returned to their boats to paddle around in the river, or perhaps to avoid scrutiny by the law. The water was public domain; the land belonged to Louisiana Pacific.

The deputy sheriff finished taking the necessary statements from both sides and finally sat down on a rock by the river to wipe his brow. He tried to sort the thing out, but he could only conclude that tempers had flared along with some fists. As far as he could tell, both sides suffered their wounds. Who was to blame? He sure wished these environmentalists would find something else to do so that he could get back to the business of arresting criminals.

PUBLIC RELATIONS

THE NEXT NIGHT

Shep Tucker, the public relations director for Louisiana Pacific, was enjoying a drink at a private men's club in Eureka. The Ingomar Club was located in an exquisite Victorian mansion on the waterfront. Its opulent velvet curtains and Oriental carpets were only surpassed by the old growth burl wood paneling and bar. Obsequious waitresses quietly attended to the needs of the members, filling their glasses with well-aged bourbon and smiling only when spoken to. They were the only females allowed in this segregated club and were hired for their pulchritude and, of course, their ability to work efficiently.

"Mr. Tucker; you have a call in the office." The comely young woman was quick to deliver the message as she refilled his glass.

"Excuse me, gentlemen. It appears that duty calls," Tucker said to the loosely assembled group, similarly dressed in handsome suits and silk ties—all purchased out of the area in exclusive men's stores. Humboldt and Mendocino are not known for their shopping opportunities; any well dressed businessman was not supporting the local economy with his clothes purchases, at any rate.

He walked across the 250-year-old Persian carpet into the Tiffany lamp-lighted hallway and out to the office. He parted the thick curtain, brushing aside the gold tasseled cord and walked over to the massive antique desk.

He sighed as he picked up the phone, knowing it was his secretary, Drew—not his wife because she was forbidden to interrupt his Tuesday night ritual with his compatriots.

"Yes, Drew."

"Hello Shep. We had a slight altercation at the Albion logging site today. It seems that those enviros came up the river in kayaks and successfully stopped the operation."

"They are getting cleverer, aren't they?" Tucker smirked and asked, "Was the media there?"

"I'm afraid so, but we don't actually look too bad this time. One enviro pushed one of our loggers and the logger actually got a good punch in— no one was hurt and even the deputy didn't file a complaint."

Tucker let out a whistle. "Well that's just dandy! I think I'd like to meet that fellow—in fact, he's got a standing invitation to have dinner at my house with me and my family. I think we owe him a show of gratitude."

Drew relaxed on the other end and responded, "Well, yes, sir. What shall I tell the media?"

"You just repeat what I said. It's about time these troublemakers take some responsibility. Our people have to be able to protect themselves. I think our local citizens will agree."

Tucker hung up the phone jubilantly. Things were progressing nicely; these idiots were even digging their own graves. It was time to put a call in to Chuck Cushman.

He returned to his friends in the lounge and relaxed into the elegantly carved wing-back chair. He took a sip of his bourbon, smiling as he envisioned his next report to Wheeler.

DIXON

"**A**RSONISTS BURN DIXON FEED LOT; EF! CLAIMS RESPONSIBILITY!!"

Robert read the headlines of the local Eureka paper as he sat at his desk in the office.

"Where do they get this crap? People actually read this to be informed? I think I'm gonna hurl." Robert's disgust propelled him to the phone to contact Isaac. Isaac always knew what was going on in EF! world.

The phone rang twice and was picked up by the answering machine. An excited voice, backed by a bluegrass band, gave the requisite instructions for leaving a message. Robert was so infuriated that he slammed the receiver down long before the series of beeps ended.

This was beginning to stink: nothing like the smell of fetid reporting in the morning.

He recalled that Isaac and other Earth First!ers had been planning to participate in a large demonstration to protest grazing on public lands, "welfare ranching" as it was fondly referred to. Part of defending the environment included saving the habitat from the "hooved rats." Big ranchers were unclear on the concept that welfare for corporate survival ignited strong disgust in the hearts of many taxpayers. The ranchers felt some god-given right to make a profit at the public's expense. Earth First! felt some god-given calling to make publicity at the ranchers' expense.

Robert considered all the possibilities and concluded that not even the EF! crowd, with their zany penchant for media spectacles, would resort to arson. Besides, it just wasn't their style to neglect to take credit for their acts.

At 8 a.m. Robert was slurping his third cup of coffee and beginning to reel from the jitters. This news only fueled his anxiety. Hannah had been absorbed for weeks in drafting the initiative that would help protect the local forests. She was determined, articulate and relentless. Her years of experience as a writer were coalescing into the most important product of her life. Earth First! was a valued associate group, but their theatrics were only the visible end of the fight to save the remaining old growth. Hannah would be livid when she saw the paper and its potential tainting of her efforts.

Robert put his mug down, picked up a pack of Camels and just briefly wished he could quit smoking. He figured he'd try Isaac again. This time the machine was cut off by Isaac's sleepy voice. "Hello." Long yawn...

"Isaac, this is Robert. Have you heard the news about the Dixon feed lot fire? The headline says that EF! is taking responsibility for it!"

"You're not serious—how can they say that?"

"It says here that 'an anonymous EF! member claims to have used arson to get their point across about range management.'"

Isaac snorted into the phone, "That's bogus. With the big demo set for next week, why would we screw it all up with something stupid like arson? Look, we may have weird names but we don't resort to violence or anonymity."

Robert laughed. He was relieved to hear—again—that Isaac would not endorse violence to property. After a big exhalation of cigarette smoke, Robert spoke out, "Look Isaac, they're at it again."

"Who are you talking about this time, Robert? Is it Hurwitz again?"

"It's the FBI. Hey, they went after the radicals of the 60s: the Black Panthers, the American Indian Movement, and now they're using the same tactics on the enviros."

"Sure, Robert," Isaac responded somewhat irritably. "I know you've been studying this crap about revolutionaries and all, but we're not exactly doing anything illegal—or even that exciting. C'mon, we stage a few protests, create some banners..." Isaac whined nasally which brought forth his native New York accent. "We're not that important—not to the FBI!"

"Wrong!"

"We're only trying to arouse public awareness."

"Isaac," Robert spoke patiently now, "you are a threat to some very big and very powerful corporations; therefore you are classified as a radical."

"Robert, this is ridiculous. How big is Big Timber?"

"Big enough to buy every Northcoast politician. Big enough to dislike lawsuits which stop them from having their way. They've been doing business their way for a long time. They're not fond of us trying to change all that."

Isaac was frustrated about having to adjust his reality. "Look, we may have radical views but we don't use violence to people or property to make a point. You know that, dude. We don't ever set up a harmful scene."

"Hey, don't convince me. All you have to do is look at the FBI's 12-step program for counterintelligence: COINTELPRO, as it's referred to. It's classic. J. Edgar Hoover designed it twenty-five years ago and it's still in use. In fact, I have a copy right here." Robert rustled through some papers and resumed speaking. "Step 11 suggests the use of ridicule in the form of cartoons, photographs and anonymous letters as a potent weapon against radicals."

"You think they'd actually fake a news event?"

"It's pretty simple to leak—in quotation marks—a hot tip to an eager reporter."

There was a big pause on the other end of the phone as Isaac considered this possibility. He sighed deeply and spoke carefully, "You think they'd use infiltrators?"

Robert laughed softly, "Gee, maybe I'm an infiltrator...or Hannah... or how about Vera? You never can tell. Their agents are experts in being inconspicuous. Pin on a ponytail, grow a scraggly beard, change your name to 'Jeffrey Pine'—you too can pass for a radical environmentalist!"

"God, this totally stuns me. I never expected things to get so serious." There was a long gap of silence while Robert smoked his cigarette.

Robert finally spoke, "There's always been concern about infiltrators. Big industry and the FBI are famous for employing that strategy. I'm telling you Isaac, if they haven't infiltrated us yet, then they're stupider than I thought."

Robert concluded his phone call and left Isaac to what would probably amount to several hours of phoning and strategy with his various EF! group members.

He returned to his coffee and cigarettes and his old, faded copy of the COINTELPRO 12-step memo. *Hmmm...Just how far would the FBI go to protect the interests of big business?* In Robert's understanding, there were no limits.

Meanwhile, Vera was engaging in her own media campaign on the phone with a local reporter who had heard about the Dixon arson. Being regarded as a spokesperson for the environmental movement was emboldening. Vera was a fluent and articulate speaker—good interview material.

Vera adamantly insisted that Earth First! had no connection to the fire and had not sent an anonymous note. She ended her conversation by stating for the record, "I do not have any knowledge of the perpetrators of this crime. But I applaud their sentiment against the corporate ranchers and resource extractors. After all, desperate times require desperate measures."

THE TERRORIST AD

Winter is so-so in Humboldt County: *so* cold and *so* wet. People who live through the rains deserve the beauties of spring, but first there is the rain. Robert stood outside the Arcata Co-op, watching a new recruit solicit signatures for Northcoast Citizens' three-county ballot measures. *The rain won't stop us,* he thought. Worrying about the hidden forces at work had been obsessing him. Robert seldom let an event occur without trying to discern its origins. Even the weather had taken on a potential sinister meaning.

Since late summer, he and Hannah had worked feverishly to devise three new ways to alter the status quo of rural politics. Northcoast Citizens was a group of democracy-loving zealots who had surprised everyone in 1988 by passing initiatives in favor of recycling, a ban on offshore oil drilling and nuclear disarmament. Humboldt County was a nuclear-free zone!

Now, a year later, they were after the dioxin spewing pulp and paper plants outside Eureka. The slogan was "Clean Air, Clean Water and Clean Politics." The other two measures further protected against oil production facilities' pollution—just in case oil drilling was allowed—and changed the law on campaign contributions.

Gathering signatures is a tough mechanical process. Robert watched the recruit until he was sure the skittish volunteer knew the process and knew how to speak respectfully to anyone, regardless of their willingness to sign. Satisfied, he began his walk in the rain to meet Northcoast Citizens' attorney Harris Collins for a lunch meeting. As he walked through he empty town plaza he picked up a copy of the *Times Standard,* tucking most of it under his jacket and keeping the sports section to use as an umbrella to protect his bare head from the increasingly strong down-pour.

"I feel like a zombie today," he mumbled, after nearly tripping over the fire hydrant outside the Szechwan Cuisine shop.

Harris was late. As expected, Robert realized. Sitting down for lunch was a pleasure if he was lucky enough to find a place where no one would recognize him. Robert had been growing a beard over the last month, and it was now beyond the scratchy state. "I am going to hide," he'd told Isaac last week in jest, but he meant it. Today he was lucky and found the lone back table at the Chinese restaurant empty. *They'd have to know where to look to find me.*

Harris had no problem finding him. Walking quickly up to the table, he thrust a folded newspaper at him. "Read the news yet? No? Check out the Fortuna paper while I make a call. I'll just be a few." Without missing a step, Harris moved past Robert and into the kitchen to beg the phone.

"Oh, Harris, it's getting too much for me. *Rain, rain, go away, come again another day,*" Robert hopelessly muttered to the too-distant back retreating through the swinging doors.

Five minutes later, Harris swung his six foot frame down into a chair across from Robert who was just slamming the Fortuna paper closed in front of him and grabbing the unopened *Times Standard*. Harris sat and waited as Robert paged quickly through the daily. Robert gasped in disbelief, "No! What crap. Terrorist!"

Silence followed. Harris knew Robert well enough to know he was ragged tired, and rightly so, but today was a truly negative day in the papers. Robert didn't need this, nor did any one of the dozen people the timber industry was obviously after.

"Robert, it's worse than that." Harris wasn't tough and arrogant, nor was he sweet and sensitive. He was matter-of-fact and self-assured, but kind. He never told his client anything but the bittersweet truth, and Robert was his client. "Let me run it down for you."

"First, there is the vandalism and the fire bomb in Dixon. No one knows who did them—probably drug dealers or speed brewers. Unfortunately, Supervisor Pritchard is blaming it all on Earth First!, and loudly. Thus the articles and editorial in the Fortuna *Beacon*."

"Second, there is the full page ad in the *Times Standard* attacking Northcoast Citizens and naming a group they call 'The Gang of Twelve' that includes all your friends. You are first. Hannah second. I did not make the cut. Not so bad except they link you to a suspected radical terrorist named Dave Foreman, who I assume you do not know..."

"Correct," Robert quietly responded.

"Really bad news is that the Chamber and the Taxpayers League are taping for the news tonight an indictment of your signature-gathering campaign. They are going to go as far as they can with it, short of calling you a terrorist.

"There's more." Harris took a breath.

"How much more?" the quickly deflating Robert hissed.

"Third, and this you can also see on tonight's news, PL is humiliating a local judge and seems to be inviting violence against him. It's Buffington." Harris paused, slowly shaking his head side to side. "He's shook."

"John Buffington shook? I remember when the timber clones We-CARE and TEAM forced him to resign from Northcoast Citizens saying he was turning radical. Let me guess. He ruled against a Timber Harvest plan. PL or was it LP closed a mill, threw dozens, maybe a hundred, instantly out of work, blaming the radical environmentalist judge. Maybe they went so far as to suggest that people might die over this."

Harris picked it up immediately. "You got it, but it's worse than that. John is going to withdraw from our cases. The only superior court judge in the state still strong enough to stand up to the bullies is going down. Not so bad for us, really. We have won at the appeals and supreme courts in the past. It's just bad for the general tenor of our times. I know you think people see you as a paranoid, Robert, but unless you are working harder than I think and you caused all these events at once, I bet you'll have some company in your delusion by the end of today." Robert listened intently, taking a sip of tea. The tea was weak.

"Thanks. I think. Let's order before they discover who we are and re-fuse us service," Robert ventured with a laugh. "Hopefully nothing bad can happen for the rest of the day."

EDITORIAL BOARD MEETING

Jerry Post's private office as managing editor of the *Times Standard* was not very impressive, unless pictures of Republican presidents and right-wing political figures shaking hands with the gnomish chief impressed you. The *Times Standard* building itself was a monument to plainness, but that was balanced by their prose style. The *Times Substandard* it was called by its detractors.

Post himself was known for his private gambling habits and his affection for the upper management of local timber corporations. The corporate owners of the chain of papers that included the *Times* were part of the good-old-boy network in the west. Thus the *Times* had a hidden corporate face and the agenda that went with it.

The *Times Standard* hired only interns from Humboldt State University, paid them the lowest allowed by law and fired them when they asked for a raise. Many former *Times Standard* reporters complained that things would appear in their stories between their desks and the printers they had not themselves written. Post would seldom mess with the copy of reporters on specific stories. He trusted his two editors to do the right thing. His control derived from the Monday board meetings which focused on the seven editorials for the week and "special problems," such as how to treat the environmentalists.

Today would see the normal Monday meeting—no different from the others, except that there was a guest. Post had been with Shep Tucker, LP's PR hack based in Eureka, for almost the entire hour before the regular meeting was to begin. The door to his usually open office had been closed so no one could hear Post's loud unpleasant voice echoing down the hall to the copy desks nearby. At 9 a.m., right on time, the two men emerged from Post's office, crossed the hall and entered the conference room to meet the two editors.

"Shep, you know Bill and Carl," Post declared while pointing to the two sitting men.

Both editors were clad in white shirts, sleeves rolled up, yellow legal pads ready in front of them. Both looked at Shep with recognition.

'Hello, Bill. Hello, Carl. Good to see you again. How's the family, Bill? Still overpopulating the earth?" Tucker thrust his clean, manicured hand across the table to each of them in turn, shaking vigorously. A friendly smile beamed from Tucker's handsome face.

"You bet, Shep. It's a hobby of mine." Bill responded, returning the smile. "Family's fine. Yours?"

"I'm a bachelor again. For better or worse. Kids are doing well though. Carl, how's Kathy and your brood?"

"Ok, here. No complaints to be heard."

"Just wanted to say hi. I'm due at the supervisor's meeting to defend our right to make pulp across the bay." Tucker leaned across the table to get near the three men. He lowered his already low voice. "The wolves are baying at us, so we're rubbing the county the right way before it comes to a showdown. Politics as usual. I'm off. Give my regards to your families. Thanks, Jerry, for the breakfast."

"No, thank your expense account." Post chuckled his lecherous laugh, as Tucker shook hands with him. Then as Tucker exited, Post turned to his staff. "Let's start. What's on tap for the letters page, Bill?" Bill Pearson handled the editorial page since he had moved from Wisconsin to head the Humboldt State University's Journalism Department.

"PL brought in the week's letters this morning. We have six yellow ribbon letters. The rhetoric is heating up nicely. For the editorials I made a list as usual." Pearson lifted two sheets of paper from under his notepad and passed one to each of the others. "We could change any of them— nothing very special, nothing about the environmentalists. It's too early to run another anti-frivolous lawsuit piece. There's this new hippie initiative coming out tomorrow, might be worth a hit. Any other ideas?"

"Carl what's coming across the news desk?" Post asked with an uncharacteristic calmness, but neither man caught it.

"Got a news conference tomorrow with this Forests Forever group. Tucker and Bullwinkle are going to be available for comment. The radicals in Garberville got another restraining order against PL…"

"Not news." Post injected.

"Not news? Yeah, sure. We reported one last week, that's enough coverage for them. You're right as usual, Jerry. Some other things, but nothing more in sight on that front."

"Got something for you both to consider," said Post. As he spoke he reached inside his jacket pocket, pulling out a small envelope which he tossed with a clunk on the desk between the two editors. Carl let Bill open it.

"Whoa. A big nail and a hand-written note. " A tone of discovery burst in his voice. "Listen to this, 'We warn all local timber companies to think about these nails every time they cut or mill a tree. Nothing less than death is good enough for the rapists in the woods.' It's signed the 'Avenger.'" Passing the note and nail to Carl, Bill asked Post where it came from.

"Hand delivered this morning. Let's make something of it, Bill. Put out something together for the day after tomorrow, something about cowards and terrorists."

"Doesn't look real to me. Feels like another fake. Whoever is doing this is causing trouble—or hoping to make us act as if it were from Earth First!. The markings say 'Earth 1st' instead of spelling it out. Hard to defend its authenticity."

"So it's fake. It still tells us spiking is going on and people might get hurt. Do what you can with it. Maybe use it as a wedge to divide the radicals from the others. You figure it out." Post had hit his stride now, barking orders to the two men and ending with "Kill the initiative story. Send a reporter, but don't run the story—any questions give the same excuse, 'Too late for today…not news tomorrow.' That's all. Questions? Comments? Good."

DEATH THREATS

SPRING

A s Robert entered town, he stopped at the local espresso and ice cream store to have a cup and catch the rumor of the day as he called local gossip. Treats was a hippie-owned store next to the hippie-owned movie theater. On the other side was the redneck gun shop. Jerry, Treats proprietor, was an old friend, and he saved the best of the gossip for Robert's ears only. Robert called him his "spy."

"Jerry? What's up?"

"Good to see you. I've been worried. Shits coming down and we need to talk. My office or yours?"

Agitated, Jerry cleaned his hands on his apron and reached for his keys when Robert replied with "yours."

"First look at this—they're coming after you." Jerry whipped a sheet of paper from his correspondence pile. It was a crudely written letter that had no address, phone number or name to identify the sender.

Caution!…Caution!…Caution! Buying products from any of these businesses supports the Country Activist which glorifies the radical terrorist group Earth First! Remember they want your job.

Following that was a list of advertisers Robert had visited every month for seven years, and yes, they supported the *Activist*. Treats was on the list.

"What's the second thing?"

Jerry cleaned his already clean hands again on his apron, then sat down. "Rainbow has been working here in the late afternoons. She got a call yesterday from some asshole who told her that unless we stopped advertising in the *Country Activist* the store would be burned and she would be raped. She quit right there and then." He stood and slowly turned around until he once again faced Robert.

"I am not as scared as I am angry at these people. They can hurt innocent people. They may already have. At least you have the courage to put your name on your opinions—they are worse than slime—slime at least has a role to play in life that nurtures us all."

Jerry sat back down with the release of a little of his anger.

"So what should we do, Jerry? You know Hannah and I will fight this with all the usual nonviolence we have in us." Robert had been expecting this; the vibes were in the air and his intuition had been screaming "watch out" for weeks.

"Double the size of my ad. Here is the copy for it and I want it to stick out like I was giving them the finger." The ad was a message to the caller with a few choice words Robert couldn't imagine printing, not even in the *Activist*.

"Okay. I'll do it," said Robert, secretly believing Jerry would cool down once it came time to set the ad into print. "I've got to get moving on this. Stay in touch." They hugged a brotherly goodbye and left the office together. One last look of resignation was shared, and Robert made it into the street past the knot of the today's CAMP victims and up to his office.

The machine held two messages from merchants who had received letters like Jerry's, and two who had been phoned; one at home by a similarly vicious anonymous caller. One said it was a woman, the other a man. As he finished writing down the messages Hannah walked in the door.

"Where have you been?" Hannah raised her voice when she was nervous. She nearly yelled to him from a foot away. Robert was too stunned by his day to rise in response, his inexplicable reaction to her stress serving only to give her more.

"Collecting bad news. Want to hear some? Oh, but first, what's bothering you...?" He almost inserted "honey," but astutely recognized the error of sweet talk when one was not acting particularly sweet.

"Look at this. We found it on the back door of the office this morning, and believe it or not, it was smeared with excrement of some kind."

The note she handed him was a photocopy of a work of art probably designed in an alcoholic rage. It contained a newspaper photograph of Vera and Isaac, apparently at a demonstration. In hand-cut letters the heading said:

Greene and Winwood: Get Out.

Below the photograph a crudely typed message stated:

The hippys up Strongs Creek Road have built a hide out for radical terrorist Vera Greene. We don't want a new HQ for Earth First! terrorists in our forests. Greene—get out of our town. Case of Coors to stud who burns her hide out—knock first if you want. Six pack for every hippy shack burned on Strongs Creek Road.

EF; kiss my ax.

Stompers

Robert let out a long sigh and laid the paper on the table. Hannah stood in front of him, waiting expectantly for his commentary. He felt blank, empty, exhausted. He stared at his shoes on the floor. One of his laces was broken, one of the eyelets was missing.

"Okay, so what're we gonna do? How do we stop this bullshit? What do we do next?" Hannah stood there with her hands on her hips and her lips tightly compressed. Robert looked up at her, then got up from the chair. He threw his daypack over his shoulder and started for the door.

"I don't know, Hannah. This time, I just really don't know." He turned to grab the door handle as her shrill words assaulted his ears.

"Don't walk away from me. I want to talk to you—NOW."

He didn't look back, but continued walking through the door, out to the stairs and down to the street. He meandered along the sidewalk to his favorite pool table and bartender. He ordered his first pint of beer and placed his stack of quarters on the table. It was going to be a long night.

BLM

First light in the forest is a sight to make anyone go spiritual for a few moments. Today was no different. Roger Crane had risen at 3 a.m. to get to the logging show before the crews running the loaders were on the job. Once he arrived he usually sat in the cab, read a novel, ate his egg sandwiches and drank more coffee. Dawn was just something that happened to him everyday while he sat waiting for work to begin.

"First in line. Last to turn off the motor for the night. Take an extra load to the mill. Make an extra $20. That's the way to go." He repeated this mantra to himself often to explain his crepuscular habits. Before dawn and after dusk he moved freely about his life. In between he belonged to his machine or to his bed.

The road up the mountain had been newly graded by BLM to allow Eel River Sawmill's gyppo fellers, skidder and loader operators, into the area where today's logging would begin. The first day up a new road was a pleasure for the kidneys; in two weeks time, when the curves turned to washboards and the pot holes had been deepened by the 25-ton traffic, the ride up and back would pound his guts. But today the ride was nearly a pleasure.

Typical logging roads into the back country left the highways on a paved stretch that narrowed as they curved up ever-steepening slopes, then turned to gravel access routes and then to a fresh surface prepared for short-time usage. The turn-offs were marked with yellow and a red ribbon. Each mile and each quarter mile were marked with signs spray painted on rocks, trees or on the dirt itself, telling the distance from the last turn-off.

As Crane passed the two-mile sign something odd in the sky confronted him—a small plume of smoke, too small for a slash burn—snaked up into the morning sky above the treetops ahead. Turning the last curve before the plume, he saw the roadway was blocked by an overturned car, then a warning sign, then a group of people scurrying to gather around the vehicle.

Weird, it couldn't be a wreck, he thought, *All those people were not in that single car. Uh-oh! Environmentalists!*

He slowed to a stop before he rammed the roof of the road-blocking car. Beyond the car was a smoldering bonfire, then a rock slide. What he couldn't see was around the next curve, where six men and women were busy digging a pit—a tank trap. He did notice that the environmentalist types seemed edgy and surprised by his early arrival.

What the hell! At least he knew for sure he'd beaten the others up the mountain, but the rest of the day is going to get strange fast. One of the blockaders, a small young woman dressed in "hippie camo" headed his way.

"Good morning. There won't be any work here today." Little Tree was always polite and Vera's training had made certain no one laid blame on the workers. She had reached the truck cab and climbed up on the exterior step to meet the driver's eyes through his rolled-up window.

Crane lit a cigarette and slowly cranked the glass into the door. "Get off my rig!" he ordered from a cloud of blue smoke. Little Tree stepped back to ground level just as the door opened to knock her off. "Don't ever touch my rig without my permission. Tell your friends to move aside and let me through."

"I'm sorry but we are here to stop the cutting of the ancient forest. We are nonviolent, but we will not move aside." She was sternly convincing. He climbed down from the seat and stood towering over her. Directly in his eyesight was the crown of her baseball cap atop her upturned head: "Earth First! No Compromise in Defense of Mother Earth," the emblazoned badge on the hat screamed at him.

"Earth First! God, have I wanted to meet up with you out here. Are any of you man enough to try to stop me?" he yelled to the fifteen scraggly-haired protesters as he swung back behind the wheel.

Engaging a low gear, he inched his big rig up to the car and began to push it to the edge of the road bed. The Earth First!ers danced in and out of his intended path. *No sweat,* he hoped.

Once he had pushed the wreck aside, he backed up twenty feet to allow him to steer around the wreck. In the time it took to make his maneuver, the blockaders muscled the car partially back into his path. With a fury that was quickly overcoming him, he blasted his horn and accelerated to pass around the car. As he moved forward he saw in the rear-view mirror a sheriff's car rounding the last curve behind him. He let off the fuel and braked to a stop.

He was shaking from his coffee consumption and the adrenaline of the confrontation. The sight of law enforcement had slowed, but not reduced his angry agitation. He swung back out onto the step and grabbed his small chainsaw from its rack behind the seat. Leaping to the ground, he moved directly into the midst of the Earth First!ers. Pulling the starting rope brought life to the saw and the sound of its roar to the otherwise quiet woods. He waved it in the air, demanding everyone back up and sit down. A citizen's arrest went through his mind.

Mem Hill stepped forward to block his path. She held her camera up to her face and tried to focus its lens to hold Crane and Crane's weapon clearly in the frame.

He dropped his saw to his side, his thumb on the kill switch, releasing it to drop to the ground. With his angry face gripped in a pained grimace, he punched the camera into her nose and eyes. With a yelp Mem fell backwards onto the ground as two male EF!ers rushed forward to grab her and pull her away from Crane, who was now struggling with her for the camera.

The sheriff pulled to a stop behind the log truck just as the fight began. Three other vehicles, carrying crews in for the day were right behind him. Bringing up the rear was another log truck driven by a young hot head named Charlie Russell.

Sheriff Satterwitte ran back to within ear shot of Russell and the crew trucks and told everyone to stay put or they would be arrested. Then turned to sprint to the action up the road. As he neared the knot of protesters, he saw Crane pull something from a woman's hands and dash it destructively onto the ground. Two Earth First!ers were trotting in his direction while pointing back at Crane.

"Arrest him. Arrest him. He assaulted one of us!" was their cry. Within yards of the knot, Satterwitte drew his pistol and ordered everyone to halt. Everyone halted.

"What's going on here?" he asked, only to be answered with a chorus of voices all singing a different song. No doubt it was going to be a tough morning. "Okay. Okay. Quiet down and let me hear you. First who called me?"

As he waited for an answer Isaac and Vera rounded the rock slide on the road past the wrecked car. They were noticed by the other protesters, and silence fell upon them as they waited for their recognized spokespersons to arrive.

Seeing the deference that was paid to them, the officer also waited for the two to reach the others. Crane, acting bored with the proceedings, hauled his saw back to the cab and sheepishly replaced it in its hanger. *Time for another cup of coffee,* he thought as he pulled his egg sandwich from his lunch box. "Time for lunch," he mumbled as he seated himself against the front bumper. He didn't want to miss this.

Vera walked right up to Satterwitte, talking fast for the last ten feet. "We're the Cahto Wilderness Action Group and we are here to keep some logging from beginning."

Satterwitte snapped back his reply, "They got a right to be here. You don't."

"Yes, we do. We are defending the forest, and we believe we are right to do it. Our lawyer called last night from San Francisco. A federal judge issued a restraining order against this logging plan, and we are waiting for it to be brought up here and served so no illegal logging will happen." Vera had it all worked out, if, as she thought, *Isaac would just stay away and let me handle it.*

Isaac slowly moved up beside her but kept his silence. *Let her talk,* he thought.

And she did, running down the schedule that she hoped would bring the order to them by mid-morning. As she talked another uniformed man, this one a BLM ranger, approached from behind the cop who whirled at the footfalls and pointed his gun in the general direction.

"Sheriff, sorry, I just arrived. I'm with BLM and I think I have a solution. My San Francisco office called and told me the court has blocked cutting until it hears a lawsuit on the Timber Harvest Plan. I'm here to make sure no work occurs on the site." Jim Welch strutted into the group shaking hands and smiling at the whoops that rang out from the Earth First!ers. *At least someone is happy about this,* he thought.

Crane could not believe what he was seeing and hearing. *How could they do that? Some judge in the flatlands sticking his fat butt into my life?* "Limbaugh is right, you bureaucrats don't know shit!" he yelled, causing Sheriff Satterwitte to yell back for him to shut up.

With the attention drawn back to Crane, the crowd burst into its original plaint cry for arrest and prosecution of the assailant and destroyer of private property. Satterwitte burst out laughing at the clownish outbursts from both sides. He holstered his gun and asked for a witness. As Little Tree began to speak he interrupted her.

"You are not a witness. You are a participant. Where is a witness?"

No one answered. "I see there are no good witnesses. And I didn't see it, nor did any of the others who came after me. Crane there has his own story, I'll bet, so you are fresh out of luck."

The protests for justice fell on deaf ears until Satterwitte ended the conversation by telling them to take it to Ukiah, where the DA might be interested. But he doubted it.

Isaac turned to Vera and shook his head saying, "At least no one was seriously hurt. Let's get a move on. This looks over. We didn't even get to sing the new song."

"A victory at any rate, and easier than we thought. We didn't get arrested and we didn't have to face using the tank trap or the boulder fall." Vera sounded truly relieved. "Thankfully, we are free to rage again another day. Let's get down the hill to reach the media—they'll love to report on this one."

THE SECOND FOREST FOREVER
NEWS CONFERENCE

They both looked exhausted, and excited, by the chance that their strategy would pay off big time. Vera, as always, bullied her way to a conclusion in a series of meetings where tempers had been high. The breakdown had fallen pretty much as Vera and Isaac had seen that it would: There were hard feelings about abandoning spiking. It was seen as a retreat by some, but they were the younger and angrier ones in the local EF! affinity groups which proved the point that Isaac was forced to make.

"People think I fucked up on the *60 Minutes* taping," Isaac had bluntly stated. "I agree. I have had to accept the criticism of just about everyone within a fifty-mile radius of Garberville. If I could undo it, I would, but it's too late. Now, with our planning for Redwood Summer beginning to take on the look of success, we have taken the extra step so that the major nonviolent action groups can feel comfortable being with us."

Vera nodded in agreement as a chorus of voices shouted for recognition. "We'll hear from you…then you…then you," Little Tree insisted, operating with the authority of group process that had made her the moderator of the meeting.

As soon as she had pointed out the order of speaking, Dan Close, who was president of Arcata's Humboldt State University student body, rose to speak, and a respectful quiet filled the air. "Face it, if we are serious about following the nonviolent action code, then we have to abandon all acts that are seen as violent by nearly anyone. If we are going to get the experienced leadership we need to pull off dozens of blockades and protests, we are going to have to have a broad expansion of our ranks.

We cannot fail to address this issue. Spiking is being used against us. And spiking is ineffective."

"Yeah, sure. How are we going to stop the corporations from raping the land if we don't make them pay a price?" a young one asked. "What about sabotaging machines? Are we going to give that up too? George Hayduke would roll over in his grave knowing we had abandoned not just spiking but the very basis for Earth First!"

Vera was next, and she began at full volume and emotion. "Let's be serious. Redwood Summer is more than Earth First!. It has to be bigger than Earth First!. If we will not limit our actions during these protests, Earth First! may not be able to participate because we did not agree to comply with the nonviolent code similar to the one used during Mississippi Summer. We can talk, but there really is no choice. We have to do what we have to do to pull this thing off."

The talking went on for hours in meeting after meeting with each of the northern California groups aligned with Earth First! In the end, a consensus was reached that spiking in northern California was no longer an official Earth First! tactic.

GREENPEACE GUY

"**Y**ou're an emotional Neanderthal," Hannah said, her eyes blazing with hatred.

Robert looked down at his hands in his lap. He noticed the cracked skin by his fingernails. *Must have been from planting all those tomatoes.* His hands were large, but well-shaped, or so he thought. He turned the left one over to reveal the soft skin of the palm. Hey, there was that scar from the time he was skateboarding. Could have been when he was twelve or fifteen years old.

"You don't even hear me, do you? You really don't fucking care what I feel..." Hannah walked over to the window and stretched her arm sideways over her head as she gazed out towards the river. She slowly straightened and then abruptly turned to face Robert. She stared intently at him, breathing forcefully through her nostrils. Finally she spoke: "I give up, Robert. Okay? I give up. This just doesn't work for me—your idea of relating is too obscure. I need a soul-mate, not a bed-mate. I'm outta here."

Robert sat in the big, old armchair looking at the floor. There were cat prints over by the door. One of the floor boards would need replacing soon. Hannah crossed in his gaze to walk the two steps to the kitchen. He saw her open the cooler. He saw a bottle. He heard the pop of a champagne cork. Hah, his hearing was just fine.

Hannah returned extending a full glass of champagne. "Cheers to the winding path of life," she proposed and gulped about half the glass. Robert gulped before he took a sip. This did not look good.

She guzzled the remainder of her glass, poured a second, drained it completely, then placed it on the table with a thud. "I'm gonna take a walk, maybe do some tai chi, get some enlightenment. Or maybe I'll drink some more champagne—you know, some instant gratification. Maybe I'll do both, get some instant enlightenment." She smirked and walked out the door, slamming it shut.

Gone.

Silence.

Robert sat up straighter in the chair. *No, this did not feel good.* Must be time to seek out other guys. Talk about things you could understand. Lawsuits. Politics. Football. He laced up his shoes, patted the cat and snatched up his car keys.

The tavern was just beginning to fill with the usual after-work crowd. He bought an entire pitcher of Redneck Lager and selected a table in the corner. Robert made sure the juke box was cued up and then deposited two quarters onto the pool table. With his favorite Neil Young tunes as background support, he concentrated on his game, effectively blocking out competing thoughts. Simple Neil reduced life's complexities to the basic elements: beer, ballads and billiards—with maybe an old pick-up truck and a dog thrown in for good measure.

His turn at the table came, and as he racked the balls he drew someone's attention.

"Can I buy you a beer—maybe you could give me some lessons?"

Robert was startled to look up and see a gorgeous blond with the world's tightest pants smiling at him. He flinched inwardly. *Oh God, this definitely smells like trouble.* "Ah, hello there. I'm ah...well...ah...I'm meeting a friend. Yeah, so I guess I better not start anything up. A game, I mean." He shuffled his feet uncomfortably and averted his gaze from falling upon what might be the most luscious woman this side of the Sierra.

She shrugged her shoulders and said brightly, "Whatever," then turned and sauntered over to the bar to seek out more fertile pastures.

Robert heaved a sigh of relief and caught himself. *What am I relieved about?* he thought. He drew the cue back and executed a volatile break. It was excellent. The balls reverberated in all directions, with three of them, all solids, landing in pockets.

He continued landing balls with a vengeance. He liked the sharp sound of the cue ball contacting the object ball. Here on the pool table he could feel a sense of control. He understood the rules of this game.

He was lining up his shot on the eight ball when a herd of hearty drinkers roamed by. They must have been loggers, judging by their cork-soled boots and rugged clothing. They must have been drunk, judging by their bloodshot eyes and the volume of their voices. Robert continued with his solo game of pool. *We're all here to escape,* he figured.

"Hey! Hey you," snarled a voice behind him.

Robert looked over his shoulder to see a tall, thin man with incredibly red eyes and a wobbling head staring, sort of, at him. Not only was this fellow drunk, but he had a "lazy eye" which further contorted his face. It made it difficult to determine his exact focus, but Robert had no doubt that the object of this snarling was him. He smiled politely, taking a sip of beer and responded, "Hello. How ya doing?"

The man grunted and turned his good eye to Robert. A bear-like grunt erupted from him before he spoke. "Hey, I know you. You're the Greenpeace guy."

"Pardon me?" Robert raised his eyebrows inquisitively.

"Yeah." The man slurred his words as he held unsteadily onto the railing. "You're that guy. I saw you at that meeting."

Robert raced through his mental list of recent meetings and narrowed it down to about five possibilities in recent weeks. He approached the man with his hand extended, realizing that this guy would have some difficulty approaching him. "Sorry, I don't recall having met you. My name's Robert."

"I don't know you," the man snarled. "I don't even wanna know you. You make me sick." He pointed his finger. "You people wanna hug trees and take our jobs away. Well I'll tell you—I'm gonna blow you away. I'm gonna defend my right to work, no matter what it takes," he proclaimed loudly, as his head wobbled on his spindly neck.

"C'mon, Brad," one of his friends hollered over. "Let's get another round."

Brad managed to turn his head from his friends back to Robert. "Yeah," he snorted, "I'm being paid to watch the equipment. You long-hairs mess with our machines and I've got orders to shoot to kill. I'm warning you, you hear me?" His voice boomed as he turned to walk over towards his friends.

Robert went back to his game. *Yeah, I hear you. I hear better than I should—though good luck convincing Hannah of that.*

UZI PHOTO BUMMER

MARCH 21, 1990

The arrival of spring in northern California was neither subtle nor ignored. The very air itself felt lighter, warmer, with the delicate fragrance of new life. The dogwoods with their radial bracts of brilliant white thrusting through the dense streamside vegetation was one of the first signs that winter was retreating. Even the banks of the freeway offered a bedazzling display of crimson clovers interspersed with brilliant orange poppies and lupines tinted the most perfect shade of purple.

The days grew longer and spirits began to lift. Laid-off employees of the timber industry, housing industry, tourist industry and even the dwindling fishing industry began to revive themselves after the sedentary months of winter. Rain could be expected until June, even beyond, but spring promised renewal: wildflowers, jobs, attitudes.

Vera and Isaac were taking advantage of a fair spring day by resuming construction on her house in the hills of Mendocino County. Vera was the carpenter, Isaac was the muse. Together they managed to create more of Vera's dream home.

"Isaac, hand me that bag of nails over there," Vera called out from her perch high on a ladder. She was trimming her windows with some used redwood she'd salvaged from a recent construction job. Her house was in that condition so disturbing to the homebuilder: livable, but obviously lacking in aesthetic details. So often in the redwood forests, one encountered rustic cabins that exhibited better intentions than craftsmanship.

Isaac handed her a small brown paper bag and asked, "Are these the ones?"

"No, the finishing nails. They're in that bucket—try that yellow bag. I need the smaller ones with the rounded heads."

Isaac looked in the bucket filled with paper bags of varying shades of brown. He scrunched his face in concentration. "I can't tell these things apart. A nail's a nail…seen one, seen 'em all." He formed a slight smile. "Hey, just like Ronald Reagan's memorial tree. You know, that decrepit one by the freeway in Arcata? I think I hear a song in this…"

Vera smiled to herself at Isaac's limitless sources of inspiration. She was enjoying his companionship, but was feeling the strain of working with him. He got so damn excited about everything and insisted that all present feel the same intensity. It was exhausting to compete with him just to get a word in. But he was energizing on those long road trips. The crowd really responded to him; he had charisma in that dark, wiry, Dylanesque way.

But Vera needed the nails more than his musings. She began to descend the ladder just as the phone rang. She climbed down and scurried to pick it up. Her ear was immediately assaulted by the voice of Bruce Anderson, the crusty curmudgeon cum editor of the small rural newspaper, *The Anderson Valley Advertiser*.

Bruce was infamous for his forthright editorials and his inventive reporting. Eccentric wasn't really the right term for this arguably off-center paper; it leaned more to the bizarre. Bruce's political views were closely aligned with anyone who had any complaints about any standing institution or procedure.

Vera laughed into the phone as she listened to Bruce tell another fine story of government waste, fraud and environmental abuses. She could just envision his beady little eyes bursting with vehemence as his rotund body remained ensconced in his office chair. The little man made a big impact without ever getting up.

When Bruce decided you were an asshole, or otherwise laudable, it got printed in *The Anderson Valley Advertiser*. He crossed all barriers and granted no reprieves. Yet he was enjoyed and accepted in these small rural communities. The locals really loved his fierce passions, and they, too, were encouraged to contribute their own outrageous opinions.

The Anderson Valley Advertiser was Mendocino County's "people's paper"—you wouldn't find it in the quaint tourist bed-and-breakfasts. BMW owners aren't impressed with other people's opinions.

"Well, sweetheart," Bruce's gravelly voice boomed into the phone, "I've got quite a flattering little photo of you here." She heard him choke on a giggle, "Though I do think a little gal like you ought to be pointing a much bigger gun, considering the people you've pissing off these days!"

Bruce was chortling loudly, almost hissing into the receiver with laughter. Vera knitted her brows in concentration. What gun was he talking about? Suddenly, she remembered the abortion demo. "Oh, did Alice give you that photo? Is that the one you're talking about?"

"Well, it claims here that Alice is the photographer, but it was Earl who brought it to my attention." He paused for a moment to shout directions at some hapless employee in the next room.

"I'll be damned if you don't make a fine poster gal for all that's needed here in Mendocino. That's it—guts—guts and guns!" Bruce was laughing again so forcefully that he had to put the phone down.

"It's the one with the Uzi, right? Those were Earl's guns. What an idiot. Don't tell me you, too, find them fascinating?" Vera was feeling slightly perturbed; amongst her friends, guns were not considered "cute."

"Well, it's not the guns, honey, it's the reaction they cause." Bruce 's voice became thoughtful. He enjoyed his friendship with Vera and wisely, sensed her irritation.

"Well, why do you talk with Earl, then? He's obsessed. Most of us think he's an overbearing ass."

"To hell with Earl. This is a hilarious photo for the cover of my next issue. How about it? You can be the Earth First! Poster Gal?"

"It's a little weird, Bruce—but, of course, that wouldn't stop you." Vera paused as she considered it. "It is kinda funny. I remember us all being in hysterics as we tried various poses." She sighed wistfully.

"Oh, are there other photos, equally as provocative?" Bruce was clearly amused, which was an improvement over his usual mood of clearly surly.

Vera laughed as she explained the derivation of the photo to Bruce: Crazy hippies pulling crazy stunts, having a typical day in the redwoods. This was right up Bruce's alley, just zany enough to amuse without being downright vulgar.

"Okay, Bruce," Vera finally said, "go ahead and use it. It'll give my friends something to laugh about." She guffawed slightly, "They're always accusing me of being too serious anyway." She also didn't mind that this time she wouldn't have to share press space with Isaac.

Vera went back outside. Isaac was hunkered down on a long bench, picking out chords on his guitar, definitely more interested in making music than houses. Vera didn't really expect him to do a lot. He was here so they could plan the strategy for their next demonstration. He looked up at her expectantly as he set the guitar down.

"What's up?"

"Bruce Anderson just called." Vera looked sheepishly at Isaac. "He asked me if he could print that photo Alice took back at your place… you know, the one where I'm holding the Uzi, wearing all the Earth First! stuff?"

"You're kidding? That's hilarious. Does he have the photo of me, too?"

"No, I guess not. He said Earl only gave him that one."

Isaac was clearly agitated—his voice raised an octave. "Well, Vera, I'm just not sure that it will do our cause any good. I like to think of us as eco-warriors, but brandishing an Uzi doesn't exactly qualify as good taste."

"Right, like you're really concerned with good taste as you ridicule fetuses, god and lumberjacks in one verse."

He glared at her over the neck of his guitar.

"Oh, Isaac, it's just a joke. Lighten up. Besides, look at the paper it's printed in. Everyone knows what a lunatic Bruce is." She picked up her well-worn leather tool belt and started to climb back up the ladder.

Isaac began to twitch his ankle, rotating it spasmodically.

Vera looked down at him and snorted. "Ha, you're just jealous. You'd think this was a great PR moment if the photo of you was being printed." She looked at him expecting retaliation. When none surfaced, she went for the kill. "Isn't that so? Frankly, you just can't stand it when someone else takes center stage."

She was sick of his moping. Every discussion had to favor his viewpoint or an endless debate would ensue.

"I am not jealous. I'm just surprised, that's all," Isaac whined petulantly. "You know how we always plan everything together." He looked up at her dolefully, his lips pouting. "I just figured we were a team."

"Shit, Isaac, I've been an activist for close to two decades now. I don't ever recall asking for anyone's goddamn permission to act, including my ex-husband." She pounded a few nails for emphasis, "And I sure as hell don't intend to ask for your permission now."

"Vera, don't start that crap. I'm not trying to direct your life and you know it. You're just so fiercely independent that you don't think you need anybody. Noooo, not you, the great warrior of the downtrodden." He looked up to see her pounding nails at a furious pace.

She stopped abruptly, hooking her hammer on the tool belt and slowly turned to face Isaac as she said, "Fuck you!"

Isaac just glared at her, then stormed off across the yard. There aren't too many effective retorts to that time honored conversation killer.

He returned a few minutes later and found her in the same position on the ladder, except instead of pounding nails, she was slumped over with her head in her hands. He so rarely saw her exhausted, much less defeated. He wondered if he had ever seen her cry; he knew she'd seen him cry plenty.

"Vera, I love you."

"Fuck you," came the feeble reply.

"Vera, please come down and hold me. I need to feel you next to me."

She remained impassive for a moment, then slowly backed down the ladder. Isaac watched her, biting his lower lip. He loved her with a passion that surprised even his poet's heart, but he could no longer deny that a feeling of separation seemed to have occurred without warning.

Isaac was growing more melancholy in their relationship. He was amazed to discover that he now lacked the words to express his love. He was a poet; he was never without words. Was he fueled by dreams and fantasies? Had he lost the ability to know her—or had she just changed without him knowing?

His mind went back a few months. He had just left the East Coast in his van, with nothing but an old guitar, a good dog and a heart full of dreams. He was heading for the Eco-Mecca of the Pacific Northwest. He had met Vera, discovered Earth First! and found a family. When he experienced the ancient forests with her and learned that Pacific Lumber was intending to cut them down, they were bonded even more deeply by their quest to preserve the last of the old growth.

Isaac was jolted back to the present as he watched Vera descend the last few rungs on the ladder. She was so small, so vulnerable, even in her heavy work boots. How could this little woman fight so hard for the giant redwoods?

She stepped over to where he stood and tentatively held out her arms to him, as if she wasn't sure who he was. He pressed her body tightly to his chest. With an unmistakable shock she realized that she no longer heard the music from his heart. As she stroked his hair and pressed her face to his cheek, she tasted the salt of his tears and was finally unable to hold back her own.

They stood there embracing under the sprawling Douglas fir as time stood still. There were no more discussions, no more arguments, no words left to share. For the first time in their togetherness, there wasn't a sound except the rumbling of the rain swollen creek and the softness of their sobbing hearts.

VERA'S CAR

Vera had driven the rural road from Ukiah to Fort Bragg many times. She was comfortable with the vertical rise and fall among the lateral twists and curves. Many an unsuspecting tourist had regretfully discovered the meaning of "spew with a view" while touring on this road. The small car maneuvered easily on the narrow road which followed the river up to the ridge, then over the coastal foothills. The scenery was pleasant and afforded serene viewscapes of forest, river and even wildlife.

Vera spoke excitedly to Alice, who was accompanying her on this trip. Alice's two small children were amusing themselves in the back seat, while the adults were immersed in rapid-fire conversation. Vera was re-laying the events of the BML blockade.

"I can't believe that logger punched her in the face! Those guys are way too macho to hit a woman in public." Alice was chuckling as she spoke, trying to envision the burly, flannel-shirted man with his sus-penders and spiked boots being so frustrated that he used force on an older woman armed only with a camera. She added as an afterthought, "Is she really okay?"

Vera responded seriously, "Well no, she's not actually. A broken nose is extremely painful. Let's get real; the trauma of being assaulted by a man will linger long after her nose is healed." Vera's face appeared pained.

Alice looked over at her carefully, wondering if she should pursue that line, but ultimately backed off.

The road took a sharp hairpin as it slowly climbed, necessitating a down-shift. Vera let off the clutch with a sigh. "I'm really disappointed in the response of the sheriff. This was clearly a case of aggravated assault. The victim was obviously injured, and there were numerous witnesses.

Evidently, we're not going to receive any support from the law." She shifted back up a gear as the road straightened out again.

Alice sipped her coffee slowly before commenting. "Look, I see your point, but I have to admit I can see where the sheriff's coming from, too." She looked crosswise at Vera, half expecting some immediate rebuttal, but encountered only concentration. She continued with her thought: "There's been so much negative press these days about environmentalists that you gotta figure law enforcement is all hyped up." Alice smirked as she said, "He certainly was outnumbered by all you long-hairs."

Vera took this in without comment and continued to drive. She glanced in her rearview mirror and noticed a logging truck some distance behind her. She checked her watch; they were making good time. They should be in Fort Bragg well on schedule to prepare for the afternoon demonstration at the LP mill. Her thoughts returned to Alice's discussion.

"You're unfortunately right—about the bad PR. I'm still relieved that we had the foresight to get that restraining order before the blockade. Those loggers were livid—it could have been worse." Vera spoke carefully, as if to review her own ideas. "I'm still dismayed that violence occurred, though at least it wasn't perpetrated from our side." Vera checked her rearview mirror again, noticing the logging truck creeping up awfully close to her rear.

"REDUCE SPEED" appeared on the sign ahead. They were approaching another small town nestled in the forest just off the coast. This one had a population of about 300 people, which supported the primary services of market, gas and bar.

A pudgy Rottweiler sauntered across the road as Vera down-shifted. Suddenly, a horrific screech of crumpled metal resounded as the small car was violently struck from behind, then smashed forward into a parked pick-up truck. The pick-up then careened onto the porch where it took out a supporting post of the building.

The children immediately began shrieking as both of them saw the blood on each other's foreheads. Vera and Alice were shaken and confused, though neither felt severely injured. Within seconds, the apparently distraught driver of the logging truck, ran up to the smashed car and cried out, "The children, I didn't see the children."

All three adults immediately focused on the injuries of the kids. Local townsfolk gathered to assist, and someone called the sheriff. Luckily, no one required medical attention, though Vera's car was mangled beyond repair.

The log truck driver was cited for excessive speed and held liable for damages. His truck, not surprisingly, only suffered minor scratches and dents to the fender.

Vera and Alice sat down in the tavern while the kids soothed their pains with ice cream. Vera drank a cup of coffee and began speaking to the owner of the pick-up truck.

"Looks like your truck got pretty smashed up. I sure am sorry about that."

The shaken young man responded, "This is really going to slow our work up, but at least no one got hurt real bad." He flashed a kind smile in the direction of the children.

Vera liked his easy manner and pursued discussion while waiting for a ride.

"What kind of work are you doing, way out here?"

"We're collecting data on endangered species—actually, spotted owls—for timber harvest reviews. They have a tight deadline, but they still need our report before they can proceed." He sighed, "They'll just have to wait. That truck isn't going anywhere real soon."

Despite her throbbing headache, Vera smiled at the irony of it all. An environmentalist gets rear-ended by a logger and crashes into the truck of biologists who are studying endangered species.

They were given a ride to a friend's house on the coast, where Isaac was waiting, practicing his guitar as usual. He listened to the whole story, relieved that no one was injured badly.

"Are you sure you're up to this demo today?" Isaac put his arm protectively around Vera's shoulders, noticing how small she really was when she wasn't ordering and orating.

She left him and walked over to her daypack, extracting a hairbrush. She thoughtfully untangled her hair, then solemnly re-braided it, ready for action again. "I'm up for this. We've put a lot of energy into planning—let's go for it!"

Isaac was relieved, but he expected her response. Vera seldom backed out of any commitments. They had a few minutes to discuss strategy before they left for the demo, and Vera visibly brightened up as the adrenaline rose.

By the time they reached the gates to the mill, she seemed unfazed by the incident earlier that day. There was already a substantial crowd of protesters busily mingling.

Isaac ran off to organize the media while Vera sought out the sign makers.

She got on her hands and knees and she joined in painting the signs. Creative juices flowed around her as people excitedly wrote their favorite slogans and messages. Little Tree was especially prolific today, as she embellished her signs with artsy images, not unlike the flowing gowns over long-johns she often wore.

In the distance, Isaac could be heard speaking over the p.a. system, expounding on the abuses of timber management towards their workers and the environment.

Little Tree handed Vera more pens as Vera snarled, "The duplicity of the corporations is so obvious. How can the workers not see that their paychecks are worth less, even as the companies that own them become richer?"

Without looking up from her painting, Little Tree thoughtfully replied, "I think people should treat each other with kindness. We all have to share this planet that nourishes us."

Vera glanced at the sweetly smiling young woman, decked out in her diaphanous dress and combat boots and marveled at the naivety. Of course, she thought to herself, it's that universal naivety that we all long for to protect us against harsh realities. Once you acknowledge it's naive, you can't go back.

She spoke directly: "Look Little Tree, LP is taking advantage of its workers. Just this year alone, three men have died in mill-related accidents."

"Oh, that's not right."

"No, it's pretty ugly in fact."

Little Tree sighed, taking this information in. "Did you hear about that guy at the Cloverdale mill—the one whose face got all cut up by the blade? Some people say that it wasn't an accident that he complained too much."

Vera stopped writing before she spoke, "Look, I don't claim to have all the facts, but it's possible. He did say he wasn't pleased with the way management maintained equipment."

The crowd became louder as it grew. People continually walked over to the sign artists seeking one to carry. News cameras arrived and everyone wanted to be a star. As Vera gathered more paper and pens, someone yanked on her sleeve, asking for a sign. Without looking up, she hurriedly scrawled in large red-painted strokes:

LP SCREWS

MILL WORKERS

and thrust the sign over her shoulder at the outstretched hand.

More speakers took to the microphone before Isaac brought out his guitar to howls of approving applause. Vera felt less lively than before and declined to join him—there were other musicians. The demonstration concluded with Isaac granting an interview to the media while Vera remained in the background. She felt a strong headache coming.

The following day, Isaac took Vera to the CHP office to fill out the papers on the accident. There were photos of both vehicles and the parked truck, indicating points of impact and travel. Vera reiterated her understanding of the incident as the officer took notes.

As she looked closely at the photos, she remarked, "That's one huge truck; it's amazing we weren't injured more badly." She continued staring at the picture and gasped, "Wait a minute—that's the same truck we blockaded on BLM land. Look, Isaac! Isn't that the one?"

Isaac snatched the photo out of her hand and peered at it intently. "Goddamn it. You're right! That asshole tried to kill you, Vera." He popped out of his chair, vibrating with anger.

The officer looked confused and tried to calm them down. "Come on folks. The driver was cited for excessive speed by the investigating officer. You know how those roads get, with all those twists and turns." He looked at the two hippies with skepticism and managed half of a smile. He couldn't really take them seriously.

"Bullshit! That driver of that rig—his name is Roger Crane, right? We need to see Sheriff Satterwitte's report from two days ago, when Mem got her nose punched." Isaac was standing at his full five feet, six inches. His wild black curls were springing off his head.

The sheriff looked at him blankly.

"You're supposed to help us here," Isaac demanded. "Someone tried to murder my friends and I want an investigation now!" He slammed his fist on the desk for emphasis.

Vera sat in the chair, stunned. Her headache still lingered from yesterday. She inspected the photos again and stated calmly, "Yes, I'm certain that this truck is the same one we encountered at the blockade. I don't recall the name of the driver or his face, but I'm sure we can locate a witness who does."

She looked plaintively at Isaac for support, but in his rage, he could only pace and grumble.

Finally, Vera spoke again, "Officer, please. I believe that's the same truck driver. He saw my car a few days ago at a logging protest. I noticed for several miles that he was following me too closely. He had time to correct, okay?" She stared intently at the photograph on the wall of Abraham Lincoln, searching for answers. She straightened up in her chair and spoke again, "Listen officer, the first words he said when he came up after the crash, were that he was surprised to see the children."

She looked the officer in the eye with penetrating steadiness. "Surprise indicates deviation from a plan. Doesn't that statement seem curious from a truck driver who just mangled a vehicle with people in it?"

"I'm sure you're mistaken, Ms. Greene. Logging trucks do look a lot alike." The officer was growing impatient with the accusations. They reeked of reams of paperwork.

"No, I'm sure I'm not—sir. If Roger Crane is also the same driver we saw at the BLM site, then I believe we have a clear case of assault—maybe even attempted murder." Vera pushed her shoulders back as she exhaled forcefully through her nostrils. She was determined to control her temper; let Isaac display the hysteria.

"Well, ma'am, I suggest you take this to the DA. Perhaps she'll be interested." The officer pushed his chair back and he stood up as he spoke.

"In fact, we still need to investigate your damaged car, Ms. Greene, to determine if your brake lights were operating properly. These log truck drivers have a tough enough job without other folks' unsafe driving."

"So are you insinuating that I may be at fault for a big rig tail-gaiting me too closely?"

"Ms. Greene, your complaints may be valid, but they are out of my jurisdiction. Like I said, the DA over in Ukiah is who you wanna speak with. Now if you'll excuse me, I have some paperwork to finish here."

"Thank you for your time, officer," Vera concluded, and calmly reached for the door handle. Isaac jerked up behind her and began whining before they hit the street.

MILL CLOSES

The sound of the coffee beans grinding was almost as satisfying as the aroma. Robert went about the business of waking up with pleasure. His thoughts were allowed to flow unimpeded and, typically, his thoughts centered on Charles Hurwitz. Robert didn't take well to losing and Hurwitz was still ahead in this game. When the old growth was saved and the taxpayers reimbursed, Robert might be able to sleep. Until then, carry on.

The sun was just cresting over the ridge tops, casting a shimmering golden glow as the light filtered through the madrones. The freshly brewed coffee was smooth and flavorful as Robert sat in the big armchair contemplating. He wondered what Hurwitz saw in the morning from his high-rise in Texas. He hoped it was other high-rises filtered through a smoggy inversion layer.

Robert got up and dressed in his uniform of Levis and T-shirt. He had long since abandoned trying to distinguish the difference between a gray sock and an olive green one, invariably selecting the first two socks at the top of his drawer. He threw on a jacket and walked briskly up the crispy dew-covered path to the car.

The air of spring was still quite chilly this early in the day and the engine mildly protested being turned over. Robert sat patiently, contemplating this auspicious beginning to a predictably uneventful Sunday. The recent memories of lovemaking caused an involuntary spark of a smile to flash across his face. Actually, across his entire body.

He walked cheerfully into the market, warmly greeting the familiar employees as he searched for the necessary groceries. He then turned to the unnecessary ones: Should he get a bottle of champagne? Would it be too hedonistic to drink champagne on Sunday morning with the woman you love?

He strolled down the aisle, pausing in front of the magazine rack. The newspaper headline interrupted his reverie with the shock of the cold champagne bottle on the skin on his hand:

LP CUTTING 195 MILL JOBS: ENVIRONMENTALISTS FORCE SHUT DOWN.

Robert grabbed the paper and marched over to the checkout counter, seething with anger. He got into the truck and immediately read the article from start to finish. The thing was that LP had been over-cutting for so long (at more than twice the growth rate, according to state figures) that they had no more timber to supply to their own mill or any other neighboring sawmills. There weren't even any environmental activists harassing LP over their stump-infested, pecker pole forests—there simply wasn't any habitat worth protecting, it had all been decimated decades ago.

Smoking a cigarette through gritted teeth, Robert obsessed. This was precisely the kind of headline that incites angry passions. Wasn't there a name for this kind of malicious reporting? How about: "bullshit?"

He continued to read over the article, turning livid purple when he got to the part about LP President Joe Wheeler: "Wheeler blamed the new round of layoffs on the 'combined effects of preservationist pressures, the uncertainty of the designations of the spotted owl and expanding parks and wilderness areas.'"

"Okay," Robert said outloud to himself, "preservationist pressures—I get it. You bastards, I get it." He looked across the seat at the lone bottle of champagne, measuring its impact against his need. Fermenting with fury, he slammed the truck door and maneuvered directly towards the liquor department. Another round of mimosas for all.

He returned to the rusty old truck and headed back up the winding road for home. He traveled in silence while his internal dialogue raged a cacophony. To give it a rest, he turned on the radio station out of Garberville. Apparently this disc jockey had also read the morning paper, for Dylan's nasal indictment blared over the airways:

> *Steal a little and they throw you in jail,*
>
> *Steal a lot and they make you a king.*

Robert smirked and threw in a snort for good measure. Sunday was supposed to be a day of rest.

Monday's headline:

LP ANNOUNCES MOVE TO MEXICO FOR PROCESSING PLANT.

Too numb to even flinch, Robert read the LP spokesperson's statement:

> *Dwindling log supplies and mounting pressures from environmentalists are necessitating this financially strategic move. We see no reason why we should mediate timber harvest plans to meet the objections from radical environmental groups.*

Tuesday's headline:

LP SHOWS RECORD PROFITS FOR THE YEAR.

ROBERT'S EDITORIAL
"TIMBER WARS?"

Timber Wars—that is the term the industry uses to describe the battle in the streets and the courts for the right to decide what becomes of the last unprotected ancient Redwood groves.

Timber Wars? What a lost world we inhabit. Imagine if the fight to save lives was called the Corpse War. The result of losing the battle to save the forests is timber. Timber is what remains after the tree has been severed from the root. A tree is part of a forest and timber is part of an industrial process that makes lumber.

What if the war was for life and not death—it wouldn't be a war at all—it might be described instead in other terms such as preservation or conservation or preventive maintenance. But it isn't our choice to call it a war, although we see it as a battle against the status quo of continuing the destruction to the end of all wildness.

Don't kid yourself: The aim of the anti-environmentalists is to destroy all nature under some dictum that its supporters describe in religious terms. Science doesn't matter because the issue is that GOD gave the timber industry the trees to turn into timber and that is all there is to it. To destroy nature was a god-given right and anyone who opposes the cutting of all old growth forests is against god, against god's will and thus a pagan, a tree-worshiper, a baby hater and a communist.

What do we believe as environmentalists? What moves us to consider a career as an outcast, as a beleaguered iconoclast in our own communities? How does a person who has been a quiet, country-home dweller come out into the nasty world of politics? What could possibly keep a person going against the barrage of name-calling? What is in it for us? You can ask the question numerous ways, but it all comes out the same.

For some it is a sense of justice, a need to fight back against the Shitheads in the world and there are quite a number in the timber industry. The Shitheads, it is their name for themselves, have been part of the industry for a long time—the racists, the cursers, the haters of women. They inhabit the timber industry and can be called upon as thugs to get angry at any perceived enemy—whatever they are to be called: Pagans, commies, feminists, longhairs, baby-haters. The list goes on nauseatingly.

These thugs are hired by the industry to keep the rest in line and to be used against critics—to "shut them up" as the industry so delicately puts it.

When we began to insist that the laws be obeyed we were turned into anti-Americans. Why? Well law and order only works for the industry if it's their laws and their order that is being preserved or imposed. If anyone wants to enforce the existing law against the industry then these hapless critics must be turned into an object of hate so the thugs can take over the "debate." It's clear to all that to be an environmentalist here, in one of the timber corporations' resource colonies, one must be willing to accept a lot of abuse in every imaginable meaning of the word.

In spite of the hatred and physical risk there still are environmentalists. Some come out of the woods with a more spiritual motive. They are not political, not righting wrongs or enforcing man made laws. They feel something is amiss and with all the humility of a monk they join the political ones in rallies and meetings bringing poetry and songs into the heated rhetoric of the moment.

There are many concerned people, people who run stores, teach classes, make products for the new age, raise children, make homes for their families who see the wrongs, feel the feelings and help with their few resources of time and money supporting the work of the political and spiritual activists.

Isaac is a spiritual one—he feels the forest call to him as he has felt other callings to be who he is best at being—a singing crusader for what needs him. He tried to join the fighters for justice and fell in love with the ancient forests. Me, an ex-catholic, fought for justice and helped the others because they were underdogs fighting the Shitheads. Hannah and Vera, ex-catholics, too, were politicals who became fighters for the forest. Alice, an ex-catholic worked for the United Farm Workers. Gus, an ex-baptist, worked for the International Woodworkers of America. Others are members of unions. Only Isaac did not have a purely political beginning. But in the end the forest has called each of us to save the last of the ancient groves from destruction. There is no better way to put it—no way to say the words so that some dogmatic pseudo-Christian would not see it as sacrilege or blasphemy or paganism. Those who fought for the forests fell in love with the forests and the forests fell in love with them, too.

If we recognize the streak in human affairs that limits our thinking about life it would be described in terms of a sense of otherness: "The others have no right to what I want," would say it. Otherness. The other is not of my group, not like me therefore not human, not alive, not really anything but stuff to kill or move or remove. Otherness is the way those who believe in the curse of Eden see creation—as an enemy—and who are dedicated to destroying it. To be otherwise, to see the woods as a friend or at times to see an Indian as a human has been anathema—a thing of the devil, to the Indian killing, tree-killing Shitheads.

When the politicals came forward and said for justice sake the laws must be obeyed, and said that "adverse cumulative effect" means loss of fish and loss of jobs so the forests should be saved to save the streams is to save the fish and to save the jobs; they were called socialists and communists. The spirituals came forward and said that their Mother called to them to save the lungs of the earth from destruction at the hands of greedy unthinking monsters and they were called pagans—less than human—a piece of trash to be swept from the mind.

One thing the politicals always rued was the apparently easy time the Shitheads had in being convinced that the politicals were the enemies of their own communities. The industry was quick to make the politicals into Cassandras whose warnings were ignored while the mob was kept busy killing the messengers. The first round of name-calling by the industry identified the environmentalists as communists and pagans. "Communists" made us un-American and a deadly enemy. "Pagan" made us enemies of the Shithead's god.

It was too easy to call us communists. Everyone who cares about the welfare of people is a socialist and likely to say something in favor of compassion—compassion is a weakness to the Shitheads. But it is not fair to point at the Shitheads and make them to blame. They were not responsible, they are just being used. They never really had a chance. The industry would close a mill and blame the environmentalists. Then, they would move the equipment to Mexico or Chile or anywhere they could get lower wages and tax breaks. The workers and the Shitheads who kept them in line are the real victims.

Look at the Oklahoma City bomber and his ideological hometown—the militias formed by those who thought the government was telling them they could not log, graze or mine. They have been lied to, cheated and schemed on, not by the environmentalists, but by the big loggers, grazers and miners.

Yes, the bureaucracy is trimming back on available timber, grazing lands and mining claims. Why? Because the environmentalists are in charge? Bullshit, it's because the Big Boys want to squeeze out the little and use the little boys' laments to change the laws. The Big Boys selectively cause the laws to be enforced against the little boys. The little boys scream and the scream is used by the Big Boys to create a smoke screen to hide the real reason to change the laws—Big Boy greed.

The environmentalists cannot stop the Big Boys unless the Big Boys are being obviously greedy; so greedy even the little boys join in the effort. The Big Boys like big profits and none are bigger than those made when dealing with the government. Big Boys like big theft. So it goes the big use the little to bring about the very thing that the little get hurt by—a cynical way of doing business but very sure and very profitable for the Big Boys.

So we are called every name anyone can devise and we are blamed for every ill that befalls the little guy regardless of how untrue it may be. The little guy hurts, the little guy looks for a scapegoat, the big guy says it's the environmentalists so therefore...and it's the rush to judgment and the condemnation of the messenger. So be it.

It hurts to be referred to by so derogatory a term—nigger, spic, hymie, pagan, commie, baby-hater. They all hurt the idealists.

Environmentalists try not to bleed in public. For years we kept the threats and violence a secret. None of us wanted to tell the industry and its PR firms what really was effective. We got angry and fought in this war of theirs even harder. But now it's not as simple as turning the other cheek, or, don't get mad, get even.

Now the war has widened and the haters who were fueled in the late 80s to hate the environmentalist-controlled government have acted to kill fellow citizens: Not just environmentalists, but timber lobbyists and government workers. Someone sowed the winds and the death of the timber lobbyist and the government workers may amount to a reaping of the winds.

The industry caused the hate to increase. There is no manner of argument that will make that truth go away. The industry paid for the hate to increase.

LOGGING CONFERENCE
EUREKA FAIRGROUNDS

The crowd was not restless. A speaker stood on the platform detailing the plans for the afternoon session. The sit-down lunch was being delivered to long buffet tables across from the large meeting room maintained by Humboldt County in its Redwood Acres Fair Complex.

People from the rural counties who made their living in the woods met each year alternating between Ukiah or Eureka. This year, the Humboldt County WeCARE group was hosting the gathering. Mixed together were loggers, mill workers, truck drivers and machine operators, dressed in their work cloths. Scattered amongst them were the corporate executives, lawyers and timber owners. Small groups of students with teachers moved about through the crowd to see the displays of logging and lumber mill scenes arranged in historical order.

Outside, timber families and other visitors toured the parking lot, littered with the gigantic machines that worked in the woods to bring the logs into the mills. The most impressive was the Feller Buncher. As big as a house, it was designed to roam the new forests of smaller second and third growth trees—pecker poles they were derisively called. Its jaws would grab two, three, even four trees at a time, sever them from their roots and load them directly onto a trailer, ready to be connected to a semi-tractor for the trip out of the mountains to the mills on the flatland below. The Feller Buncher would replace ten men in the lumbering operation, yet the excitement it drew from the timber workers and their families did not indicate that they knew what its effects on their future might be.

Candy Black, the wife of a third generation old growth timber chopper, walked across the lot with three similarly shaped women. They were heading towards a small meeting room complex, 500 feet from the assembly hall.

"Chuck's going to be here to meet with us in ten minutes. We'll have time to compare our notes from last week and have a few laughs." Black rolled across the pavement, her legs working hard to move her polyester clad bulk. Her hands were full with a clipboard and a full quart of Diet Pepsi. She was trying to quit drinking the stuff since Pepsi might be supporting the Sierra Club, but the boycott had not been called yet so she simply tried to hide the label from easy recognition. She had already taken a razing from her husband who had joined Candy's boycott efforts like it was a new religion.

The four women entered a room to join two men slouched in lounge chairs near the coffee pot. Immediately, the old friends greeted each other with howls of recognition. Chuck had already taught them to be enthusiastic, and they responded to each other like football players after a score.

"Look at this. It's my new Van Gogh." Candy waved a crude drawing in the air. "It's the announcement for Earth First! National Tree Shit. What a yuk."

In the midst of the laughter, a tall, heavy, redheaded, definitely-in-charge man walked into the room talking. "Hi, sorry I'm a bit early. Can we get going now? You look like you are all here. The man strode to the end of the room and, like a grade school teacher, herding his flock into the seats around him. "I'm Charles Cushman with National Inholders Association spreading the word on how to fight terrorists. Candy, I know you. Why don't the rest of you introduce yourselves?" He pointed at a woman sitting next to Candy. "Okay. I'll start with you. What do you know and what do you want to know?"

"I'm just a housewife with two kids—just like Candy. We've known each other all our lives. We used to steal boyfriends from each other. Not any more. I am enthusiastic about fighting back. My husband is worried about losing his job. He works for Candy's father-in-law. They say it's dangerous to go into the woods with these radicals running all over spiking trees. I will work with Candy and I'm glad to meet you."

"What was your name?" Cushman snapped.

"Lynn Nelson." She turned to her friend Candy who smiled and nodded approval. Lynn would do anything she was asked to do, dear girl.

"And you? Please start with your name." Cushman pointed at a medium-sized man who looked as if he might have some of the ambitions Cushman sought.

"Gary Gundlach. A family man working at Mill A at PL. I'm a Christian with a journalism degree. I'd like to see godless environmentalism destroyed." Gundlach was a serious fellow. Well groomed as they all were, with a little something more. Cushman imagined Gundlach in his work clothes walking along a tree-lined road with his wife and children in tow. That would make a good piece of propaganda. Cushman was good at this and knew he had something here.

"Next."

As the others described themselves, Cushman roamed the room looking every bit the mad genius. He thought himself a hero, a warrior. Outside, the crowds churned around the equipment. Inside, this handful of loyal workers would chart a path to defeat the enemies of the corporations. Cushman felt the pulse of these people. He knew what they liked to be, how they liked to act. After so many meetings around the West, he knew what he would find in each stop. A small group of dedicated local bullies to put the screws to the longhairs and the outsiders. It was territorial. *We were here before you. We're going to be here after you are gone.* That was their motive and he knew how to exploit it.

"Okay. Look. You got to make this fun. These people have been making your life hard. Make their life hard. Turn their tactics against them. Say you know who they are. Where they live. Tell 'em. Send a note to tell them you are watching. You are the mothas who're on their tails."

Candy leapt from her seat. Her feet left the floor as she twirled a few degrees in the air. "I got it! I got it!"

Cushman stood opened mouth, unable to believe the energy she had for this. *God, what a woman. She probably makes her husband give her head in the morning.*

"Mothers watch their kids and these guys probably are all hung up about theirs. What if we told them their mothers are watching them. They'd freak."

"So what?" Cushman snapped. "Mothers watch?"

"We'll call ourselves Mothers Watch. What a yuk." Another leap, another yelp and she sat down. "Excuse me."

Her friends went wild. "See why we love her!" someone exclaimed.

CATCH AND RELEASE

Isaac was hopping around like a speed freak after three espressos. He and Vera had driven for two hours to attend this meeting in Eureka. He got impatient with all the planning; it was the action he understood. They'd started business slightly early, and the entire meeting progressed so smoothly that it was burnt out as a joint was lit up. Natural death of a meeting is always a good thing. Vera wisely abandoned business as the sweet scent of marijuana filled the air. It was late anyway.

After cleaning up the paperwork (Vera insisted on clear directions and consistency), they headed to their car, needing two trips to pack everything back in. They grabbed their musical instruments last and drove from Eureka to Arcata, 12 miles up the highway.

They both loved Arcata—great restaurants, coffee, bookstores, music. The town actually had the guts to declare itself a "nuclear free zone" following the Northcoast Citizens success making the county a Nuke Free Zone. Thanks to the university, Arcata was a haven for progressives and eccentrics. Lawyers in three-piece suits walked comfortably across the town plaza while clusters of tie-dyed college kids played hacky sack to the hypnotic rhythm of drum beats. This small town on the bay was nestled defiantly between Eureka and McKinleyville—both havens for conservatives, K-Marts and cable TV.

Nearing the off-ramp to Arcata, Vera was so immersed in discussion that she didn't notice the flashing red light in her rear-view mirror, not until she heard the blaring siren.

"Oh shit, we're being pulled over." Vera scowled into the mirror as she down-shifted. "I was under the speed limit. I always drive slowly."

"I've told you," Isaac said tersely, "being stoned makes you drive too slowly. They look for that, you know." Isaac whined nervously in a high pitched voice reserved for chaos, "We aren't carrying any stash are we?"

"Of course I'm not carrying. Just calm down, goddamn it. We haven't done anything wrong."

Vera pulled the car onto the shoulder while Isaac sat twitching in the front seat, half expecting a pair of giant loggers with oversized chainsaws to assault them in the darkness of Humboldt Bay. His imagination was gratefully relieved when only one uniformed CHP officer walked up to the passenger side window with a flashlight.

"Evening folks," he said pleasantly enough. "Can I see your driver's license, please?" He passed his flashlight briefly through the car, before taking Vera's license.

"Hmm." He inspected the driver's license and then Vera. "Well, the problem is, ma'am, that you've got expired registration on this vehicle. I noticed your old tag back at the stoplight in Eureka."

So why did he wait to pull us over on the freeway? Isaac wondered. *So he could catch us at speeding…two for the price of one? Law enforcement must be bored tonight.*

Vera quickly responded, "That's not possible. I distinctly remember paying my registration. I know I put that sticker on. Could it have fallen off?"

"Hmm. I'll need to call this in. You two sit tight." He backed away from the window and walked to the rear of the car to inspect the plate before returning to the patrol car to make his call.

Isaac nervously drummed his fingers on his lap as he spoke. "This is bullshit. This is harassment, Vera. They're trying to scare us."

"Well they're succeeding with you—so just shut up." Vera hated it when Isaac panicked, which he seemed to be doing a lot of lately. "See, he's coming back and his gun isn't even drawn." She flashed him a feigned look of relief, then rolled her eyes back in disgust.

The officer returned to the window and stated, "Well ma'am, it appears that you are legal. Everything is in order, though... I think you might want to take a look at this sticker."

Perplexed, they followed him behind the car. Sure enough there was an expired sticker but it obviously was not an official DMV one, as it had been crudely colored and glued on. They peeled it off to reveal the legal one, then examined it under the flashlight.

The officer spoke first, "Looks like someone wanted to play a little joke on you."

Isaac was infuriated, "Isn't there something we can do about this? Are you going to investigate?"

"Well sir," the officer spoke slowly. "Without direct observation of the perpetrator, I don't see a whole lot we can do. I'll file a report and get back to you if anything comes up."

"I demand justice..."

Vera cut him off in mid-sentence, "Thank you, officer, for your patience. We appreciate your help."

The officer returned to his vehicle to write out his report, as a mystified Vera and Isaac got back in their car.

"Dammit, Vera, why shouldn't we insist on justice? That has to be forgery, or vandalism, or..."

"Mockery."

"...or some sort of crime! You can't just duplicate government documents."

Vera patiently drove on before responding, "Okay Isaac. You're doubtlessly right, okay? But haven't you learned your lesson from our last encounter with the law? They aren't interested in protecting us. In case you've forgotten, one of our goals is to cultivate positive relations with law enforcement—not badger them."

Isaac glared at her like he was going to pounce. But after a few deep breaths, he decided he was too blasted tired to get into an intense discussion with someone else who knew it all. When he could trust his voice to return to the proper octave, he spoke.

"Look, I'm not paranoid. Someone is watching us and screwing around. I need to call Robert. I wish I had a cellular phone." He was silent for a nanosecond before excitedly questioning, "Where do you think they did it? It must have been tonight at the meeting. We would have noticed, or the CHP would have noticed had it been done earlier today before we left home."

"Yeah, I think you're right. I've considered the possibilities and I have to agree with you. It must have happened tonight. Whoever it was knew our itinerary, or else they had to be following us."

They arrived at the Earth First! house—a rambling old farmhouse set out in the cow pastures of the Arcata bottoms—to find everyone asleep. They gratefully unrolled their bed gear on the living room floor and retired, exhausted.

After a short night's sleep, Isaac woke abruptly to a thick blanket of coastal fog swelling in visible waves across the nearby pasture. He rolled over to inspect Vera's inert body for any signs of consciousness and detected not a one. His head was inundated with ideas, lyrics and visions. He slid out of bed and crept into the kitchen.

He was steeped in concentration with a wicked cup of coffee when Vera walked in. While still rubbing the sleep out of her eyes, she immediately launched into a logistical discussion. Listening to her discourse caused his head to throb even more. *She was disgustingly perky first thing in the morning. How could someone segue so easily from horizontal non-consciousness to vertical vitality?*

They arrived at the demonstration site, the Pacific Lumber mill in Scotia, along with about 30 other activists. The placards were already made, and people were beginning to form marching lines. Vera had the bullhorn and started organizing the protesters, while Isaac checked his memos to verify which media representatives would be covering the story. He immediately proceeded to the nearby pay phone to attempt to rouse two more reporters for today's event.

The noon whistle blew and the curious workers came out to the tables, watching the spectacle of tree-hugging longhairs performing their theatrics. They opened up their lunch coolers and sat back for the show. Repetitive factory work was inherently mind dulling. A little noontime diversion was always welcome.

The protest was going well. Several TV cameras had arrived to catch images of the workers clustered on their lunch break, while a parade of hippies was chanting in the background. Suddenly, someone yelled, "Hey, it's the PL president, John Campbell. He's coming in that car." All eyes turned to the gleaming luxury sedan which was moving steadily towards the gate.

"Citizen's arrest! Let's arrest John Campbell for crimes against the forest!"

The protesters immediately congregated around the moving vehicle, yelling chants and thrusting their signs. They proceeded to move in front of the car, walking with it since Campbell evidenced no sign of slowing down. The security guards were nervous now, anxiously awaiting the arrival of the county sheriffs. Campbell rolled his window down a crack and shouted angrily, which caused those nearby to laugh and mock his Australian accent. The mill workers were loving the show.

"You're under citizen's arrest for violation of the Forest Practices Act." A swell of cheering and clapping followed—from both protesters and workers. Campbell was married to the boss's daughter and had few friends on either side of this fence.

Like an amoeba encircling its prey, the protesters surrounded the vehicle on all sides. Campbell, in a panic, sped up through the wall of shouting and waving people who were running alongside the car. One woman was knocked over to the side of the road and several protesters were clinging to the sides and back of the vehicle in an attempt to force it to stop.

The security guards jumped in and attempted to pull people off the car. One of them yelled at Campbell, "Get out of here—NOW!" as the frenzied crowd screamed and clung tighter to the vehicle.

Campbell sped up through the human barricade as people scattered on all sides.

Isaac looked over at Gus and flashed a smile of pure delight; action was happening. Gus waved back at Isaac and continued pacing the car. Running in front of it he realized that Campbell was not going to stop for him or any of them. With his long ponytail flying behind him, he leapt onto the hood, yelling, "No compromise!" and lay there spread-eagled, grasping the windshield wipers as Campbell accelerated through the gate.

"Look, John Campbell has an Earth First! hood ornament! It's Gus!" someone gaily cried as the cameras excitedly lapped it up.

About seventy-five yards up the road, Campbell pulled over and asked the man to get off of his hood. Gus looked back over the roof of the car and saw a group of protesters running to catch up, immediately followed by the camera people clumsily lugging their equipment. Isaac, of course, was behind the media waving his arms and shouting directions like the master of a grand chariot race. Gus smiled defiantly at Campbell and said, "My friends are coming. We're going to arrest you!"

Campbell turned his head quickly to see a convergence of shouting, running activists and, in a frenzied panic, hit the accelerator. Gus, his belly pressed to the hood, glared at Campbell's face through the windshield and said pointedly, "Bad press, dude."

The car drove another hundred yards until a sheriff's car blocked the road ahead and Campbell pulled over. The pursuing protesters with their attendant media crew were just in time to see Gus being pried off the hood by three officers. He was immediately arrested along with a group of the more vocal and persistent protesters, including Isaac.

Isaac didn't go down without seizing the moment to capture more media exposure. He waved and shouted to cheers of applause. He yelled out something about "arresting John Campbell for vehicular assault," but was silenced as he was loaded into the back of the sheriff's car with the cameras frantically clicking away. He was too busy congratulating himself on the great press event to be concerned about his potential jail term.

John Campbell eluded arrest of any kind and proceeded onward.

Vera and Hannah were laughing so hard they were almost in tears.

The millworkers were in hysterics. The security guards were awe-struck. No one had anticipated such a melee, such a grand diversion on just another lunch hour. The factory would be buzzing with more than machinery for that afternoon.

Isaac, Gus and three others were booked into the Humboldt County Jail, where they were briefly read their charges, their rights and then locked in cells. Isaac alone was detained for questioning, as he had a prior record for trespassing and a reputation as an activist leader. He was forthcoming in his answers and gave the law enforcers no resistance. When absolutely necessary, he understood the value of being courteous and respectful; after all, they did hold the key to his cell.

He made his one phone call to Harris Collins, Robert's stand-up lawyer, who had already spoken with Vera and was arranging for bail.

It was Saturday night and he sat alone in the sparse room, wondered where the others were. He could hear voices down the corridor and the cells surrounding him seemed to be occupied by derelicts and druggies—lots of moaning and incoherent grumbles. The pervasive odors of vomit and sweat, mingled with excrement, were enough to make anyone incoherent, even without using drugs.

Isaac slept fitfully through the night. The groans and rumblings in his cell block kept him awake just enough to remind him where he was. He wondered if they made tapes of "jail mood noise" to have on hand just in case the real noise wasn't sufficient to drive the prisoners crazy. As the first light of dawn filtered through the high window bars, he heard the jingling of keys. He sat up as an officer stopped before his cell and barked, "Winwood?"

"Uh, yeah, that's me. Isaac Winwood."

"Says here that your lawyer posted bail. You're free for now," the officer stated, as he selected the proper key and undid the lock.

Isaac shook his head incredulously and rubbed his eyes. *Must be early Sunday morning. Great to be outta here. I hope the others are doing okay.* It was weird to be let out so early, but due to a pounding migraine, he didn't dwell on it long.

He walked out the front door of the jail onto the deserted main street of Eureka. He scanned the scenery for the nearest phone when he caught sight of a jumbo-sized woman leaning against a rather small car. He never realized Hondas were so little. She waved to him and beckoned him over.

Isaac walked hesitantly towards her, curiously considering the possibilities. She looked like a typical Eureka housewife, her leviathan-like body stuffed into clinging polyester. *Hmm, maybe this is a Fellini dream...?*

"Hello, Isaac. My name is Candy Black. I'd like to have a word with you. Join me for a cup of coffee?"

Isaac stared at her for several seconds before responding, "Coffee? That would probably help. How'd you know my name?"

She smiled agreeably as she motioned him to get into her car. "Oh, let's just say I have a lot of friends." She returned her attention to driving the few blocks over to the Denny's.

Isaac followed Candy into the garish restaurant, feeling his headache reverberate with disgust. He slid into the orange plastic seat across as she arranged her bean bag-like bulk into the opposite booth. They say that the colors red and orange are appetite stimulators. Candy's shiny red blouse just made him want to hurl. The waitress arrived and poured Isaac a watery, tan liquid which she identified as coffee. Candy ordered a Diet Coke.

Having revived herself with caffeine and sugar, Candy finally spoke. "So, I've heard a lot about you—seen you on the news. I figured I might as well get to know this guy I already don't like." She smiled just a bit to show she wasn't entirely serious.

"Do I know you, Mrs. Black? I'm sorry, but I really don't remember. I'm sort of groggy from a pretty bad night."

"Call me Candy. See, I'm one of the founders of 'Mothers Watch.' I'm interested in the battles that you're fighting because, see, you Earth First!ers are causing our community a lot of trouble. I intend to keep you from too much more of it." She slurped her Coke noisily, as if to emphasize the importance of her last statement.

Isaac tried to rev his mind up to her speed. "Candy, do you understand what it is we're fighting for? Don't you see that the only real villains here are the corporate owners of the timber companies who don't give a damn about you, me, or the workers?"

Candy smiled. *Nice try.* "I'll tell you what I do understand. Earth First! isn't offering my husband a job to dance around and screw up hard-working people's lives. You environmentalists don't give a damn about making a living yourself because you suck off of welfare. You suck off of this hard working community." Slurp, slurp.

"This isn't about jobs versus forests." Isaac looked at Candy imploringly. "This is about people being treated with respect and dignity—the same way we need to treat our resources. These ancient forests are rare. Once they're gone, so is the unique habitat for several species...and so are the timber raper corporations who'll never be back in our lifetime." He grimaced as he sipped the coffee-esque liquid in his mug. Somehow his canned speeches didn't go over so well in a Denny's restaurant.

"So who's going to pay our bills? Who's going to feed our children? If you people have it your way, this whole area will become a big, useless park." Candy slammed her drink down on the table as her squinty eyes blazed. "You better just go back to your caves and leave the rest of us responsible folks to take care of business around here."

"Candy, please. We're not trying to take away jobs." Isaac was exhausted and suffering from the migraine attack. He tried to focus. "We just want you to understand that the timber industry is fooling you. Your husband and all the rest will be out of jobs when they're done savaging the forests." The smell of fried bacon emanating from the kitchen only increased his discomfort.

She seemed intrigued. "Well, how come this here forest has been providing for us for generations. That is, 'til you environmentalists showed up needing more spotted owls, or whatever?"

Isaac swallowed hard. "Look, technology has wiped out more jobs than any environmental laws ever will." He noticed a blank look on Candy's face. "We can work together to create jobs and a healthy forest for all the species that live here."

Candy snorted excitedly, "Chuck Cushman, who helped us start our watch group, says that spotted owls are like aspirin: Two are good for you. One hundred will put you in the hospital." She smirked and sat up straighter as she glared defiantly at Isaac.

Isaac nodded his head and closed his eyes to take another deep breath. "Candy, I really wish you could hear what we say, instead of being brainwashed by these big public relations firms." He folded his hands together on the table to reinforce his sincerity. "This Cushman guy doesn't live here and doesn't even care what the issues are. His job is to convince you that environmentalists are bad so that you'll be afraid and angry—so that you'll fight the timber companies' battles for them."

"Well, I believe him, see. See, he's helping us protect our families. I'm going to keep on fighting to help my husband keep his job. We're all going to fight. Besides, what do you long-haired, big-mouth activists know about keeping a job?"

Isaac felt like he might as well have been trying to sell tofu burgers to a cattle rancher. "Look, none of us wants to fight. But the environment can't speak for itself, so we have to speak up." He slid out of the booth and stood up, extending his right hand. "Thank you for the conversation and coffee, Candy. I've got to get to work."

She shook his hand and smiled as she watched him push open the big glass doors and step outside. She'd never gotten that close to a hippie before. Kind of exciting to meet their leader; he was a lot shorter than she expected. She wanted to talk to Chuck. Isaac Winwood didn't seem very dangerous at all.

DIRTY TRICKS

Candy Black was in the back bedroom, now her "office." She laughed as she opened up the latest box of bumper stickers. She just knew all her friends would get a cackle when they saw them: *Earth First!: America's Favorite Speed Bumps.*

"Well," she said out loud to no one in particular, "if those crazy earth Nazis lie down in front of our trucks, then we'll be happy to oblige them." She chuckled at her own wit as she straightened out all the new electrical cords—such a network, such a tangle. Louisiana Pacific had given her a photocopy machine and Pacific Lumber had found a good typewriter for her. Good old John Campbell of PL had even installed another phone-line with an answering machine.

She liked this. She liked the importance of saving her community, her friends' way of life, her own husband's job. With the kids all grown up, she found herself with too much time on her hands and a very active mind. Now people were actually calling her for information and advice. She was the center of the eco-resistance on the Northcoast and she proudly flew yellow ribbons to flaunt it. She even bought a new yellow sweatshirt with a hood to wear to meetings and rallies.

Candy sat down at the typewriter to compose a flier announcing another yellow ribbon rally. Her creative juices were flowing like the Eel River at flood-stage. She called for another boycott of any local businesses which supported Earth First!. She perused the pages of *The Country Activist* and the local environmental center's newsletter, to see who advertised there. Let these green obstructionists feel it right where she and the rest of the timber community felt it—in the wallet. She hadn't felt this much power since she was head cheerleader in high school.

Her indulgent reverie was interrupted by the cheerful ringing of her new phone line.

"Hello, this is Mothers Watch," Candy proudly spoke into the phone.

"Good morning, Candy. This is Chuck. Glad I caught you in." Chuck Cushman was always organized and constantly looking for other avenues to advance his programs. He had unlimited ideas and zero patience. "I'm checking to see that you're ready for Rick Siemens and his 'dirty tricks' workshop scheduled for this Friday."

Candy excitedly popped opened another Diet Coke. "Oh yes. Everyone is looking forward to this." She sucked in a quick breath. "Rick is such a nice man. He told me about using the expired sticker—you know, on license plates—and anyway, the girls and I already tried it. We had so much fun!"

"Uh, yeah, that's great. I'm sure you and the girls will learn all sorts of new things at this workshop. Now, I just spoke with both Galitz and Campbell and their companies have agreed to give their employees the afternoon off to attend this workshop." Chuck grunted to clear his throat. "Of course, they are to be commended for being so generous with their companies' resources."

Candy smiled into the receiver, "Oh that's fabulous, Chuck. Those enviro weirdos haven't got a chance now that we're all working together. Golly, we even have strategies and plans, don't we? This is just like a battle, right?"

Chuck grimaced into the receiver. *This woman is a moron. Why do I associate with such idiots?* "Yes, Candy. This is indeed a battle. Now let me say that I appreciate all the good work you're doing. I've given the FBI that video you made when those radicals assaulted Campbell's car—they were very pleased. Yes, indeed, very pleased."

"Really? I didn't think the FBI even knew where Eureka was. This is exciting; sort of like *Unsolved Mysteries!*"

Chuck was about ready to lose his breakfast into the receiver. "Hmm… well, very good. I also want to remind you to keep those letters to the editor coming; especially about this nonsense that the radicals say they don't do spiking. The public must be informed."

"Oh, the girls and I love to get together and write all those letters. Of course, I do most of the writing and they just sign 'em." Candy chuckled with glee.

"Keep up the good work, Candy. I'll check back later in the week."

"Goodbye, Chuck. And, thanks."

Cushman hung up the phone and stared out the window at the horses in the pasture. He loved this ranch in the finest area of Washington State. He also loved his other three ranches, and needed to move fast if he was going to be able to swing the creative financing required to maintain his lifestyle.

Candy slurped loudly on her Diet Coke in a state of sheer exhilaration. She flitted about the office, her face beaming as she stacked posters and filed memos. She was saving newspaper clippings relating to anything on the timber issue, or radicals in general, and was constantly urging her friends to submit letters to the editor. This was really a full-time job, trying to keep up with the environmentalists. They were turning up all over the place. Maybe there was something to all that tofu they ate.

Candy fondled the new Mothers Watch T-shirts with an uncommon reverence as she spoke on the phone to one of the girls. Her husband, John, wandered into her office, eating his fourth straight night of TV dinners. He leaned against the door frame, watching his wife at work.

"Candy," John asked, "do you mind if I go out and play some pool tonight with the guys? Doesn't seem like you've got much time for me anyway."

She looked up and smiled. "No way do I mind. I'm up to my eyeballs in preparing for this big workshop on Friday, and you know I just have to be ready." Her face glowed. "I might even lose a few pounds at this rate."

John let out a huge sigh. He was generally a somber man; patient, kind and reliable. He was a respected logging contractor and ran a tight crew. He wasn't one to make sudden changes, and this woman before him was not the same wife he had a few months ago.

"I miss your good cooking, Candy."

"Oh John, you're just saying that. Besides, cooking is how I keep this outrageous figure." She giggled, patting her polyester-clad rear.

"I like you the way you are. I am real proud and all, of the stuff you're doing. The guys at work all talk about Mothers Watch. I just wish you had more time..."

"Really? They talk about me?" Candy beamed up at her husband of twenty-two years.

"Sure, honey. Those environmentalists haven't got a chance with you and the other girls on top of their crap." John put down his fork before he spoke again. "In fact, I heard some of the guys talking today and they were saying that the timber companies have promised to back us up. They said that if any of us just happen to catch an environmentalist sabotaging any equipment or property, and we just happen to kill them to defend ourselves, well, then, we're guaranteed $40,000."

Candy's eyes got big. "$40,000? Oh my gawd; that sounds like a bounty."

"No, not really. See, the money is for legal defenses—or a guy could use it to get out of the country."

"That's pretty big money. Wish I could catch one those hippies monkey wrenching. I'd buy a new Camaro, a bright red one." Candy chortled at the image, then stopped short. "John, I was just kidding. You're not thinking about carrying a gun into the forest now, are you?"

He rolled his eyes at her and snorted, "Honey, I've been carrying a gun for the last five years now."

John put on his baseball hat emblazoned with "I eat spotted owls for lunch" and headed into town in his pick-up truck. The smoke in the bar was thick enough to forgive even the most grievous of fashion insults. Some indistinguishable country twang emanated from the old jukebox as John ordered a draft Bud and joined the rest of the guys near the pool tables. He was warmly welcomed and joined in the next game.

"Alright!" John squealed as he broke the balls sending the number three and number six into the pocket. He executed a clean bank shot and a fair left English to pocket two more before he missed. As he stood back waiting for his turn, he asked the other guys, "Have you heard about the reward money for catching those environmentalists messing around in the woods?"

"Goddamn—it's $40,000, isn't it?"

John slowly nodded his head. "Yeah, the big bosses are getting a little ticked off by all these protests. They got it coming from the courts and the woods now. If it gets too hard, maybe they'll all pack up and move to Mexico."

"You mean the Bahamas? Shee-it. Like their salaries don't cover their tropical vacations as it is."

Another logger spoke up: "Hell, they might just have declared open season on long-haired hippies. Maybe catch me a trophy size—one of them vegetarians in a VW bus!"

"I wonder how much you get if you catch a whole bus full!"

They all laughed and swigged their beers, ordering another pitcher for the next game of pool. They bantered about the ten best ways to catch a hippie, but were drowning in fits of laughter and beer suds by the time they reached number six. Hard to take much seriously when you've got a good pool game and a full mug of beer before you.

Brad Douglas, a logger well known for his bravado and his bragging, jumped off the barstool. He grabbed his mug of beer and, executing a robust swig, proclaimed, "They aren't gonna get past me; I'm ready for them nature lovers." He was quite tall and thin, with a ruggedly handsome face. He had as much of a reputation for handling heavy equipment as he did for handling other men's wives—heavy or otherwise.

"Yeah, Brad. Too bad those hippie chicks aren't ready for you. Why you just might chafe your face on their bristly thighs!" Brad momentarily considered the possibility of making it with a natural woman, but quickly realized that he preferred his women to look real, like the ones in the catalogs.

Brad continued strutting as he puffed up his narrow shoulders. "If I catch one of them long-haired radicals spiking a tree, goddamn it, I'll crucify them and take the whole friggin' tree to town with them still attached." He stomped his spiked-soled boots for emphasis, while his comrades hooted and hollered for another round of beer—another round for the great warrior logger.

Back at the Mothers Watch office, Candy was on her third pint…of diet Coke. Her pudgy little fingers were flying over the typewriter keys with fervor. Her latest composition was destined for the Bay Area, the *San Francisco Chronicle*. She was intoxicated with glee.

Dear Editor:

Earth First! renounces tree spiking. Get real! Are there really people dumb enough to believe this? That would be like letting everyone in jail out if they said they would never commit another crime. I would like to believe the world is not that stupid.

This is a group of spoiled children. They do not work, pay taxes or own property. They don't even believe in private property. Most of them come to the Northwest from the East Coast and none have the qualifications to tell us how to manage our resources. Do you really think we are so dumb, we would not manage the forest for our future? Reforestation was not thought of by Earth First!, the Sierra Club or Forests Forever. Trees are America's renewable resource.

If the people in the Bay Area think housing is expensive now, wait and see what happens if any of the initiatives pass that want to stop logging.

—Candy Black, Eureka

OPD: SERGEANT BOB CHEWART AND OFC. MIKE DIMMS

The sergeant hung up the phone and put out his last cigarette of the pack. He stood up, stretching his back, and glanced out the window onto the street.

He gazed at the usual display of humanity: Traditionally dressed lawyers hustling with their briefcases while clusters of young black men swaggered and swayed, wearing colossal belts cinched tightly over their pants which, by unspoken law, must be at least three sizes too large. Belching, fuming automobiles choked every possible intersection, giving the captive drivers a chance to take in the ever-changing array of billboards.

Ah, Oakland; the busy city by the Bay.

Oakland, California, is really two cities, neither of which has managed to pull itself out of the shadow of its neighboring municipalities: San Francisco and Berkeley. The west side of Oakland is a flat sprawling collection of ghettos that mirrors every major industrial city in America. The disadvantaged, the poor who shuffle down the hideously cluttered streets, seem oblivious to the trash and debris strewn about their lives.

Just a few miles away to the east, lie equally sprawling but gentle hillsides covered with expensive homes, elegant gardens and world class views of the spectacular San Francisco Bay and the city for which it is named.

Oaklanders have a lot of pride, but one gets the unmistakable sense of bravado—the kind that conceals the ripped-off feeling of envy. To the north is Berkeley, a town famous for its radical elements, trend-setting thought and politics. Berkeley: where street people in cast-off clothing freak freely with the erudite and pseudo-erudite while exclusive dress shops display their extravagant wares next to homegrown ethnic food stands.

To the west, directly across the Bay is The City—so much a cosmopolitan center that the reference to it is capitalized. San Francisco was the West Coast's roaring, glowing core of international art, commerce and culture when Oakland, and even L. A., were just tiny villages.

Oakland's politics have always been reactionary—responding to the progressive flow of its neighbors. It became the fortress of conservatism and the source of police might whenever the radical fringes on its borders encroached. The activists in nearby Berkeley created consternation since the civil rights movement of the 60s and continue to plague the conservative/corporate interests vested in Oakland.

Sergeant Chewart pulled away from the window and walked over to peer through the Plexiglas partition where officers were chomping on their phones, their files, their burgeoning piles of paperwork. He craned his neck to look for Mark Dimms, his most recent partner in this division: Domestic Terrorism. He spotted the lieutenant leaning against the soft drink machine, yukking it up with some of the guys.

"Officer Dimms, I'd like to see you in my office, please."

"Yes, sir, I'll be right in," Dimms quickly replied, patting his buddy on the shoulder as he passed him by. He was honored and impressed with being asked to participate in this investigation. Working with Bob Chewart and the great FBI agent Fred Boyle was the young officer's chance to make a name for himself.

Sergeant Chewart was rummaging through his desk drawer when Mark Dimms entered his enclosed office. The younger officer sat down and waited attentively for the sergeant's attention. He gazed politely at the display of awards, honors and badges dominating every wall. Wow, the sergeant has really seen some action. Chewart apparently found what he needed and looked up at the expectant face of Mark Dimms.

"Well Dimms, we've been handed a videotape of some interesting suspects. These are some people we're going to get to know up close." Chewart smirked. "We're expecting a visitor, Mendocino County Sheriff Sam

Satterwitte, to join us and uh, narrate for us." He laid the video down on his desk and checked his watch.

"Yes, sir."

"Now, you've been briefed and have reviewed the materials regarding this terrorist group—Earth First! they call themselves—so you fully understand the extent of their activities, correct?"

"Yes, sir."

"Just to update you, here is a copy of their terrorist manual. I believe you've already been briefed with excerpts." He opened up a large, stuffed folder and extracted a document showing a cross-section of a bomb placed in the ground. The accompanying description gave detailed explanations of materials and methods for producing the bomb.

Dimms reached across the desk to examine the page. "Whoa, this is the kind used to maim vehicles, right?"

"I believe the specific target is dirt bikes...ah...in the desert, or the wilderness, as the environmentalists like to think of it. Their particular psychology is based on preserving all things in their natural state." Cough. "Obviously, they have a large assortment of 'enemies' if they're determined to defend the wilderness on those terms."

"Ah, sir, do we have any evidence of these environmentalists attacking humans? I mean, all the information we have on this group indicates that they focus on machinery and man-made structures. I've read a lot of background material on environmentalists, and most of these types are very nonviolent. I mean, if I have read the files correctly." Dimms nervously looked up at his superior, hoping he didn't sound too naive.

Chewart lit up a cigarette, inhaling a hearty draw. He exhaled forcefully, then spoke. "You are correct. I assure you, though, that we have good reason to observe their actions and, of course, the anecdotal evidence is overwhelming."

"Yes, sir. Are you referring to this manual?"

"Precisely." Chewart slowly tapped his ashes into the ashtray and smacked his lips decisively. "The FBI has asked for our cooperation in monitoring the environmentalists over the next few months."

"Yes, sir. You worked on the civil rights protests in Berkeley, right sir?"

"Indeed I did. We've established a good history of cooperation with the Feds. Keeps our...ah...network of information flowing smoothly."

Just then a knock resounded on the door and Sam Satterwitte entered. "Good afternoon, Bob, Mark, pleased to be here in your fair city."

Chewart guffawed. "Right, Sam. Nothing like a stinking city filled with low-life scum." He reached out for the big sheriff's hand and they shook heartily. The sheriff reached over for Officer Dimms' hand before sitting down.

"Yeah, Bob, you can't escape it. I've got my own form of scum hiding out up there in the redwoods." Satterwitte smiled easily. He loved his work.

Chewart smirked also and held up the video, pushing his chair back. "I believe, gentlemen, that we have some work to do here while we've got the good sheriff's attention. Let's check out these...what are they called?...eco-terrorists," he said with a laugh.

The men retired to the viewing room and were joined by two more Oakland Police officers. As they were setting up the VCR, Chewart explained the source of the video. "A timber community activist named Candy Black has been documenting their activities. Her husband runs some logging business. Apparently she's got a lot of time on her hands and a lot to lose if the environmentalists get those initiatives passed. The timber companies are pretty concerned about all of that."

The TV screen came to light showing a crowd of protesters in front of the Pacific Lumber mill. The crowd parted to reveal a car driven by John Campbell. The Sheriff narrated the action, describing the events leading up to the arrests.

"Now Sheriff," Chewart interjected, "who is the core group organizing Redwood Summer?"

The Sheriff picked up his notes. "Well, we've got these activists, Earth First!, who are doing all the planning. And I believe we've got all the main leaders here on film." The screen was frozen on two laughing women and one man. "The one on the left is Vera Greene, one of the key organizers of the Earth First! group. She's the brains—does the meetings, coordinates with agencies—a damn good speaker. The other woman is not of interest; she's an industry mole. The man is Lou Giaccalone; doesn't seem to be a main leader though he often appears at their meetings and groups often congregate at his house down on the river."

Captain Rudsitter spoke up: "Do you know the location of the hideout for this Vera Greene? Seems like she's one we should be keeping a close eye on."

"Ah, huh. I believe we should be able to find her place." The Sheriff stroked his chin thoughtfully, "If I got my directions right, she lives about half a mile, maybe three-fourths, up Strong's Creek Road, off of Highway 101. There's a group of houses—nice neighborhood."

The video continued on, revealing more shots of Vera, Hannah, Lou and others. Both the Sheriff and Sergeant Chewart supplied information about the progression of events. Finally they froze it again on Campbell's car, where a man could be seen almost plastered to the hood, while in the background Isaac was running next to the camera crew.

"The guy on the hood is Gus Russell. He's almost always with that Winwood fellow you see in the back there. Russell engages in most protests and is a former reporter for some big city paper. Now he does freelance. He was arrested, as you see in the next frame."

They moved ahead to show Isaac being handcuffed. "Okay, this is the main spokesman for Earth First!" Someone sniggered. "Yeah, I know, he doesn't look too formidable, but apparently he's quite a nature fanatic. Sings these outrageous songs and gets the media all stirred up. Actually, he's a pretty interesting fellow, once you get to know him," Satterwitte added, shaking his head. "Anyway, he works closely with Vera Greene and they were lovers, maybe still are."

The officers continued to study the video, pausing to discuss as they took notes. The PL protest segment ended and another one began, this time at a Planned Parenthood clinic in Willits.

Sergeant Chewart took over the narrating. "This is an older protest—let's see—ah, almost six months ago. This one was filmed by another timber community supporter, a mill worker named Gary Gundlach."

The camera panned the opposing groups of activists, coming to rest on Isaac and Vera. "As you will see often, those two rely on their musical talents to enrapture their audience." A general chuckling ensued at the sergeant's sarcasm. "Now, besides our two musical friends, we have another key player, a Hannah Caine, who is much more behind the scenes."

Chewart pointed to the attractive woman with the long hair, standing discreetly behind the crowd. "She was one of the primary authors of their forest initiative. We don't have much footage of her, or even much information other than that she works at that newspaper."

The camera panned to a rather large man shouting and hoisting his fist. Chewart stood up and gestured with his pencil extending toward the screen, "Now that's Earl Sutley. He's been involved for years with the eccentric political factions—Peace and Freedom Party, for one—the FBI has a thick file on him."

"Ah, yes," said Captain Rudsitter. "I've heard of Mr. Earl. Seems like he's involved in all sorts of unusual politics—a weapons collector, I'm told."

The camera moved onward and froze on another woman. "This female is Alice Kaufman. She apparently roomed with Earl Sutley and has been a longtime friend of Vera Greene. She and Greene were involved in an altercation over on the coast with a logging truck a few months back. You'll see her at many of the Earth First! events. Appears to be a savvy one."

New footage appeared on the screen, this time of the town of Garberville. The camera panned the city street, showing a quaint collection of shops and businesses with a busy stream of people and auto traffic. The camera zoomed in on a rather inconspicuous man (for Garberville) with a long graying ponytail, less than six feet tall, carrying a green day pack.

"Okay, gentlemen," Sergeant Chewart spoke, "that fellow over by the crosswalk with the day pack, smoking the cigarette, is Robert Devine.

He's the owner of that hippie newspaper, *The Country Activist,* and another author of those forest initiatives. Our sources tell me that he's quite sharp—former stockbroker, ah, let's see…"

Sheriff Chewart looked briefly down at his notes. "…Okay, here it is: he used to be a math professor." Cough. "Anyway, this guy is hard to find, hard to follow. He seems to lurk in the background, if you catch him at all."

Captain Rudsitter interjected: "We've just been informed that Devine has filed a rather clever lawsuit against Charles Hurwitz of Maxxam. While his friends are off playing merry pranks in the woods, this guy is raiding computer files and picking the brains of every legal consultant he can reach. He files for Freedom of Information Act papers about once a week—a real scholar." Smirk. "Could be a dangerous guy…"

The camera continued to follow Robert, and ended with him entering the coffee house. New footage opened up, obviously of a more professional quality, showing the press conference at Redwood National Park. Again the camera found Robert in the crowd amongst the reporters.

Sergeant Chewart picked up the narration. "Okay, here we have a televised press conference where you'll see Hannah Caine, who is the wife/girlfriend of Devine, speaking at the podium. Devine is, as usual, in the background, while Winwood, also true to form, is up front and center with the media."

Mark Dimms spoke out, "Look, sir, that Devine is carrying that day pack again. In fact, in every picture we have of him he's got it with him. I wonder what's in it?"

"Good question Dimms…good question…"

"He also has a cigarette in each photo. He smokes Camels," the Sheriff laughingly pointed out. "What do you think that means?" he asked, cocking his head towards Chewart who was just lighting up another one.

"It means he's got good taste."

Turning the lights in the room back on, Captain Rudsitter addressed the group: "Remember, gentlemen: it's possible there's no mastermind here. Regardless, we've got excellent inside sources. In some cases we've even got their trust. I believe we should have no problem in keeping an eye on this group. So let's do it."

The officers got up from their chairs and were about to depart when the Captain interrupted them. "Oh by the way, the FBI has arranged a special seminar for us. We'll be joining them at their annual Bomb Investigator's Training Course up in Eureka the day after tomorrow. I'm sure it will be instructive. I'll keep you posted with the details."

BOMB SCHOOL

Special Agent Fred Boyle leaned against the corner of the desk, looking quite comfortable in his khakis and denim shirt. He chatted amiably with the other officers, sipping decaf from a vending machine cup. Saturday at the junior college campus in Eureka was dead. Various civic groups used their spacious facilities on the weekends, and today's "Bomb School," hosted by the FBI, was well attended and well disguised as just another class.

The Oakland contingent comprised of Sergeant Chewart, Officer Dimms and Captain Rudsitter. They had just arrived and were settling in with their vending machine coffee and plastic wrapped donuts. There were only twelve bomb schools held each year throughout the nation and the sites always changed, so this one attracted various law enforcement agencies from northern California who considered it an honor to work with the esteemed Fred Boyle.

S.A. Boyle took his official place behind the podium, waiting patiently for the class to quiet down. He noticed S.A. Dick Smeld, from the San Francisco office, lurking near the back of the room, and nodded his head in salutation. Things were moving right along.

"Good morning gentlemen." Boyle quickly surveyed the small sea of faces, regrettably noticing one woman, "...and ladies, of course." As the last of the stragglers found their places he proceeded. "Welcome to the Bomb Investigator's Training Course here in lovely Eureka, California." The class nodded deferentially, awaiting the master's direction.

Boyle introduced himself, "As most of you know, I am Special Agent Fred Boyle. I have been trained as a hazardous devices technician and I'm currently a police instructor in terrorism and bomb matters. I have been assigned to the International/Domestic Terrorism Squad of the FBI for the past twenty years. Having processed over 150 bombing crime scenes in the United States, I can safely say that I have seen the range of terrorist techniques."

He motioned to the stacks of paper waiting at each desk. "As you'll notice from your agenda, we'll be spending the first part of the day here in the classroom, discussing the physical components of the bomb devices. Upon completion of the textbook component, we'll caravan out to private property, loaned to us for this occasion by Louisiana Pacific, to partake in some…ah…fieldwork." He smiled at the assemblage. "I think you'll enjoy this session—it will provide you with hands-on practice should your agency need to respond to a bombing. Now, are there any questions?"

The class leafed through the syllabus, asking few questions before launching into the first of several video segments showing the array of bombs most likely to be encountered. They were shown incendiary devices, pipe bombs, anti-personnel bombs, fragmentation bombs and motion sensitive detonators. They were shown devastation to buildings, cars and bodies. Boyle led the class expertly through the maze of explosives, answering questions patiently and proficiently.

The class broke for lunch and reassembled at the parking lot to complete the afternoon with on-site training. The short drive out to LP's clear-cut was an education in itself for some of the non-local participants.

"I never saw this kind of forest the times I've driven through here," one man exclaimed, pointing at the blur of stumps and ragged shrubs through the windows. "You always see those nice tree-lined freeways and parks from the road."

"Yeah, it looks pretty bad right now, but they manage these forests for generations to come. A few decades from now it will be thriving and lively, right Sheriff?" Boyle looked over at a Humboldt County Sheriff's Officer, who merely smiled noncommittally.

The caravan came to rest in a deserted clear-cut where three cars were already parked. Boyle, looking ever like the consummate agent in his mirrored aviator glasses, spoke: "You'll notice, first, that we have gathered different vehicles with varying potentials for sabotage. Since most of our bombs are placed in everyday street cars," he gestured towards the awaiting automobiles, "we wanted you to attempt to locate the devices on these vehicles here."

The class proceeded to the first car and examined its locks, doors, engine compartment—every inch. They discovered the explosive device, a pipe bomb, strapped to a piece of plywood and concealed under luggage in the back seat. A student questioned: "If this car were locked and secure, would the perpetrator break the locks to place the bomb inside of it? I mean, wouldn't that indicate sabotage to the victim?"

"Yes, that brings up an interesting point. Bombs are seldom placed in the passenger compartment, so we always check the engine compartment and under the vehicle itself. In an instance such as this one, we can assume that the perp is either the driver of the vehicle or had access to it."

"But what kind of fool would drive around with an armed bomb?" The class erupted with sniggering.

Boyle smiled benignly. "Remember, you're dealing with a criminal element, and though they may be devious, there's a reason they're doing crime, right? But, seriously folks, as a rule, when transporting a device, they will disarm and or segregate its components to avoid accidental detonation. Let's look at the next victim." He swept his arm towards another car at the top of a small knoll.

The class gathered around the vehicle and was carefully guided through the proper procedures while searching for possible hidden explosives. This time, they discovered a motion-sensitive device placed behind the muffler. Upon successful dismantling, the bomb was reassembled, replaced under the vehicle and detonated.

As part of the exercise, the students were then to recover the parts of the bomb and reconstruct the placement. S.A. Boyle was clearly enthused, as was most of the class.

The third car awaited. This bomb had already been detonated and the class was assigned the task of determining the exact kind and placement of the bomb. The car, though functionally destroyed, was still intact enough to be thoroughly investigated. The students went diligently about their work, reconstructing and salvaging various components. They amassed a pile containing a 9-volt battery, a light switch, some residue of powder and a 2-inch galvanized pipe.

Suddenly one student cried out, "Look; it's a watch—probably a pocket watch." Boyle just smiled.

They spent the remainder of the afternoon reconstructing what was a simple, motion-sensitive, detonated pipe bomb. Boyle addressed the class as they were taking notes. "All of you are aware of the impact of the shrapnel—in this case, finishing nails? Most of the homemade bombs we encounter are of this type. Can you determine where and how these nails were affixed?"

The students dutifully examined the galvanized pipe and concluded that the nails were taped to the outside with duct tape, judging by the fragments of silver. Because the vehicle was not totally destroyed, the class was readily able to determine the placement of the bomb. There was a large, gaping hole on the floorboard behind the front passenger seat. This type of explosion would have severely injured those in the car.

The class gathered around the famous instructor as he wrapped up the day's lessons. "This concludes our seminar on bomb investigations. I trust it was both informative and interesting," Boyle removed his sunglasses and grinned at the assembled officers. "Now let's just hope you'll never need to apply your knowledge."

CAMPBELL AT THE ROTARY

John Campbell, the president of Pacific Lumber, sat erect in the folding metal chair, clapping and nodding his head at the appropriate moments. The old stage was liberally sprinkled with other timber industry luminaries, among them Dave Galitz, also of Pacific Lumber and Joe Wheeler from Louisiana Pacific. The speaker from Blue Lake Forest Products had captivated the audience with his eloquent description of the hard-working forest industry workers and his provocative portrayal of the annoying environmentalists.

Campbell had an impassive smile affixed to his otherwise very expressive face. Here, at the Rotary Club, he was expected to behave with the utmost decorum. Many of Eureka's influential figures would be watching him. With all the attention thrust on the recent takeover of Pacific Lumber by Charles Hurwitz, Campbell's composure was required. He could not let Charles down. His mind wandered to his upcoming fishing trip, only to be returned to the stage as the audience broke out again in thunderous applause.

"Furthermore," continued the speaker, "one out of every four jobs in this county depends, directly or indirectly, on timber." He paused to give his impressive mathematics time to sink in. The audience swelled with a collective sigh and he pushed forward, "The industry is being attacked by environmentalists, the government, even the public. We intend to fight back by creating our own initiative." Ooh, aahh.

Campbell smiled and clapped as the audience came to its feet. The timber industry had the best public relations firm their substantial money could buy. The advice to counter the environmental initiatives? But of course—a timber initiative. And to add wit to deviousness, they would name it "Global Warming." Perhaps the name could even fool some of those dim-witted enviros. Campbell smirked as he recalled the meeting with Hill and Knowlton where the idea was introduced. A brilliant inspiration—but that's what H&K was paid so handsomely for.

The speaker finished his presentation to thundering applause and Campbell was called to the microphone. "Good day to you, ladies and gentlemen," Campbell intoned in his pleasant Australian accent. "We're honored to have you here as we announce our initiative for continued good forest practices. We're all environmentalists," he said dramatically, for maximum effect. "Yes, we're in total agreement with everything that Earth Day stands for…it's just the approach we don't agree with.

"The Forests Forever initiatives may have the right sentiment, but they definitely have the wrong approach. We also want to preserve old growth, but restricting logging practices is impractical and short-sighted. We need vision, not hysteria, to manage our forests." The crowd swelled with approval. "Those environmentalists' initiatives will hamstring our industry and cause recession in our communities. We think we have a better approach. We offer Global Warming to the voters of California."

Campbell smiled and bowed his head slightly over the applause. Hurwitz should see him now. This company was in good hands. As the crowd was settling back in, Campbell reached behind the podium and retrieved a box. He placed it on the podium as the audience waited expectantly. Opening it with great ceremony, he extracted a large piece of redwood.

"Ladies and gentlemen, I ask for your attention here." Silence prevailed. "This is a part of a redwood tree taken from our mill in Scotia. As those of you near the front can see, there is a large spike—eight inches to be exact—protruding from this chunk. This iron railroad spike caused substantial damage to our equipment. The headrig saw was destroyed as the log went through it. Work was held up for hours replacing the saw. Several more man-hours were spent in inspecting all lumber taken from that site." The audience was mesmerized.

Campbell continued, "This time no one was injured. We were lucky. Just in the last two weeks we have discovered three incidents of spikes in our old growth redwood. We have no idea when the spikes were placed and we have no suspects." Smirking emanated from several audience members. "We simply don't know, and we would like to believe that our local group of environmentalists, Earth First!, stands by their denouncement of such dangerous activities.

"Our people—professional foresters, skilled millworkers and contractors—could all do an excellent job of taking care of our resources if these environmentalists would just get out of the way and let us do what we do best: grow trees." The audience hooted affirmatively and exuberantly applauded.

Dave Galitz took the microphone. "Thank you, John," he said nodding at Campbell. "Now to satisfy a few of your questions. No report was filed with the local sheriff's office. We, the management of the local timber companies, met to discuss this issue and agreed unanimously that a public declaration of this act of terrorism would only create publicity for the perpetrators. We don't want to encourage such actions, but we do want to let other mills know the possibility for danger exists.

"What we as a community can do is band together to promote the timber industry's own reforms in the package of the Global Warming initiative. Let's put our energy into positive public relations and insure that the health of our forests is in the hands of the professionals." Galitz nodded his head, signifying that he was through, and the audience applauded again. The camera crew at the side of the room captured it all for the six o'clock news.

SHERIFF SATTERWITTE'S MEETING

"We have all been here before," Vera wryly stated to Sheriff Satterwitte as they sat down in his office. "This harassment is actually becoming a daily occurrence. What can we realistically do about it?"

The Sheriff shook his head slowly from side to side and smacked his lips as he concentrated. Finally he rested his hands on his desk and spoke: "Vera, okay, I've worked with you for awhile now. We all appreciate your attempts to involve our department in your organizational plans. But," he sighed, "I just don't know about these death threats. We don't get much of that." He looked sincerely perplexed.

Robert spoke up, "Sheriff, excuse me for intruding here, but when one of your citizens is routinely threatened, you are required to take action." He looked pointedly at the Sheriff, "It's not as if we're clueless as to who might dislike our politics...are you?"

The big Sheriff flinched, then leaned back in his chair. "No, Mr. Devine, I believe we can safely say that the timber community is not pleased with your particular politics. You must realize, though, that you are talking about tens of thousands of suspects here." Robert looked unimpressed as the Sheriff continued. "More than half of my deputies have family in the area, and half of them work in the woods or the mills or drive trucks for the companies. Just what would you have me do?"

Vera looked over at Robert, "Robert, we can't expect a 24-hour security. The Sheriff's right. There's not really much he can do—we have no verified suspects."

"Frankly," the Sheriff spoke up, "death threats do not actually fall within my jurisdiction. They're more properly a matter for the Ukiah Police Department."

"C'mon, Sheriff," Vera implored, "that's ridiculous. All we want is to insure the safety of all the participants. That chain of command stuff is absurd."

Sheriff Satterwitte shook his head, "No, it's the law. This county's extremely low on manpower. We're already stretching it just to keep the peace. What with all of your plans to bring in thousands of more folks, well…we can't keep up." He turned up his palms in a gesture of futility.

Even Vera's patience was being exhausted. She responded sarcastically: "So, you'll keep the peace like you did when Mem's nose was broken, or when my vehicle was assaulted, right?"

The Sheriff stood up and leaned against his desk, "Look people, you've put us all in a difficult position. We simply don't have the manpower to investigate these threats." He reached for the door handle, indicating it was time for them to exit. Seeing the three hostile faces before him, he added with a snort, "If you turn up dead, then we'll investigate."

Robert smirked.

Isaac stared, slack-jawed.

Vera just shook her head and pulled her shoulders back. Resuming her organizer's zeal, she let go of her fear and spoke: "Then let's deal with an issue that I do believe is in your jurisdiction. What about the safety of the summer demos? You've already promised that we'd have this department's support for peaceful assembly. In this context, what can be done?"

"Ah, you're not actually going to be dealing with us—I mean directly. We'll…ah…be dealing with the Oakland Police Department." The three stared incredulously at him. He hastily added, "We've got some sort of inter-agency cooperative agreements for large activities like this one."

PCBS AT THE GP MILL

V era was approaching the Environmental Center in Ukiah. Ukiah's network of carefully aligned streets and linear buildings gave the feeling of being caught in the vortex of California's worst concrete nightmare—somewhere like Anaheim. Ukiah was the county seat and, being conveniently located on Highway 101, was the main artery through the redwoods. That was enough to justify its existence.

The plans for Redwood Summer were compounding daily, as was the need for organization. Vera was planning a meeting for next week in Oakland with the organizers who would provide food and other camping equipment. Experienced activists from the Bay Area were expected to conduct the mandatory nonviolence training workshops.

A discernible hush came over the room as she walked in the door of the Center. Everyone quickly lowered their heads and immediately became engrossed in the tasks in front of them.

"Hello, everyone. How's it going?" Vera tried to sound nonchalant, thinking that maybe Isaac had been here earlier, whining about their floundering relationship. People expected her to be unemotional. Right, she was the tough one. Yet Isaac, who was an ambulating mass of expression, could readily elicit sympathy.

"Uh, hey Vera. What's up?" came a rather feeble reply from one of the volunteers.

Vera scoffed in the general direction of all the bent and busy heads and walked over to her desk space. She was followed by Gary, the director of the Center. He looked her solemnly in the eyes and stated, "Vera, I've got to talk to you about something. Let's go out back on the deck."

Gary grabbed an envelope and followed Vera out the back door. She sensed the weight of all the eyes upon her back as the door closed behind them. Gary gulped and handed Vera the envelope. "This arrived yesterday, addressed to the Center. There's no return address; just a North Bay postmark."

Vera opened the envelope to expose a newspaper photograph in which she was smiling as she played her fiddle. Drawn over her face were the markings of the scope and the cross-hairs of a rifle sighting. Stapled to the page was the now infamous yellow ribbon of timber solidarity. She unfolded the attached note which was crudely typed on an old typewriter.

vera green

get out And go back to where you come from

we know every thing

YOU WONT GET A SECOND WARNING

She looked at it carefully before responding. "They spelled my name wrong," she stated impassively. "Okay. I assume I've pissed someone off. I'm supposed to be surprised? C'mon, I knew it would come to this." She threw her braid over her shoulder. "I'll live with it."

"How can you be so sure? Vera, please? This is serious; this is as good as a death threat." Gary pleaded with her.

Vera snorted slightly and closed the envelope. "Sure, I think it's serious, but that doesn't mean I'm going to stop—it doesn't mean Redwood Summer demos are going to stop." Gary looked intently at her, stifling his breath. She smiled slightly, placing her hand on his shoulder. "Hey, our protection is in numbers. When we go out in large groups with the eyes of the nation upon us, we'll be okay. This threat stuff just doesn't play well outside these little timber towns."

Gary followed her towards the door and tried again to get her attention. "Vera, I'd like to report this threat to the police." His arms were crossed protectively over his chest; his eyes registered fear and fatigue.

Vera smirked, "Yeah, sure. If it makes you feel better, then get it documented. Like it will really do a lot of good."

Gary shuffled away, shaking his head. At his desk he looked up the number of the Ukiah Police Department and dialed tentatively. He resented that being a political activist had come to threats and fear. He spoke to the officer in charge and arranged for a time to drop off the offending letter.

The following day, Vera came in even earlier to the Center. She convinced herself she wasn't worried and was determined to be cheerful. By ten a.m. she had secured a few thousand more dollars in pledges and had alerted environmental groups in three other states of the plans for Redwood Summer. She sat back, pleased with the morning's progress as she sipped a cup of coffee. The phone rang a few times and she leisurely reached forward. It was Isaac, from his place up in Humboldt County.

"Vera, how's it going?" He felt like an idiot. What a lame thing to say to the woman you just spent the last three years of your life with: loving, holding and missing her like crazy for the past week.

"Just great. I've managed to secure more funding. You know, I have a really good feeling about this summer. I think we're really going to pull this off!" She sounded sickeningly cheery. "Now, if we can just get that initiative passed…"

Isaac replied quickly: "Robert and Hannah are working furiously to gather signatures. Even the Sierra Club is showing support, so we must be good!" Isaac took a deep breath and closed his eyes. "But hey, the reason I called—well, there are two reasons." He lost his courage and, after a pause, spoke again into the phone. "Is that meeting with the Seeds of Peace still on for next week?"

"Absolutely, I just spoke with them and we're all set. They're quite experienced at organizing provisions." She tried to maintain a neutral, even joyful tone, despite the deep ache and sadness she felt at hearing his voice. They hadn't even seen one another for over a week, and by tacit agreement would continue to avoid physical contact. She had sensed their relationship being over for months now, but Isaac was less willing to acknowledge the inevitable. Isaac was a dreamer. Vera was the realist and she felt real pain.

"Um...so are you coming up this way soon? I mean...um...do you wanna get together for dinner or...something?" Isaac was fumbling in the worst way. Unfinished lyrics resounded in his head as he nervously twitched his fingers, his palms sweating with anxiety. *Nothing but a woman can make you feel so dumb. There must be a blues rift here...*

Vera completely ignored his question. "So, what was the other reason you called?" She had no patience for bothersome emotions, especially ones like heartache and longing. Save those for the poets.

Isaac stalled a bit, collecting his wits, "Oh, yeah, a phone call. Some guy from Georgia Pacific in Fort Bragg is trying to reach you. It's not management or anything. I think he's a mill worker. He said it was real important to talk to you, specifically. Something about union issues. I told him I'd pass on his number."

Vera got a brief chill, recalling the scope and cross-hairs photo. Why was this stranger looking for her? Warriors can't stop to feel, so with just a little trepidation she took the number from Isaac, then closed their conversation in a businesslike manner, avoiding entirely any further allusions to intimacy.

She called the number Isaac had given her and spoke with a man named Eric. He briefly told her of some concerns about the use of PCBs that he and some of the other workers at the mill had. He had heard that Vera had experience with labor unions, and some success in defeating unfair labor practices. He asked Vera to meet with him and to discuss the possibility of helping him organize the workers to take action.

Vera was complimented, and quite pleased. *This is a perfect opportunity to bridge the separation between environmentalists and workers.* The separation, she had always maintained, was clearly exploited by the timber corporations' yellow ribbon mania and its spawning of groups like Mothers Watch.

After finishing up business at the Center, Vera drove the 30 miles north to meet Eric at a restaurant in Willits. Fred's Frontier Room was decorated with logging regalia: old fashioned chainsaws, black-and-white photos of timber men hard at work and an assortment of stuffed animal heads arranged in descending order. She half expected to see a mounted "jackalope" head, followed by, perhaps, a trophy rat. At least the gleaming leatherette booths were large and well lit.

She arrived early, as was her style, and began examining notes she had made about PCBs back at the Center.

Shortly after she sat down, a young man came through the door, looking like most of the other patrons in his worn blue jeans, soiled shirt and heavy work boots. He scanned the room until his eyes fell on Vera, and a slight smile of recognition appeared. He had seen pictures of her in the paper.

Vera smiled back and stood up to extend her hand. "Eric? Hello. Pleased to meet you."

"Yes ma'am. You must be Miss Greene? Thank you for meeting me."

"Call me Vera, please."

Eric took off his baseball cap to expose a greasy flattened mass of hair, molded by days of wearing the cap. Judging by the slight lines around his eyes and his tight, muscular body, he looked to be in his late 20s.

The waitress appeared and they each ordered a cup of coffee as they exchanged polite conversation about family, the weather, local road conditions.

Vera finally got down to business. "So Eric, you said that workers were exposed to PCB at the mill. Were they offered medical treatment by management?"

He snorted slightly. "Well, the company says the damaged capacitor wasn't leaking PCB, only mineral oil. Yeah, right, so my buddy only sucked in mineral oil when it burst right above his head." He gulped a sip of the brew and looked fiercely at Vera. "No way. We know that stuff was toxic. We know what they fill capacitors with."

"Did you go to the hospital?" Vera was taking notes.

"Yes, ma'am. We said they should pump his stomach, but GP had gotten to the emergency room before us. They told the doctors it wasn't necessary."

"Did he suffer any symptoms?"

Eric fiddled with his cap on the table. "He was as sick as a dog—barfing and heaving. Hey, I have to be straight with you. We're scared. We've heard all sorts of bad shit about that stuff, about how just a little bit can cause cancer." He slurped the coffee loudly and thumped the cup on the table. "The guys at the mill—we know that management is lying to save their asses."

Vera smirked as she nodded her head in agreement. Eric wiped his brow and continued speaking: "We know they've been burning PCB in the atmosphere, at night—you know, when they think they won't get caught. Hey, my wife is pregnant and my neighbor's got kids. What's gonna happen to us if we're all breathing in this cancer stuff?"

"Did your union help?"

"Yeah, sure. They reported it to Cal-OSHA. Those assholes rejected the claim." He shook his head incredulously. "I swear to God, GP must have paid someone off—we've got a lot of evidence. But we don't want to lose our jobs. We just want our workplace to be safe." He drummed his fingers nervously on the table and looked over both shoulders. "Uh, management's already told us we don't need to be poking our noses into their business, if you know what I mean."

"Uh, yeah, I think I know exactly what you mean."

Eric looked at her, bewildered. He wasn't used to receiving support for his grievances; people don't like squawkers in company towns.

Vera stopped writing and turned to face him. "Okay, we need to talk to every employee who has any knowledge of this incident, and then we're going to take it to the Feds."

"What difference will that make?"

"Fed-OSHA had stricter standards. Most importantly, they aren't impressed with these small town manipulators."

Eric sighed with relief. "I've been ready to lose my job over this. I really didn't know where to turn next."

"Eric, I'm gonna help you get organized and fight back. But you're going to receive a lot of flack—even from your own friends. No one likes to see their lives disrupted."

"Yeah, I know. Believe me, I know. I gotta admit, this stuff really scares me. Either I lose my job, maybe my friends, or my wife and kid's gonna get sick," Eric replied cautiously.

"If enough of you show up, then management will be forced to listen. Trust me, I've been through this before."

Eric smiled and reached for Vera's hand. "I'm real pleased to meet you. I've heard some lousy things about you environmentalists, but maybe everything I heard ain't exactly true."

He reached to put on his cap and stood up to leave as Vera closed her notebook. She smiled to herself as she watched him exit the restaurant. She loved nailing the ass of the corporate world.

Vera drove out to her place in the hills above Willits, negotiating the winding mountain roads with agility. A sliver of a new moon was just visible on the eastern horizon as an almost garish glittering of stars graced the violet sky.

She parked the car in the flat by the house and grabbed a few things from the piles on the back seat, cursing as a bag of nails spilled onto the floor. Walking up the steps to the front door, she hummed contentedly, glad to be home at last—even if the roof still wasn't quite finished.

Vera stopped short when she noticed her cat, Kunda, slumped against the door. She stooped to look closer and saw the blood on his chin. Recoiling with horror, she jumped back and dropped her bags, choking back a sob.

Breathing rapidly, Vera unlocked the front door, turned on the porch light and examined Kunda's inanimate form. Poisoning. How else do you explain a perfectly healthy three-year-old feline bleeding from the mouth? In an attempt to regain composure, she lamely inspected the nearby road for clues, knowing full well that nothing could be determined in the darkness. She turned back towards the front door and glanced solemnly at her dead cat deciding to bury him now, by starlight.

The physical exertion required to dig a hole was a welcome relief from the exhaustion of the mind. Someone really was trying to scare her. When Vera had spoken earlier to Bruce Anderson about the death threat at the Center, he had offered her the use of one of his guns. She scoffed at the idea of using violence to counter violence. Right now she had good reason to question her belief that violence could be thwarted with truth.

She covered the grave with more fresh dirt and gathered a few rhododendron blossoms to lay on top. A cascade of tears trickled down her cheek. Sitting there on the deck, beneath the infinite sky twinkling above, she felt very frail, very alone and much to her surprise, very afraid.

EARTH NIGHT POSTER

Hannah was in the office shrieking. She held out a piece of paper to Alice and demanded, "Look at this! This is disgusting. Why do I have to endure such indignities?"

"Uh, this may be difficult for you to grasp but this isn't entirely about you. See Hannah," Alice held out a similar piece of paper, "I have my very own copy. I'm equally as screwed as you are, okay?"

Miffed but undaunted, Hannah marched into Robert's office, standing impatiently against the door while he completed a phone conversation. He held his hand out, palm up, in a gesture of "stop," when he saw her approaching. Hannah was beautiful, intelligent, persistent and reliable. She also was spoiled, demanding and imperious. She made a damn good environmental activist. She could disarm the sleaziest of corporate heads and sweet talk the hat right off a sheriff.

Robert concluded his phone call and slowly hung up the receiver. "Okay, Hannah. What is it?"

She thrust the paper at him, her mouth quivering. Alice stood behind her in the open doorway, rolling her eyes. Robert looked curiously at the two women and accepted the page. He read the first sentence and smiled. Ah, finally, some political writing which didn't take itself too seriously.

Dear Hannah,

It has come to our attention that you are an Earth First! lesbian whose favorite pastime is to eat box lunches in pajamas.

Hannah, this kind of behavior is to be expected of lesbians like you, since we have been observing Earth First! freaks like you for some time. Not only have we been watching you Hannah, but we also know and have distributed your phone number (707) 485-8778 to every organized hate group that could possibly have hostile tendencies toward ilk of your kind. No longer can sleazy dikes like you operate with impunity through the guise of anonymity. We know who you are, where you live and continue to home in on you...but do you know who we are. How does it feel eco-freak, to have the tables turned?

Rest assured, Hannah, that we shall not be indiscriminate in our actions against the spineless, invertebrate members of Earth First!. To the contrary, we will specifically hunt down each and every member like the lesbians you really are.

Sincerely,

Committee For The Death of Earth First!

Brought to you by Fed Up Americans for Common Sense

Robert laid the letter down on the desk and rooted around in a pile. He plucked a piece of paper out and smirked, "At least they didn't call you a 'fellatio expert who sucks dicks in outhouses'. Of course it wouldn't make sense if they did." He stifled a chuckle when he noticed the woman's icy stare. "Hannah, get a grip. Someone is trying to scare us. That's all they can do."

Hannah stood there in abject silence.

Robert continued in his most convincing voice: "I've already reported this to our kindly sheriff," cough, "and it appears that our little threatening homophobe has been busy. Every environmentalist from Ukiah to Crescent City stands accused."

Alice handed her letter over to Robert. "Here, add it to the files. I'm too busy to listen to this crap. 'Operating with impunity'...someone's exhumed a thesaurus, huh?" she scoffed, walking back to her desk.

"There's nothing we can do about this?" Hannah persisted.

Robert shook his head and spoke softly, "Yeah, actually, we can feel honored. Someone is bothered enough by our success to be afraid."

"Then why do I feel so debased? Why do I feel like someone has violated my rights? Whatever happened to freedom of speech? Thought? Expression?"

"They are expressing themselves. Unfortunately they're misguided in who their enemy is." He smiled warmly. "These people are cowards. They can't confront their own demons any better than the rest of us can."

She looked deeply into his eyes, about to express something, then pivoted and walked out the door. Robert shrugged his shoulders and put his bifocals back on. Sitting down he noticed the volumes of paper in front of him. Lawsuits were a demanding mistress.

The darkness settling in through the windows roused Robert from his work-induced stupor. He realized with a jolt that the rest of the office was empty. Some people actually restricted their work day to eight hours. He rubbed his temples and removed the glasses, leaning back in his chair to stretch his legs out. Glancing at his watch, he noticed it was 8 p.m. Time for a game of pool and a beer—well at least it was time for a beer.

He wandered sluggishly into the nearby tavern. He ordered a beer, a burger and a newspaper and slumped down on a stool at the end of the bar. He was oblivious to the boisterous patrons slowly filling up the small room. He ate his greasy burger and relished each oil-drenched French fry as he read the latest news. He was startled by a tap on his shoulder.

"Dude, have you seen this shit?" Isaac was holding the, by now, too familiar piece of paper that Robert had already spent too much of his day anguishing over.

"Yeah, buddy, I've seen it. So has Hannah, Alice, Gus, Lou and every other 'eco-freak' south of the Canadian border. We've been discovered," Robert replied wryly. "Cheers."

"This is outrageous shit. They can't do that…can they?"

Robert inhaled another French fry and a huge gulp of beer. "They? You mean the timber corporations? The FBI? Yellow ribbon zealots? C'mon, Isaac, we can't sneeze on the streets without it being reported as eco-tage." He gulped the rest of his mug and ordered another. "As usual, our detractors remain faceless."

Isaac ordered a beer and resumed, "Robert, I'm not gonna sit here waiting. I've had it with these macho sickos." He slurped his beer contemptuously, then unzipped his pack, pulling out a crudely drawn poster. "See; two can play this game. At least I know how to have fun without hurting people."

Robert looked at the poster carefully. "Are you so sure about that? Some people would consider this very hurtful."

On the paper was a drawing of a large bulldozer framed by a foreground rendition of two longhairs. One guy held a crudely drawn oversized wrench and the other held a jug with the words, 'Karo' written clearly on it. Emblazoned at the bottom were the words:

EARTH NIGHT 1990: GO OUT AND DO SOMETHING FOR THE EARTH...AT NIGHT.

"Don't you think this is cool? Don't you like the hippie dudes with their enviro T-shirts? This is perfect—Earth Day's only a week away, right?"

"Right, Isaac," Robert sighed, blowing onto the beer in his mug, "a week away. I had no idea you were such an artist." He tried to smile up at his old friend.

Robert's lack of enthusiasm wasn't lost on Isaac. "But, Robert, they can't just keep threatening us and get away with it. I've got to retaliate somehow." He held the poster up at arm's length. "This works for me."

"I'm sorry, Isaac, I just don't agree with inciting volatile passions."

Isaac jumped up and stuffed the paper back into his pack. "Okay," he said, "we don't have to agree on everything. I'm still gonna put this thing out. I think it's fun. Can I use your copy machine?"

"Sure, buddy, you know where the key is." Robert heaved with exhaustion as he watched Isaac skip excitedly out the door.

As the stars resumed their places in the night sky, Candy Black was just finishing up her own office work. She tidied her desk and turned off her machines. She smiled lovingly at the computer, marveling at its ability to change just a word in a paragraph, to "personalize" letters, as she liked to think of it. As she reached for her Diet Coke, she accidentally knocked a book on to the floor. She retrieved the thesaurus and returned it to the bookshelf.

Life was so incredibly interesting now. She actually needed to buy a new outfit—there was a formal dinner tomorrow night. Sure, these were just timber men, executives really. Chuck said that some big public relations firms would be there, too. As she covered up the computer she thought, *Aren't I in public relations, now?*

Oh well, she turned out the lights, *they would never really notice what I'm wearing but still—Joe Wheeler, Dave Galitz, even Charles Hurwitz would be there. I really need to make a good impression. Maybe I should get something in black? Hmm…with those nice pearls.* She shut the door behind her. *No, too fancy, too subdued. Maybe that new store at the mall?*

She padded down the hallway, slurping on the Coke, dreaming of the possibilities. I know, something in pure silk…maybe in a luscious green…yeah, something outrageous that I can wear with… impunity! Yeah! She smirked to herself.

SANTA CRUZ POWERLINE

The normally peaceful, idyllic, coastal community of Santa Cruz was propelled into sheer chaos in the early morning hours following Earth Day. A wooden transmission tower lay severed on the ground, the legs having been ripped off by a chainsaw. Hospitals and emergency services were powered by generators, and more than 90,000 people were forced to endure several hours off the grid. Just as PG&E crews were rerouting power, another line went down.

This time, a 100-foot steel tower had been toppled by someone who removed the bolts. Hysteria reigned in the community as utility crews and sheriff's investigators searched for clues to the incidents. Investigators did recover a metal chisel, an axe with a three-inch handle wrapped in black electrical tape, and bolts which had been bent, beaten and their threads stripped. They also discovered partial shoe tracks in the mud along with a package of cigarettes.

The FBI was enlisted to investigate this act of domestic terrorism. They began by scrutinizing the source of the leaflets which had showed up at UC Santa Cruz campus on Earth Day. The leaflets contained a crudely drawn bulldozer and a couple of hippies brandishing tools. The wording suggested that people do something for the earth—at night. It wasn't signed by the local contingent of Earth First!, though a similar poster had been distributed earlier that day by Earth First! on the campus.

By the end of the day, every newspaper within 200 miles of Santa Cruz was rocking with the news. They had been contacted simultaneously with a hand-delivered letter claiming responsibility for the power outages. The group called itself, "Earth Night Action Group." No one in the environmental community had ever heard of them—not even Earth First!.

The Earth Night Action Group submitted their letter filled with misspellings and written in block printing. They asked the public to endure the inconvenience and to consider the destruction that the earth must endure. They stated, "In defense of Mother Earth, we say NO to lip service from the corporate earth rapist PG&E. We will use direct action not words. Earth Day is every day."

The media was entranced. For the next week, the front page of every northern California paper was dedicated to sensational stories revolving around the power sabotage. Women who gave birth by candlelight and people who cooked without their microwave ovens were interviewed. Heroic feats off the grid were sensationalized. Some people couldn't even use their computers.

Naturally, Vera and Isaac were sought out. Vera went to Santa Cruz to attend a press conference with the local Earth First! group. She was quoted as saying, "The environmental community denounces this Earth Night Action Group. We know of no individuals or people who are involved in this form of sabotage. We feel that if anything, it was committed by a group dedicated to sabotaging the goals of environmentalists by casting us in a negative light."

Vera spoke up as the interviewer asked for comments. "None of us has any idea who did it, but whoever did it is a hero in my book. PG&E's participation in Earth Day is particularly odious. They are operating a nuclear power plant on an earthquake fault that would kill hundreds of thousands of people."

A PG&E spokesman defended his company: "PG&E feels that we have a better environmental record than most big companies. We know improvements are always needed but criminal activity is not a solution… certainly acts of terrorism are not a solution."

Vera scoffed audibly and said, "Who's the terrorist? The person who takes down a couple of power lines or a corporation that operates a nuclear power plant on an earthquake fault?" Her fellow environmentalists looked over at her with trepidation. She continued, "Hey, I'm real sorry that some people's ice-cream melted. I think this group made a good point."

Down the road just a few miles, the sheriff in Santa Cruz was jubilant. He was off-duty, on his way home from a grueling night, when he apprehended an obviously drunken driver. He noticed the black electrical tape on the back seat and the chainsaw oil. When he looked in the trunk, he was further rewarded by a large chainsaw and an incomplete set of wrenches—several of which had been badly scratched and bent. The driver was almost too incoherent to hold a match to his cigarette. He surrendered without resistance.

The sheriff immediately called the FBI to inform them of this suspicious connection to the power line sabotage. The FBI arrived within minutes, but not before the drunk driver admitted to the downing of the power poles. The sheriff sure felt fine. He proudly smiled at the agents and said, "So I guess it's a wrap?"

The agent in charge glanced at his fellow agents and clicked his tongue. "Uh, well, Sheriff. We have a little problem." The agents twiddled their thumbs. The sheriff looked perplexed. "You see, this man is ah… ah…part of an operation. We can't really arrest him for this sabotage or it would adversely influence the success of crucial covert activities. You do understand?"

"Of course," the sheriff somberly replied as he surveyed the small office packed with agents shuffling their feet and casting glances at the ground.

The chief agent firmly shook the sheriff's hand and, looking him directly in the eye, said, "Thank you, Sheriff, for your cooperation in this matter of utmost security." The agents departed and the sheriff released the drunk driver to their authority.

GOLDEN GATE BRIDGE

Immense spiral clouds of mist surged across the Bay and hung suspended, eclipsing even the great bridge. At 4 a.m. the 101 was already besieged by the commuter flow into the City.

The headlights from the moving vehicles dispersed eerily through the fog, casting distorted shadows. Four cars pulled up to the Marin side and parked in the turnout.

"You got the bag with the carabineers?"

"Uh…no. It's over there—in Lou's car."

"Okay, people. Let's check our equipment one last time and synchronize our watches."

The group of two women and nine men, dressed in army fatigues and wearing technical climbing shoes, hoisted their backpacks and ropes and approached the bridge.

Isaac called out to the others, "I'm gonna try to reach a couple more reporters—I'll catch up." He skipped excitedly into the phone booth. Looking at his notebook, he plunked two dimes in the slot and quickly dialed. He listened impatiently as the phone rang five times, keeping his eyes on his group assembling equipment near the base of the infamous structure. Finally, on the sixth ring, a sleepy voice spoke into the phone, "Hello…?"

"Good morning. This is Isaac Winwood calling from the Golden Gate Bridge and…"

"Who? What the…it's…four a.m. What's going on?"

"Isaac. Isaac Winwood. Remember, you interviewed me about the old growth redwoods?" There was a long pause before Isaac continued. "Hello, we're here in Marin and we're minutes away from making headline news. I just thought you'd like to be in on it."

"Okay," the voice responded heavily. "What exactly are you doing?"

Isaac chuckled, "You see, Josh, we're honoring Earth Day. Thousands of commuters will watch our demo. You'll definitely want to get this scoop."

Isaac heard a huge sigh coming through the phone line as he hung up the receiver. He checked his notebook and deposited two more dimes, dialing as he glanced back towards the bridge. He reached this reporter on the second ring and elicited immediate interest. Environmental activism was hot news in northern California. Just the name, Isaac Winwood, was sure to arouse passions. Satisfied, he hung up the phone and darted across the parking lot to his comrades.

Gus and Lou applied the bolt cutters to the padlock on the chain-link fence. The lock was easily severed. They quickly traversed the narrow walkway spanning the Golden Gate Bridge. Through the densely swirling fog they could see the icy waters of the San Francisco Bay 300 feet below.

The first group ascended to the top platform in the tower elevator. They were quickly followed by three more people who exited the elevator, then glued the doors shut behind them. Alice and Vera climbed up the stairway to about 30 feet above the sidewalk bordering the roadway and chained themselves together to the bridge cable. The ladies arranged themselves comfortably above the moving traffic below and sat down to watch the others high above them.

From the roadway, the specks 500 feet above could scarcely be discerned as small people with big plans. Isaac and three others grasped the side of a huge banner while Lou extended it to its full 100-foot length. With the help of two others in the middle, they unfurled the banner over the side of the bridge.

DEFEND ANCIENT FORESTS.

NO TO FOSSIL FUELS.

SAVE THIS PLANET.

The message was thrust in the face of any commuter awake enough to be driving a vehicle.

Gus huddled back against the supports of the upper platform and extracted a cellular phone. He excitedly dialed the number of the local radio news station. "Good morning," he intoned pleasantly from his perch. "This is Gus Russell representing Earth First! from high atop the Golden Gate Bridge."

Barely missing a beat, the perky reporter quickly responded, "Mr. Russell, we were expecting your call. But," she said breathlessly, "according to our sources, so were the sheriffs and the police department. We understand that your group has unfurled a large banner over the roadway, Mr. Russell. Just what is the point of this elaborate action?"

"The banner says…" and he enunciated carefully what the commuters below couldn't help noticing.

"But, Mr. Russell, surely you realize that you're violating Federal property by climbing the Bridge? The fact that you called this radio station indicates you understand the severity of your actions."

"What we're trying to do is indicate the severity of the crisis the planet faces," Gus responded, looking distastefully at the bumper to bumper traffic on the deck below, noticing that many of the cars contained only one person. "Temporary discomforts are our offering to the Earth. We have a message and immediate publicity is the best way to promote it."

As Gus looked down at the bridge deck below, he saw the congregation of flashing red lights and smiled over at his comrades. Speaking into the cell phone, he continued, "Earth Day means we recognize the planet that nurtures us…every day."

"How can you advocate no fossil fuels when you yourselves drive in vehicles?" the reporter pressed on.

Just as Gus was about to respond, a voice boomed through a bullhorn. The police were ordering the protesters down under threat of imprisonment. The protesters held fast to their positions, with determination and climbing equipment. Meanwhile traffic on the bridge was backed up and crawling, due to one lane being closed off so that law enforcement could get closer to the violators. The slowly moving commuters now had ample opportunity to view the huge banner which had cursedly caused a kink in their morning travel.

For three hours the CHP and the Marin Police and Sheriff Departments attempted to convince the protesters to abandon their position. The violations were mounting against them. Finally the ironworkers for the Bridge were called in. First, a blowtorch was used to sever the locks on Alice and Vera, who were quickly shuffled into the back of a police car. Next the ironworkers scaled the towers and reached the group at the top. After several minutes, Isaac and the others rolled up the banner and were escorted down the cables by the ironworkers. When they reached the bottom, where law enforcement was eagerly awaiting, they turned to the workers and several rounds of hand shaking ensued. *Fellow climbers conquering the same heights. Thanks for the overtime.*

The protesters were handcuffed and immediately taken to the Marin Police Department for booking on charges ranging from vandalism and trespassing to interfering with a police officer and creating a public nuisance. All protesters were released on promise to appear for arraignment at a later date. Isaac was accustomed to this aspect of being an activist. Vera just considered it a necessary nuisance. The Golden Gate commuters were overwhelmingly irritated at spending more time in their venerable vehicles. Love/hate relationships abounded.

Before the activists had even been apprehended, Hill and Knowlton, the public relations firm hired by the Northcoast timber industry, had already conferred and then distributed an extensive information packet to the media. Besides the timber industry's self-promotion, the packet contained distinctly unflattering stories about Earth First! and a press release from one, Isaac Winwood.

The media from San Francisco to the Oregon border were flooded with reports of the huge banner and the heroic arrests of the protesters.

Recordings of Gus's call to the radio station were playing almost hourly. The traffic from Marin to San Francisco flowed smoothly now. Fossil fuels belched unimpeded.

Isaac and Vera waited patiently in the lobby of the police station while the officer on duty attempted to locate the proper release materials for their vehicles. He finally uncovered the paperwork and gave them the address of the tow lot in Marin. When they arrived at the garage, the owner informed them that their cars had been there earlier, but were then towed to another lot across town.

Isaac threw his arms up in exasperation. "I don't believe this. Why the runaround?"

"Let's go, Isaac. I've got a long drive ahead of me." Vera motioned for Isaac to get back in the car.

They arrived at the second lot and found this operator to be surlier than the last. At first he didn't seem to recall any cars being towed in earlier that day. Gradually his recall improved. He led them around the huge lot, searching for their cars among the staggering volume of decaying and demolished vehicles. Finally they spotted their cars in the very back. As Vera approached her 1981 Subaru she gasped.

"Oh my God. What have they done?" Inside, the seats had been cut apart, the dashboard torn away from the frame in places and her baggage strewn everywhere. Clothes and books lay huddled together in pathetic heaps. Isaac peered at the destruction, speechless. Vera sifted through the rubble and exclaimed, "My film...look at this!" She held up two exposed rolls of film which had been unraveled onto the floor of the back seat.

"Did you take those today?"

"Hell, no. Those were of my sister's birthday party. This is unbelievable," she whimpered. She poked around some more and exclaimed, "Oh great, they took my new binoculars. I distinctly recall placing them in the glove compartment before we got out today."

It appeared her car had been thoroughly groomed and then thrashed by a deranged primate. The other protesters' vehicles had apparently also been subjected to the same manner of detailed search.

Isaac marched back to the lot operator's office. "Did you see the condition of the cars when they were brought in? Didn't you have to authorize, for the police, I mean, the condition?" Isaac added sheepishly, "See, I've had my car impounded before and that's what they do."

"Well I wouldn't know about that," the man responded warily.

"C'mon, mister," Isaac whined, "Our cars got thrashed. We just want to know who did it. Don't you have any paperwork?"

The man peered cautiously out the window and gulped. He looked up to the gaze of Vera's deep blue eyes. Even in army fatigues, her feminine form was obvious. She smiled slightly and stuck her hands in her pockets. He looked flustered and said, "Well, okay. I guess I can show you this here report." He pulled it out, spreading the grease-stained papers on the cluttered desk. Other than random trash or decaying seat covers, none of the reports noted poor condition.

The operator looked confused as they quickly scanned the paperwork. "Maybe you should talk to the police," he finally suggested, "them guys was here a while ago looking at your cars."

"But that doesn't make sense. They would have searched them back at the headquarters," Isaac mused, scratching his beard. "Did they say anything to you?"

"Nah, not really. They just showed me their badges." He shrugged. "They were from Oakland."

"What? The Oakland PD searched the cars? What's Oakland got to do with this?"

Vera stood up, tucking her T-shirt into the waist of her pants. She wrapped her arm through Isaac's and said, "Thank you for your time. We'll take our cars and leave now. C'mon, Isaac, we're done here."

They walked out of the grimy office and across the lot toward their cars. Vera touched Isaac lightly on the shoulder. "Isaac, has it ever occurred to you that maybe we're drawing too much attention to ourselves?"

Looking perplexed, Isaac said, "No…why?"

"Think about it, Isaac. Look at our cars." She brushed off the front seat and adjusted the seatbelt. "See you in a few days," she called out as she drove away. "Take care." Isaac shuffled over to his van and leaned against the side. When he opened the door, hundreds of feet of cassette tape cascaded onto the pavement. An entire collection—no, era—of music lay mangled at his feet.

"This sucks," Isaac said to the luminescent ribbons twitching slightly in the breeze. "You can have my car, but don't touch my tunes."

HEAD SHAVINGS

Hannah awoke without reluctance to the sound of the blue jays squawking. She savored her coffee in bed, then slipped on her nightgown before stepping into the yard, where she encountered Robert, reading.

"Look, I'm still hurt that you never found the need to contact me, but there's no point in dwelling on it now. Besides, I'm glad to see you. Let's do something interesting today." Hannah bent down, throwing her arms around Robert's shoulders and kissing the back of his head.

"Well, I am interested in reading through this lawsuit," Robert replied, while absently patting her hand and trying to refocus his attention on the papers in front of him.

Not so easily deterred, she continued kissing him lightly behind his ear. "Honey, I was sort of thinking of something that doesn't require your reading glasses…"

Slowly, Robert put the papers down on the table next to his pen and turned to face her. "Do you think that men just have an infinite supply, or what?" He grabbed her and playfully nibbled on her nightgown. Hannah threw her leg around his waist and melted in his arms like chocolate fondue. She felt the earth move with a deep, penetrating vibration. Abruptly, she pulled back and heard the unmistakable whirring of helicopter blades.

Through the distant trees, they could see the khaki green marauder cruising up the river canyon. This wasn't a search and rescue mission, this was a CAMP raid and, by now, every cultivator within a 20-mile radius was breathing hard and creating an instant connection with some divine spirit. Hannah squealed when she spied the approaching copter.

She ran out onto the grassy flat by the river and threw her nightgown off, twirling it around her head like a deranged flamenco dancer.

"Do you think they'll notice me?" she asked breathlessly as she flitted about the grass, leaping and pirouetting with naked abandon.

Robert stood there transfixed with the sight of this naked woman dancing for a paramilitary helicopter about to harass and torment his friends and neighbors. He smirked, "Yeah, it's safe to say that you'll be duly noted."

The helicopter flew right overhead and, sure enough, doubled back for a closer look. Hannah waved and twirled, the huge black dog jumped and cavorted with her and Robert stood lamely by, feeling rather unimportant. The helicopter made a few more circles overhead before it took off, upriver and over the ridge where they could hear it land.

Robert peered up to the ridge-top where the helicopter was last sited. "Isn't that Jim Hoover's place?" He pointed up the hill as he walked over to harvest some early blackberries.

"Oh, no. I think you're right. Poor guy."

"They're gonna screw you no matter what, aren't they?" Robert snarled as he shook his head in disgust.

Jim Hoover was a 57-year-old laid-off mill worker from the Potter Valley Mill. Since the mill had closed down and moved business to Mexico, Jim had joined his sons in cultivating to make a living—he saw it as more morally correct than taking public assistance.

"I'll be right back." Robert yelled at Hannah. "I need to go to town anyway for a newspaper." He ran into the house and grabbed his car keys.

"Bring back some beer," she yelled back at him.

Hannah put on her nightgown and went back inside. She lay back on the couch, stroking the cat and dreaming. What if they could leave home and the office for an entire week? What if they had enough money to stay in a nice hotel, even a cheap motel, instead of on someone's living room floor? What if she could buy a totally new dress instead of "getting creative" with second-hand finds? She closed her eyes against the tears, not sure if they were caused by the insistent itching or by the realization that her life was spent in anger and acrimony: a Catholic guilt complex divinely channeled into martyrdom.

Robert drove into town and stopped by the office to check messages. He was hotter than a bee bite when he heard Isaac's explanation of the bridge caper. The other four jailed protesters had been released earlier that day. The bad news was that the sheriffs had forcibly shaved all four of their heads. They claimed the activists were infested with lice and that shaving their heads was a health precaution.

Robert smirked to himself and thought, "Right, classic schoolyard logic. If you can't defeat your enemy, then at least you can humiliate them. Hmm, isn't that COINTELPRO point number 5?"

He proceeded to the newsstand and grabbed a *Eureka Times* to further dampen his day. Sure enough, the headlines confirmed his suspicions:

ENVIRONMENTALISTS' HEADS SHAVED: LICE THREAT-
ENS SANITATION OF JAIL

He read on, too disgusted to groan.

Attorney for the four protesters, Harris Collins, said that the demonstrators, who wore their hair in dreadlocks, were not even checked for lice before their hair was cropped. He called the forced shavings, harassment.

Humboldt County Sheriff, Dennis Lewis called the charges, "....ridiculous. In this case the hair was so badly infested, knotted and unwashable that there was no way they were going to get any critters out of their hair," said Lewis.

Attorney Collins said one demonstrator attempted to resist and "three officers held him down, cuffed him, carried him from the holding cell into the barbershop and shaved his head and beard."

"He had massive bruises to his upper left arm and hand," Collins said. "There's a lot of hostility toward the protesters in this county jail from officers."

Robert shuffled up the street to the store, overcome with sadness and frustration. He selected a few six packs of good beer—for Hannah, of course—and walked somberly to the car.

DAY OF THE LIVING DEAD HURWITZES

"**L**ook at these photos! How could anyone dress up in that get-up and parade around? These were taken in front of PL headquarters? What in God's name did they hope to do? Look at this. People dressed like trees. This is absolutely ridiculous. What a waste of our time. Which one is that Winwood?"

Campbell moved over to the desk and pointed to the tree holding the guitar.

"These are laughable. Where did you say you got these photos?"

"One of our workers support groups—I believe they call themselves, Mothers Watch—have been active in keeping an eye on these radicals. Of course, so far everything has been rather harmless, but we feel it's time to hire professionals to photograph and be involved from now on."

"Yes, always go with the pros." Hurwitz thumbed through more of the photographs, then paused. "Absurd. Look at this! They're wearing masks that look like my face. What did they call this event again?"

Campbell cleared his throat, "Day of the Living Dead Hurwitzes." He cast a furtive glance at his boss, wishing desperately they were discussing flow charts or bottom-line profit margins.

Mystified, Charles Hurwitz looked over his glasses at Campbell. *They just didn't do business like this back in Houston.*

"Charles, that Winwood fellow is a macabre bastard. He associates with a woman named Vera or Valerie—someone who's just as weird. My sources tell me that she's the brains in the outfit, a former labor organizer. Apparently, some of our own employees are rather taken in by her clever speeches. I've received a written report if you'd like a copy."

"Of course, I always maintain that it's just as important to understand your enemies as it is to understand your friends. Helps us all do business better." Hurwitz smiled up at Campbell who was now pacing in front of the window. "Now John, just how bothersome can these people be? Their pranks are amusing to some, I'm sure, but we have a business to run here."

Campbell turned to face the photos and picked up a few. "These people are incredibly effective at reaching the media—which, if I do say so myself, is really our only obstacle in keeping the business going. I'll tell you Charles, they've cost us countless days, even weeks, and, of course, dollars, in retaliating those frivolous lawsuits. That Winwood fellow is like a persistent mosquito; he seems to be circling around here all the time. I'm getting a bit of a hatred for him."

"Now John, I always operate from the positive perspective. Hatred won't take you or Maxxam where we need to go, now will it? Your job here in California is to see that our properties are put to the best possible use for the company's profit. We provide jobs, the forest provides us with timber. It's really quite simple."

Campbell was fuming. *What did this big city banker know about living with the workers, living on the job?* He and his wife had to face these people in the grocery store, the post office. Their kids all went to school together. He couldn't have his position ridiculed in public, or questioned.

Plus, these Earth First! protests were drawing a lot of workers out and they were drawing out some complicated issues with them. Pacific Lumber's board of directors was meeting here in Scotia. Hurwitz and other Maxxam directors were working with various company executives such as Campbell to improve "working relationships." Hurwitz asked him questions about production and the likelihood that the environmental lawsuits would stop production. It was then that Campell had pulled out the pictures of the Earth First! demonstration.

Only last month, Campbell had requested a better security force to guard the equipment in the woods. Hurwitz had passed the request on to Maxxam's public relations and private security firms. *John has a refreshing naiveté,* Hurwitz thought. *He's thick-skinned, but not shrewd enough to plot for his own private gain—a man capable of loyalty.* Hurwitz cared about his relationship with John Campbell; he needed his dedication and perseverance to oversee operations here in the northwest. Maxxam needed ready capital fast to pay off its junk bonds.

Hurwitz also cared about his image amongst the employees. He liked to believe that he was a fair and honest man. He was consulting with Campbell, in part, to figure out what to do so that the name Hurwitz might not be synonymous with thief. Last time they talked, Campbell had shown him a copy of the wanted poster the radicals had distributed. It offered a reward—$8,000—for the prosecution and conviction of Charles Hurwitz.

The two men concluded their business discussion and readied themselves for lunch at the Ingomar Club. As they were putting their jackets on, Hurwitz turned to Campbell: "What about those endangered owls or frogs or some such creatures? Do our lands really have such a thing on them?"

"Hmm," Campbell smirked, "that's not what our biologists say, but those bloody environmentalists are determined to analyze every blasted feather. No worries. They've lost their only ear in court, I'm told."

"And who would that be?"

Campbell fastened his button and finished stuffing his briefcase. "It appears that this rather addle-brained old judge, who seemed to listen to the forest whiners, has had to step down from hearing any of these timber cases. His family received some ugly pranks threatening them if he ruled favorably for the environmentalists." Campbell smugly adjusted his tie. "I can't imagine who would threaten a judge."

"Hmm, now that's a stroke of luck, isn't it? All these legal concerns— let's talk about making a profit. It's a subject I understand."

SUPERVISORS' MEETING

"Okay, Sheriff, this time it really is 'deja vu.' Check it out," Vera commanded as she thrust the paper at Sheriff Sam Satterwitte. Sitting back in the chair, she pulled her legs up under her. She was getting pretty comfortable here in the sheriff's office.

Sheriff Satterwitte reached across the desk for the paper and frowned as he worked his way down the page. He finished and tossed the paper onto the desk with a big sigh. "I suppose this narrows our suspects down."

"Right, Sam. And now we can have a real shoot-out at the downtown corral." Vera leaned forward on her elbows. "Seriously, I'm getting scared. My choices are to run away and hide or wait for the next onslaught of hatred. Either way I lose. And you're just as powerless as I am."

The Sheriff sat back in his chair and studied the note again. It was short. Its intent was clear.

TO VERA GREENE AND ISAAC WINWOOD

IF ANY TIMBER WORKERS ARE INJURED DURING THE PLANNED PROTESTS YOU WILL BE HELD PERSONALLY RESPONSIBLE. WE KNOW WHO YOU ARE AND WHERE YOU LIVE. IF YOU WANT TO BE A MARTYR WE'LL BE HAPPY TO OBLIGE.

—HUMBOLDT COUNTY EMPLOYEES OF THE FOREST PRODUCTS INDUSTRY.

"I don't know what to say, Vera."
"Yeah, that's pretty obvious."
"We have a situation here…"

"We have a situation here?" Vera smirked. "Sam, these people are threatening my life and you want to refer to it as a situation? Let's get real. Call it what it is: death threats." Having spoken it out loud, she felt better, cleaner, as if by recognizing the demon there'd be a chance to conquer it.

The Sheriff looked over at the small woman curled up in the chair across from him. Right now, his constituents were living in fear of losing their jobs, their homes, their way of life. Technology reared its ugly head across the small towns of America and its wake rendered the laborer obsolete. It took many forms. Here in the Pacific Northwest it was a long-haired, organic gardening, peace-loving, ethnic shirt-wearing hippie. It was Vera.

He looked again at the note on his desk and gave it a quick punch of his fist. "Tell you what we're gonna do. I've been meeting with some of the independent loggers around here. They seem real sure that you people are threatening them." Vera rolled her eyes and opened her mouth to protest, but he gestured his hand forward, palm up to stop her. "See, the Board of Supervisors has asked me to invite you to their meeting next week for a presentation. You can explain your plans so these folks can hear you."

Vera clicked her tongue in the side of her cheek before responding. "Okay, Sam. That sounds fine, but you do know that some of the Supes and I have…ah…had some fiery interchanges. Marilyn Butcher would never invite me to a meeting unless she had to."

"Let's just say she had to."

Vera looked over at the Sheriff with raised eyebrows. "See you at the showdown, then."

Vera and Robert discussed the supervisors' meeting and he agreed to accompany her. They both agreed to keep Isaac away. In light of his Earth Night Action Poster and his other tactics—or lack of tact—he was considered a liability. It wasn't that he was responsible for the Santa Cruz power sabotage, he just wasn't responsible period.

The night of the big meeting arrived. Robert met Vera at the Environmental Center in Ukiah. When Vera walked out of her office wearing ragged blue jeans and a rather volatile political statement T-shirt, he cringed. He had at least changed into a clean pair of khakis and a semi-pressed, button-down shirt. It's one thing to sell out, it's another to reduce tension. He strove to keep himself unremarkable. Not that he would cut his ponytail, but he always kept it clean and brushed. Vera's could use a little of both.

Vera put her attention into her work, not her appearance. For a man that made perfect sense, for a woman that was downright threatening. She didn't accomplish things by looking good, she did it by being good. She simply refused to give power to appearance. "Hey Robert," she called out cheerfully, grabbing her flannel shirt off the back of the chair. "Are we ready for this, or what?"

"Yeah, I'm always ready to be raked over the coals," he smirked. "I don't think Hannah's gotten to me this week, so I'm overdue."

Vera laughed and patted Robert on the back. "Being in love is rough, huh? I wonder when I'll ever have time to do that again," she said wistfully. This time Robert patted her on the back and they walked up the street to the supervisors' chambers.

The parking lot was packed. Every possible place along the street was filled. Judging by the preponderance of pick-up trucks, Willie Nelson might be in concert. Unfortunately, it was only the supervisors' agenda and every citizen from every gravel road in the county had arrived for this one.

From half a block away, the environmental contingent could be seen waiting out front. Rakish hand-loomed berets and comfort sandals made for Flintstone feet dominated their dress. What remained in between was fairly indistinguishable from the rest of the crowd: jeans and flannels— always in good taste north of Santa Rosa.

The crowd squeezed into the chambers as latecomers took their places in the hall. The meeting progressed through the usual dry business as more people arrived, creating an oozing line of attendees out into the street. The audience's patience was being pushed as the temperature in the small room rose. The shuffling of feet intermingled with audible murmurs. Soon conversational whispers hissed in the background.

And now, the moment they'd all been waiting for. "For our next order of business," the chairman adjusted his reading glasses, "we will hear from Ms. Vera Greene regarding the organization of the planned summer demonstrations in our woods." Whispers ceased immediately, followed by a low hum.

Vera approached the podium, smiling. "Hello people," she brightly called out. Her buoyancy didn't appear to be contagious. "I'm glad to see so many of you are interested in the facts."

"The fact is you're destroying our jobs!"

"Yeah, get out of Mendocino," the crowd yelled out, fists raised.

The chairman pounded the gavel for attention. "The audience will await their turn to speak or this meeting will be canceled."

Vera held up a piece of paper. Audiences love a good visual image. They quieted down. "Look at this poster which we found attached to our office door. Just take a good look, will you?" She thrust the poster forward so those in front could clearly see that a photo of her was covered in the scope and cross-hairs of gun siting. "This is not violence being directed at timber workers; the violence is being directed at us!"

The crowd bellowed.

One man in the front of the room stood up and said, "Yeah, well, I run a logging crew and I tell my workers to use whatever reasonable force is necessary to restrain protesters." Waves of approval undulated throughout the room. Emboldened by the attention, he continued: "If they want to demonstrate peacefully somewhere else, that's fine. If they come onto my logging site, THE SHIT HITS THE FAN."

The audience raged with hoots of enthusiasm.

"C'mon, folks. One day of lost work isn't going to prevent you from making a living."

The crowd erupted.

"What do you know about work?"

"Get out of our business."

The chairman demanded order from the audience.

Vera was unfazed by the anger. "The only way there can be safety is in our numbers and our nonviolence. Your timber industry officials have created this lynch mob mentality. These death threats could have been made by someone in this very room."

Marilyn Butcher, a supervisor and ardent supporter of the timber industry interjected, "Vera, you've brought it on yourself."

"Well Louisiana Pacific and Pacific Lumber have brought these protests on themselves," Vera retaliated.

The crowd went totally out of control. They were on their feet yelling and name calling. Another supervisor spoke into his microphone over the crowd, "I'll be quite honest with you, Ms. Greene. I don't like your politics. I think you and your friends are terrorists. If you don't stop taking food out of people's mouths, one of you is going to get killed!"

"Yahoo! Right on!" the crowd raged.

"We have a right to work!"

"We'll protect ourselves any way we have to!"

The walls of the room reverberated with voices. Outside, the streets were plastered with people carrying placards and chanting. The chairman looked overwhelmed as Marilyn Butcher said to him, "I can't sit here and listen to her. Either you bring order to this room or I'm leaving."

Sheriff Satterwitte finally took to the podium to quiet the audience. He suggested to Vera that she return to her seat. It seemed like a good idea to her.

The Sheriff spoke into the microphone, "None of us wants to see violence. And we've got to start here tonight." The crowd shuffled and mumbled. "There's been people hurt at these protests," he continued.

"Our department simply doesn't have the manpower to patrol all these demonstrations."

Robert listened carefully to the Sheriff talk. Having dealt with him over the years, Robert knew him to reside in the pockets of big timber. Right now he sniffed the lint.

"We believe that a few precautions can help us better control the crowds." The Sheriff quickly glanced at the tightly set face of Marilyn Butcher, then said, "The Sheriff's Department is proposing an ordinance for all demonstrations that would limit the size and material of sign handles. The handles could be no greater than one-fourth of an inch in thickness and could only be constructed of plastic or wood."

The crowd was momentarily confused. They were ready to react, not consider details. Suddenly a chorus of hisses arose from the environmental contingent. Vera stood up, seizing the opportunity to speak. "Sheriff Satterwitte, do you seriously believe that enforcing such an ordinance is a productive use of your department's limited resources?"

The Sheriff cleared his throat. "We feel this would limit the availability of a weapon should violence break out."

"And limiting the size of sign handles will contribute to open dialogue between all parties?" Vera responded.

The audience was rumbling with sneers and laughs. Marilyn Butcher leaned forward into her microphone, pointing her finger at Vera, "You people need to be held accountable. Someone is going to get hurt."

"Marilyn, I have outlined in detail for you the scope of our mandatory non-violent training." Vera spoke clearly and calmly. "It's not the size of a sign handle that will insure safety, it's the obliteration of ignorance that permeates these discussions."

Marilyn snorted audibly, pushing her chair back with a jerk. "Mr. Chairman, I've given up." She strode defiantly out the door. General mayhem and major disorder prevailed. The Sheriff recognized the swelling of antagonism and, in his wisest move of the evening, ushered Vera, Robert and their friends out of the chambers and into the street. The mob parted for the badge, but would have absorbed these job-killing, tree huggers if given the chance.

Robert, raising his eyebrows, looked over at Vera. "I guess small signs tell a big story."

"Yeah, the big Sheriff can't limit our enthusiasm, so he'll resort to our sign handles."

Robert responded with a round of sarcastic clapping.

BOGUS SMEARS - TIMES STANDARD

Carlton sat at his desk in the office of the *Times Standard,* staring despondently at nothing in particular. All around him, the staff scurried madly about, hurtling towards the next deadline. He fixed his gaze on the press release on his desk and then back into space. Slowly pushing his chair back, he grasped the paper in his hand and, deliberately controlling his breathing, he walked across the hall to Chief Jerry Post's office. He knocked once and was motioned to enter.

"What's the big news, Carlton?" Jerry barked out between redlining copy and tossing paper into the overflowing waste basket.

"I'm just not comfortable with this...this..." he gulped, "ah, press release. I think we ought to hold off until someone verifies." He looked over at his boss's impassive face and spoke quickly, "Dammit, Jerry. We let the last one go out and it hurt. I know you've got friends in high places who'd love to see this in print, but that's not journalism. At least not the kind I understand."

Post straightened up in his chair and pursed his lips. He reached across for the paper Carlton was clutching in his hands and examined it. "Okay, so a contingent of earth Nazis says that they still want to do tree spiking. That's news, Carlton. People want to hear this."

He thrust the paper back at Carlton. "Print it."

"Jerry, people are getting scared out there. Loggers are feeling threatened by environmentalists; environmentalists are feeling threatened by loggers. This is getting serious. As journalists I believe our job is to seek the truth, not the news."

Jerry scoffed. "In case you forgot who pays our bills, we have publishers to answer to. They pay me to print what they want the public to hear." Post looked over at a horrified Carlton. "C'mon, this is the real world.

You want to play ball in this field," he cocked his head back, lighting up a cigar, "you'll have to play by the rules of this game."

Carlton shook his head from side to side. "I've got some calls to make, Jerry. And yeah, you want it printed, it gets printed. Just don't use my byline."

Jerry watched the door close behind Carlton and relit his cigar. "Julie, get me Shep Tucker," he commanded into the intercom.

The following day, mill workers were greeted with stacks of the press release announcing the renunciation of the renunciation of tree spiking. The placard in front of the stacks said, "Warning." Similar stacks appeared at the mill sites, grocery stores and local gas stations of every small community from Garberville to Orick.

Having covered much of the county in the wee hours of morning, Candy Black was putting the miles on her little Honda and her big photocopy machine. Before distributing press releases, she had worked much of the previous day developing her latest creative writing piece and was certain that her mentor, Rick, would add it to the "Dirty Tricks Hall of Fame."

Candy giggled as she added the finishing touches.

FIGHT BACK: SOME THOUGHTS ON STRATEGY

We know who the powers are that are trying to destroy all wildness. To dance, play, laugh and avoid work as much as possible and to steal from the rich and powerful, to undermine authority every chance we get, this is the life we choose. We do whatever we can to FUCK UP the workings of the megamachine with an apparent randomness that confounds their orderly plans.

Please send donations to Earth First! c/o Isack Winwood P.O. Box 14334 Garberville, Ca 95467.

"Hmmm… Now that does sound good, doesn't it?" she asked herself outloud. She had tried several versions, and to the best of her recollection, the Isaac she had met would have said it just like that. The ringing of the "hot line," as she referred to it, interrupted her.

"Hello. Mothers Watch."

"Hello, Candy. Chuck here. I wanted to let you know that Shep Tucker and Dave Galitz are both quite impressed with the impact your work is having. The workers are informed now, thanks to you."

"Oooh, super! I've been having such a great time," she replied exuberantly into the phone. "The girls and I are getting so good at writing," she was giggling breathlessly, "and we don't even have college degrees!"

Chuck cleared his throat. "Yes well, that's what we need—enthusiasm. Now the reason I called is to remind you that these…ah…these press releases should also be distributed to the environmental groups. It seems the last few times you neglected to drop some off at their offices and it would appear to be a tactical oversight, wouldn't you say?"

"Oh," Candy gasped, "oh my. You're right. We want everyone to wonder where they came from, right? Oh, no. I'm so sorry, Chuck. I won't forget the next time. I promise."

Chuck rolled his eyes and exhaled with a whistle as he listened to her speak. *What a pathetic character*, he thought. *She really is involved in these little tricks.* He let her unwind before consoling her. "Now, Candy. You know that we all make mistakes. This one is easily corrected. Just be aware. I'll let you go now. We're all rather busy."

"Sure Chuck. I think you'll really like this latest masterpiece. I'll be sure that it gets distributed to all the right places."

"Very good. Take care."

"Bye, Chuck."

Candy hung up the phone feeling scolded and embarrassed. She had tried so hard to please, and now she felt the weight of inadequacy propelling her with an urgency to succeed. This time she would impress all of them. She walked into the kitchen to retrieve a Diet Coke and flopped onto a chair, slurping pensively. Three ounces down; six ounces down;

eight. Halfway through the bottle it struck her. *What brilliance, what sheer genius.*

She bounced up with considerable agility for one toting an extra 70 pounds, and pattered quickly down the shag-carpeted hallway to her office. She eagerly grabbed the family address book and went straight to her husband's list of employees. *One of these guys would be mad enough to help me with this brilliant, but definitely dangerous plan.* She leafed quickly through the names. *Who's got the balls to pull this off?* As if by divine intervention, a name on the page suddenly glowed with promise.

Leaping to her feet, Candy seized the phone from its cradle and dialed eagerly. She left a message on the answering machine to come over to her office this evening, then gently replaced the receiver with a satisfied sigh. She went back into the kitchen in search of more Diet Coke. Pacing heavily, while slurping with great contemplation, she surveyed the contents of her office. With a flash of insight, she raced to the stacks of Sahara Club newsletters, then snatched the press releases she had designed, wrapping them all up and covering the bundle with butcher paper and duct tape. Ah…the perfect package.

COUNTRY ACTIVIST EDITORIAL: HEDONISTS

Controlling natural resources has been the aim of empires throughout human history. Arable land, water, forests, mines, sites for cities that can be defended by land and sea, uranium, space, oil.

The means of control are as old: Pyramidal power structures, ideology, armies and war.

Nothing has really changed for as long as known human history stretches into our past.

Christians, Catholics, Lutherans, Methodists, Islamists, Confucists, Judaists—name your poison—have been created for the role of assisting the power structure in devising an ideology that leads to war. The details do not matter. Everything that could ever be said has been said.

The key to it all lies in the "religious" war against Hedonists. Hedonists are pre-ideological people. No ideology is possible because Hedonists do not know good from evil. They are nonbelievers. The war is clear in the words of the religious that Hedonists are evil and in whatever form they take, including heathens and witches, they must be driven away from the believers.

The significance is that in order for the power structure to control natural resources it must murder and rob to gain control. It needs armies for war. The greatest good is the sacrifice for King, Country, Faith, Freedom, the Flag, you know what I mean. "Onward Christian Soldiers."

The argument is always one of good and evil. The power structure is in communication with god. The new enemy is evil. The priests say it's god's will. The greatest good is to serve god and country.

There is no greatest good. There is no communication with God. There is no evil enemy. There is no god's will known to a human being: it's flimflam, a show for the believers and soldiers.

One does not have to be Lao Tzu to recognize the need to know your enemy. To know your ideological enemy study their philosophers. To know your Religious enemies study their sacred scripture.

If you ate from the tree of Knowledge of Good and Evil, you have been banished from the Garden of Eden. I say, "I have not eaten from that tree and do not agree things are good or evil. I see the garden and one day I will leave off fighting those who are destroying one of its manifestations—the Ancient Coastal Redwoods" and return home.

We prefer to be called Edenists and we will save a bit of it, but only because a sale to the government will enrich its present controller.

Meanwhile we are testing the strength of love against the system of pyramidal control.

We Edenists will continue, too.

BOGUS BOMB

The Arcata Plaza was pulsating with people on this unusually sunny day in early May. The shops lining the perimeter of the plaza basked in the steady stream of customers. At the center, the park-like grassy lawns were filled with lunch hour relaxers and the ubiquitous drumming, sunning, hacky-sack playing post-adolescents.

Isaac was scurrying from his van parked on a side street, lugging his satchel stuffed with papers and computer disks to the Environmental Center. Oblivious to the rest of the world, he pushed the door open loudly to find just one volunteer filing away in the back corner.

"Hey, have you seen Hannah or Gus today? I've got some disks I need to show them," Isaac called out as he slapped his bag onto a desk. He immediately proceeded to the computer.

The volunteer looked up from her filing and smiled. "Hi, Isaac. Um, no. No one's been around since I've been here—maybe two hours. But you know how it is on a sunny day in Arcata." She shrugged her shoulders and cast a glance outside.

Isaac grunted unintelligibly, now fixated on the computer screen in front of him. The volunteer returned to the filing heap which, after so many months, should be steaming, ready to compost. The only sounds in the office were the clicking of the computer keys and an occasional whir or beep as the machine processed material. Outside, cars moved slowly on the one-way streets and periodic shouts and laughter drifted lightly through the open window.

Suddenly the front door thrust open and a man stepped defiantly into the office. The hard clack of his cork-soled work boots reverberated off the linoleum, startling the volunteer who looked up to see a stocky, bearded man. He glanced furtively at her, scowling, then stepped toward Isaac, who was obliviously clicking away on the keyboard.

"Hey, you! Are you Winwood?" The man stood square before the desk, holding his body in an aggressive, horse-rider's stance.

Isaac continued entering his data, hesitating as he watched the screen. "Ah yeah," he responded without really giving his attention. "Can I help you?"

The man held out a package secured in silver duct tape at arm's length. "Yeah, you can. You can get the hell out of our forests and leave us honest men to our jobs."

Isaac immediately stood up, staring incredulously at the man before him. "Do I know you, brother? Do you want to talk about this?" He reverted to his best "conflict diversion speak."

"Hell, no. You don't know me, but get a good look at my face because I'm the one who's gonna kill you!" The man then heaved the package towards Isaac's desk and turned quickly, bolting out the door.

Isaac screamed, "Bomb!" as he looked over at the stunned volunteer. They both scrambled towards the front entrance and out onto the street. Isaac then yelled out again, "Bomb! It's a bomb!" while startled passersby stopped in their tracks, alarmed at the two horrified people racing by. Isaac ran into a dress shop on the corner and excitedly commandeered the phone.

Located one block off the plaza, the Arcata Police were on the scene in less than a minute. They cordoned off the surrounding area and evacuated adjacent businesses. Isaac, ever the opportunist, had contacted three newspapers and two television stations, with an urgent hysteria. An hour later, the police had retrieved the bomb package and by that evening had decisively determined that it contained a generous stack of Sahara Club newsletters, some apparently bogus press releases and little else.

Isaac schlepped across the plaza to meet Robert at the nearby brewery. Over their first pitcher of beer, he relayed the entire incident. "Robert, this guy was obviously a logger. He was mad as hell, maybe even hopped up on something. I don't know, I don't know..." he shook his head from side to side. "What's going on here?" He savored the cold beer, seeking ablutions.

Robert straightened up in the booth, placing his mug down on the table. "Well, times are getting rougher. Hmm," he smirked, "why, I can remember a time when just being known was all you craved. Now it's a hazard to have your face on the front page."

"Goddamn it, Robert. We swore off spiking, and then some crazed timber droid with a yellow ribbon up his butt plants fake press releases. We endorse nonviolence, and death threats greet us everywhere we go." Isaac took a generous swig of beer. "I don't get it."

"I get it alright. We're being warned. This just reeks of the FBI in the 60s." Robert looked over at his despondent friend. "I know, call me paranoid, but I was there. They're after us and...apparently...they'll stop at nothing." Robert drained his glass and immediately refilled it. He slouched back into the booth, his mouth set in a hard line.

Isaac slumped forward with his elbows on the table, holding his forehead in the palms of his hands. He sighed and stared at the mug of beer resting in front of him.

"What do the police say this time?" Robert gently asked.

With his face still resting in the palm of his hands, Isaac mumbled, "They asked me to stop by later tonight."

"Okay. I'll go with you."

Isaac looked up, exhaling deeply through pursed lips. "So what do you make of the 'bomb'? You know, the 'we hate enviros' newsletters."

"It's pretty obvious. They're primarily a southern California group. Someone up here has enlisted their help—or at least their tactics."

Robert tapped his finger on the side of his glass, then resumed his train of thought: "You know, I have a friend down in Riverside who's crossed paths with these cretins. These guys can get pretty serious."

"What do you mean? What's more serious than threatening to kill me?" Isaac whimpered, then sipped his beer, quickly comprehending that the actual act would be worse than the threat.

"No, I agree. That's pretty serious. But this hate group once published—get this—in their newsletter they once published the license plates and addresses of environmentalists. Then they'd send their cronies out to meetings to cause mischief. I believe they refer to it as 'dirty tricks.'"

"What?" Isaac whined. "That's pure harassment. They can't do that can they? Freedom to assemble is a constitutional right."

"Yeah, well, these guys think ripping up the desert with gas-guzzling machines is their constitutional right." Robert picked up his mug, draining it in one huge gulp. "And guess what, buddy?" He looked over at Isaac who was slowly slurping his beer as if it were some healing elixir. "It appears they've got comrades around here who think it's their constitutional right to destroy our forests."

Isaac sighed heavily. "You're right. I just forget that such a mentality exists."

"It looks like you got a good reminder today," Robert wryly responded.

Isaac hoisted his mug in a feeble gesture of bravado. "Let's get to the bottom of this," he said, pointing directly at the pitcher of beer, "and maybe I just won't give a damn."

Robert smiled at his friend, eagerly joining him in this endeavor. They ordered another pitcher to accompany their tastefully greasy meal, and after several robust cups of coffee they wandered over to the police department. They were immediately ushered into a private room.

"Mr. Winwood?" an officer asked, extending his hand in a shake. "I'm the officer in charge of this case, and you know Deputy Shaye from Mendocino?" He gestured towards the other uniformed man.

Isaac shook his head affirmatively. "Call me Isaac, please. This is my friend and advisor, Robert Devine," he said, indicating his companion.

The police officer picked up a piece of paper. "Well, Isaac," he said, looking directly at the obviously distraught man, "our culprit has confessed." Isaac's eyes were huge with wonder. The officer continued, "Some witnesses saw the guy running to his car and they were able to describe it well enough to track him down. You know how twelve-year-old boys are about cars," he said, smiling.

"Who is he?" Robert quickly asked.

The deputy spoke up now, and coughed to clear his throat, "His name is Tim Whittacker. He's an employee of John Black's."

"Wait a minute," Isaac piped up, suddenly revived. "John Black—isn't that Candy Black's husband? He runs a logging crew, right?"

The Arcata police officer shrugged his shoulders, glancing warily at the deputy.

Isaac persisted. "I met this guy's wife—the logging crew boss, not the bomb guy. Anyway, I met the wife—Candy Black—when I was let out of jail." He flinched and looked sheepishly at the two officers. "See, I was arrested for civil disobedience and, anyway, this Candy Black lady was there to greet me when I was let out early in the morning."

Robert was snickering, watching his friend explain this provocative circumstance to law enforcement. The officers listened politely, somewhat bewildered by the bobbing black curls and thick beard of the victim before them.

Isaac continued, "Her husband was a logging guy. She told me that." He looked at the officers, "Could that be just a coincidence? I mean why was she there to meet me? Why was this guy threatening me?" He began to hyperventilate. "Why am I being harassed? What are you going to do about this?"

Both officers looked embarrassed. They didn't really know how to comfort this kind of victim.

"You gentlemen do know that threatening someone with a bomb is a federal offense?" Robert asked with all the subtlety of a sharp pointed blade.

"Yes, ah...Mr. Devine," said Deputy Sheriff Shaye. "We have reported this to the FBI. We don't take bomb threats lightly."

"And why is a Mendocino County sheriff called in to investigate an incident here in Humboldt County?" Robert rapidly fired back as Isaac sat there stunned at the turn of conversation.

"Mendocino is the primary site for your planned protests this summer, as I understand from your spokespeople," Deputy Shaye responded tersely, inclining his head towards Isaac. "Mr. Winwood frequents our county and has made previous contacts with our department. We feel that the situation requires inter-county cooperation."

Like an observer at a ping pong match, Isaac stared wide-eyed, shifting his glance from the deputy to Robert. He wished they hadn't ordered that second pitcher of beer.

"Oh, I see…cooperation," Robert intoned. Like a boasting barrister, he rose from his chair to strut imperiously across the room. "So the counties are now cooperating in preserving the peace." He smirked audibly. "And do your Federal friends consider this 'situation' crucial to national security, too?"

The deputy straightened up against the wall where he had previously leaned so casually and imperceptibly pushed his shoulders back. The Arcata police officer lifted the corners of his mouth in a perplexed grimace, about as confused as Isaac was.

"Mr. Devine, we are doing everything in our power to secure justice," Deputy Shaye responded.

"Hmmph. So this Tim Whittacker is a logger. Will he be prosecuted? Even though he works for a good ole boy?" Robert raised the volume of his voice as his body visibly stiffened. He was outraged and highly emboldened by two pitchers of beer. "Will the local papers report that environmental terrorists were mixed up with bombs? Is that what we're going to read tomorrow?" Robert was furious as he turned towards the deputy, "Is it?" he demanded.

The Mendocino sheriff's deputy took a good deep breath. "Look, we report the facts to the media. They write the stories." He softened his tone as he once again leaned against the wall. "Let's face it, manipulation of the media is behind a lot of this. We'll certainly investigate."

"I sure as hell hope so," Robert replied, shaking his head. He looked over at the alcoholically subdued Isaac and inclined his head towards the exit. "C'mon, let's bail. It looks like they're done with us—for now."

CHICO

L ogging is violent work. Many loggers have violent tempers and short fuses. Greene and Winwood are risking creating martyrs of innocent, idealistic college students. The innocent student engaging in this summer of nonviolent disobedience may escape without injury or he may not.

"Say what?"

"I'm not gonna read the whole thing over again, Isaac," Vera snapped.

"Okay, okay. Who's the guy again? The guy who said it?"

Exasperated, she unfolded the paper and scanned the article. "Let's see…It looks like he's the rep for the International Woodworkers of America in Mendo County."

"That's just great. So he's out there telling college students that we represent violence. Once again, we've been slandered."

"Yeah, so it's bullshit, so don't get your underwear in a bunch. Look, it's not like this podunk paper gets read anywhere even close to Chico," Vera scoffed.

"Dammit," Isaac whined, keeping his eyes on the road in front of him, "we don't need that kind of press."

Vera pursed her lips together, stifling a laugh. "If I recall correctly, you're the one who told *60 Minutes* that you'd strap a bomb on your body. That's not exactly the kind of press we need either."

Isaac accepted the tongue lashing in silence. Driving somberly, he focused on the twisting, turning road around Clear Lake which would ultimately lead to Interstate 5 and then Chico. Slowly cruising through Cache Creek Canyon, he noticed an object on the horizon. He pulled the car over onto the narrow gravel shoulder and peered out the window.

"What is it? Is it the fan belt? Shoot—I knew I should have changed it."

Isaac's gaze was transfixed: Up in the sky just above the treetops was a golden eagle. The raptor was leisurely floating on the warm rising air from the canyons. "Shh, talk about getting your panties in a bunch. It's a golden. Up there." He pointed ahead to the large brownish bird with the six and a half-foot wingspan. "See the white tail band and the wing patches—there—on the underside? It must be a juvenile."

Vera craned her neck to catch a glimpse. The uncommon bird, though not rare, preferred these steep, remote canyons. The somewhat treacherous drive through Cache Creek was well worth it for a chance to spot these magnificent birds.

Subdued from this hit of wildness, they drove on in comfortable silence. Their relationship had survived the initial awkwardness of changing gears from lovers to comrades. They had managed to salvage a respect and appreciation for the other's being without resorting to manipulation and blame. A sense of freedom and even deeper respect now permeated their connection. Vera reached in her satchel and extracted a joint.

"Care to join me in a toke?" she asked, pushing in the cigarette lighter.

"Sure. A golden eagle is always cause for a celebration."

Vera smiled to herself. Isaac was, in some ways, everything she needed in a man. Unfortunately he was also too much. She let her mind drift to David, the peace activist...now there was a man to dream about...

When a cloud of smoke fills the car, the natural response is to turn on the radio. Isaac tuned in a classic country station from the valley. It was the perfect compliment for this remote canyon back-road. Within minutes, they were both singing along to a country tune neither of them knew, but could easily second guess the lyrics.

A loathsome advertising jingle punctuated their contentment and Vera looked at her watch. Two hours to go and then the rally was on. Enticing college students to become politically active was her forte. Sure, they were idealistic, so why not give them some ideals worth having?

Arriving at the university in Chico in the early afternoon, they set up their stage, adjusted the PA system and took out their instruments. Vera's fiddle always attracted a fair amount of attention. There was a strong crowd of supporters, as well as some of the just-curious enjoying their performance on a sunny April afternoon. To hoots and laughter they sang their rousing political ballads, borrowing from the best of John Prine, Arlo Guthrie and even Rush Limbo. Sure, Rush had methods of moving his audience that any speaker could learn from.

Vera outlined the premise of the summer of defense to the crowd, emphasizing the mandatory nonviolence training for all participants. Isaac handed out fliers and shook hands. He finally took the microphone and proclaimed: "Real changes only come when the whole world is watching. We all must learn that the planet is not here for the exclusive use of the human species. This is a civil rights movement for the earth."

With resounding applause, the students cheered them on.

Remembering the nasty article warning idealistic students of violence, Isaac spoke up again: "Listen folks, our tunes may be lighthearted, but this is not a dinner party. You may encounter some violent tempers and some short fuses. The question is, Are you prepared to meet violence with nonviolence?"

"Yes!" the crowd roared. "Nonviolence for the earth!"

Vera and Isaac, pleased with the support, smiled at each other. She grabbed his hand and walked over to the microphone with all the ceremony of an Academy Awards starlet accepting her statuette. She enunciated clearly, "Do what your hearts tell you. Do it for Mother Earth!" They raised their joined hands in a universal salute.

ISAAC CRIES

MAY 10

"**Y**ou're here," Isaac said, as he swept into the *Activist* office, "Great to find you awake at this hour."

"Yeah, we are under a deadline. It's 1:30 a.m. and the printer wants our galleys by five. I'm working on no sleep and two beers. Robert and I have been arguing off and on for hours, with no end in sight. You are the only one who is glad we are here," Hannah growled. "So, add to my misery Isaac; what have you got to say?"

Isaac had come to the *Country Activist* office looking for Robert.

"I need a break, Hannah," Robert said. "Isaac, pull up a stool and tell me what's on your mind."

"Robert, I need help. I have hit a wall. Vera is done with me. I am getting death threats almost hourly, all day and all night. Vera, too. Here is the latest one I found under my windshield wiper blade tonight."

Isaac pulled out a yellow piece of paper from his pack.

"Oh, look! Another cross-hairs over your pretty face," Robert quipped.

"You can be a jerk sometimes," Isaac said, slumping onto the battered couch. "Vera and I have been building affinity groups to help organize Redwood Summer. We're headed to Oregon this weekend for a rally. Vera is giving a speech and we'll sing a few songs. That's the plan, but I am getting nervous and jumpy about this trip. Vera says I am losing it. But I think things are getting dicey, and with every threat comes more proof. So, I came to ask you what you would do."

"You mean what am I doing now? I get nasty phone calls, our advertisers get threatened with rape, undercover cops and infiltrators come through the front door on a regular basis..."

Hannah burst out laughing. "Listen to you two. Everyone needs sleep. Everyone needs a good meal. We are working too hard and enjoying it not at all. I am tired of everything and everyone. When the elections are over this fall, I'm quitting. I am quitting, Robert, everything. I have seriously lost my sense of humor."

"Not me," Robert sighed.

"Robert, I'm serious about Vera. She stopped talking to me about anything but work. She said I had become so grouchy that..."

"Wait a minute. Who has $10? I'll hustle across the street and score a six-pack before they close."

"Good idea." Robert pulled a few mangled bills from his front pocket and handed them to Hannah. "I'll finish the editorial while you are gone. We are close to it, Isaac. Give me five minutes and I am all yours."

Beer or not, the night never rose above rock bottom. Isaac sobbed real tears for the communal pain they shared. Nothing more needed to be said, yet they couldn't stop repeating all their sorrows.

"Vera has been getting an increasing number of death threats. She is speaking tomorrow at a union meeting in Oregon and she has been getting calls warning her that if she shows up she won't leave town alive.

"Robert, I'm scared she will get hurt. I have been dreaming nightmares about her. She says she must go to prove that bullies won't win." As he spoke, fresh tears formed in his eyes. Reacting to Isaac's body language of fear and defeat, Robert stepped forward to offer a brotherly hug.

"Hannah, Isaac and I are going for a walk." She did not respond with more than a wave of acceptance, or dismissal.

An hour later, Robert returned alone. He walked quietly to his desk and dug in. As the light from the dawn began to soften the harsh glow from the street lamps, the two publishers walked their now finished copy of the next *Activist* to the printer two blocks away.

"Okay, Robert. End the silence. What did he have to say?"

Robert had obviously resisted discussing it. He had his reasons, and Hannah thought they were reasons about getting the work done on time without much emotional penalty to pay for pulling another all-nighter. She was right about that.

"Isaac is scared about Vera, and maybe himself. He wanted to know if I would try to talk Vera into staying away from that meeting in Eugene. He cried on my shoulder—really cried—and I told him to stay home if he felt he should, but Vera should go. Hannah, someone is going to get hurt. Isaac'd just feeling the pain before it happens."

Hannah walked along in stunned silence until they had slipped the portfolio with the next *Activist* under the printer's door. She had a little dance she did as a matter of habit. That done, she turned abruptly toward Robert.

"I don't want to do this any more. No more *Activist*. No more activism. I mean it. I need time to think and to plan a new life for myself." She waved her arms in hacking motions, punctuating each word with the slap of her hands on her hips.

"Okay," was all he said.

"I want six months to relax and plan my future—with or without you. Do you hear me?"

Robert nodded, while he entertained thoughts about the limits of people under siege. "I am too tired to think. Let's talk later."

She looked like she was holding her tongue. "Yeah, maybe something new would do me good."

After airing it out, they became resigned to their situation. The Shitheads would not be allowed to win so easily. They had walked into many lions' dens together and alone, so what was new about this time? They could not quit, but they could change their strategies and tactics.

They agreed to stop publishing the *Activist* with the December issue. Hannah wondered if she was capable of feeling anything for anyone or any thing—Robert included.

"You know," she said one day, "we are being traumatized, turned into sobbing paranoids, jumpy and fearful, snapping at each other, forming a dysfunctional mess instead of a coherent political force. We only have one simple choice to make—when will we seek mental help?"

IMAGINE

He heard voices.

He stood silently listening for them again. Nothing. He moved slowly, with his attention shifting from his ears to his eyes. "Now where was I?"

He consulted the manual in front of him. "Subaru 1981."

He took a ruler and measured his right hand—first this way, then that. Taking a pencil he entered numbers into his calculator. Twice he stopped to make notes on his yellow legal pad. "Looks like four and a half inches under the seat from the frame to the floor. No more than twelve inches wide. Okay." As he talked to himself he began to draw a series of rectangles and circles. Suddenly, he stiffened, halted movement. The pencil he was using to make notes stopped in mid-stroke.

He heard a voice.

"What?" he muttered. He remained still. He had not slept in almost two days—since the voices began.

Yesterday he lost track of eight hours but it wasn't sleep. He remembered going on a walk in the morning. It must have been morning, but he could not clearly recall. Then, at sunset he found himself in the parking lot at the S.F. Giant's stadium. "Subaru 1981" was in his mind and there was one right in front of him.

He had a door jimmy in his coat sleeve. Leaning near the Subaru's front passenger door he opened and entered the car. As soon as he closed the door he slid into the driver's seat. "Why am I here?" The words hissed from his mouth and with a sense of renewed recognition he reached down under the driver's seat, measuring the opening with a wave of his hand.

"Not good enough."

He left the car through the driver's door, turned and opened the back door latch. He closed the front and entered the back seat. His shoes slid under the front seat and again a sense of recognition struck him. "There."

His hands descended to the floor and he spanned the opening under the seat with his hand, from first finger tip to thumb tip. "One and a quarter."

He turned his hand sideways, palm towards his shoes and measured the height of the slot. "Five knuckles." He sat back in the seat and glanced around the car, looking for something else, something he might have missed. A minute passed, then he opened the door and wandered towards the front of the stadium, thinking about how to get back to the East Bay and home.

That was last night. Then the voices began again.

They tormented him all night. He was afraid of going to sleep in the dark. He never could be sure he would awaken in his own bed. Once—more than once—he had found himself awake hundreds of miles from home without a clue about how he arrived there.

There had been voices before. In recent years he heard them off and on. But the last few weeks it had gotten worse. They distracted him—sometimes causing him to talk out loud to answer them.

Someone had been bringing food to him. He never saw who, but the refrigerator always seemed to have frozen dinners and fruit juice—the kind he liked with lots of sugar.

Other things were appearing from nowhere.

He found a box of wire and finishing nails, some duct tape and a pocket watch one day. He thought he might have brought them home. No memory existed of doing so. He found a piece of paper on his kitchen table once three weeks ago—a drawing of a bomb and these new things, the wire and watch, were in the drawing.

The drawing was of a two-inch galvanized pipe, eleven inches long with black iron end caps: one drilled for wires to go to the match-head igniter bottle. Epoxy glue in the drill hole. Explosive 3:1 potassium chloride:aluminum powder. Three sizes of finishing nails taped on the outside pipe, taped to a piece of paneling that fit under the seat. And the paneling had the pocket watch and also a motion switch of two bent wires and a ball. Nine-volt battery and safety switch and test socket empty.

He took a small piece of paneling from the floor under his kitchen table, measured it, marked it and with a small handsaw he laboriously cut the wood along the lines he'd drawn. "Eleven and a half by eight. Good." Dropping the measuring tape to the table top he sat down to study the drawing.

He grew lost in his thoughts.

He wondered if the voices and the bomb stuff were connected somehow, but his thoughts were spinning around and he could not hold them long enough settle on an answer. He turned back to his work. "Pipe is about two inches. Paneling is one eighth. It will fit, but I better try." He took the duct tape from his box of tools and wrapped the pipe down on the newly cut paneling.

Taking out his backpack he placed the pipe and paneling inside. He left the house carrying the pack on his shoulder and the car jimmy in his hand. He had located another Subaru in a hotel parking lot nearby. Probably the night clerk's, he had concluded. It had taken him three hours round trip to Candlestick and he had immediately begun the search for another car closer to his home. He had entered the new car twice so far to re-measure the rear opening under the seat. Now he would try the fit of the paneling and pipe.

As he walked the two blocks to the hotel, he wondered if his memory was correct. He felt he had built another bomb not long ago. He just didn't remember where he had put it. The voices didn't mention it, so he might have made it up. He wasn't sure.

The new one fit just right and he returned home to put the wires and the battery and other things together as it showed on the drawing. Again he felt a sense of déjà vu. Had he done this before?

He worked until he was done, except for the last connection which he left undone. The ticking of the watch was silenced by a piece of yellow sponge. The wires were red and black and well soldered to the battery.

"Hide it." he muttered. "Maybe sleep now." He threw a blue towel over the device, drank some lemonade and slipped down on his couch hoping for sleep. As the sun rose he slept.

When he awoke he heard voices again. Clearer now. Something didn't feel right. His hands were tied behind his back. Struggling he found he could not free himself.

The voices were not loud.

"He's coming to."

"We are almost there. He'll last."

He felt the van turn right sharply as he slid across the cold steel floor. Then it stopped and doors opened and slammed shut around him—once, twice—then the cargo door glided open, bringing bright lights into the interior. "A straight jacket," he muttered. The male forms in the doorway grabbed at his arms.

"You're going to be alright. You are back at the clinic. This is just to calm you down." The voice was reassuring. The pin prick in his thigh brought him to full awareness.

Then the voices.

"He's ready."

Then silence.

Hannah put her book down with a heavy sigh, muttering, "Why do I read these kinds of books?"

Robert, awakening, said, "Sorry, couldn't hear you."

She blew out the candle, bringing instant darkness to the loft they shared. She rolled over until her hips were against his back. Her voice and movement had brought him back to consciousness.

"Just a bad spy novel I won't finish." She quivered a little as she spoke, then stopped as he turned to face her, gathering her up in his arms.

"Want to think about something real?"

CLOVERDALE

Just before sunrise, the natural world sleeps. Today, even the birds are silent. The distant sounds of the highway are muffled by overgrown fields. The air is still and dense. The molecules in a state of torpor wait to be aroused. He has no reason to be wary, or even quick in his movements. The mill is deserted at this hour. Not even the security guard would arrive for two more hours.

He arranged his materials in a cardboard box. He wasn't concerned with the usual duffle bag. He brushed a stray hair off his forehead and wished briefly that he had a cigarette—not that he smoked, but just for the effect. In movies, he'd seen guys smoke before they performed an intricate maneuver.

Looking around the side of the old mill he noticed the weed-covered pasture. Even in May it was beginning to dry out; the bright blue chicory gray in the somber light of pre-dawn. He surveyed the opposite field. He could still make out the yellow star thistle. *Nasty stuff on bare legs.* The soft cooing of a dove interrupted his thoughts, mobilizing him to continue onward with his plans.

He reached into the box and fumbled around until he found the metal pipe. He turned it over in his hands, searching for the small hole to ensure that the epoxy glue had held. He made sure that the wires were still soldered well to the 9-volt battery: A Duracell battery—*A name you can trust.* He inspected the timer watch, synchronizing it with his own. 4:30 a.m. *Plenty of time.*

The gasoline and oil mixture in the can sloshed as he picked up the box and moved it around to the back entrance of the mill. He sat down, leaning against the door, and began to position nails around the outside of the pipe, using silver duct tape. He liked the gratifying rip as he pulled tape off the roll. After inspecting the pipe to verify that it was sufficiently covered in nails, he connected the final two wires using a small screw. He followed the diagram to the smallest detail.

He checked the watch again and stepped back to admire his hand-iwork. *It should work just fine. The morning security officer would have something to write home about.* Suddenly, he remembered the most important detail of all: the sign. He sprinted over to his vehicle and pulled out the crudely constructed sign, placing it just out of the radius of the bomb. *The sign must be read.* He returned to his vehicle. Driving slowly down the dormant main street of Cloverdale, he merged back onto the highway. There was a faint glow in the eastern horizon.

An hour later, just as the sun crested over the hills of Clear Lake, a brilliant flash erupted from behind LP's mill. Carefully propped up against a nearby phone pole is a plywood sign.

Hand-scrawled in red paint, it simply stated:

LP SCREWS WORKERS

THE STAKEOUT

Berkeley before dawn is a quiet town. The darkness is complete, except for the glare of the street lamps filtered through the tree limbs arching across the silent streets. The late model Chevrolet with its two passengers is hidden by the darkness, parked at an intersection of two streets choked with the parked cars of local residents. At 4:30 a.m., this middle-class neighborhood was at its quietest. Nothing moved in any of the four directions, as the men in the car could easily see.

A third man, turning a corner a block away, moved toward the Chevrolet from the rear. The men in the car were watching for movement in front of them. Only when they saw the third man's reflection in the side view mirror did they come to a state of alert.

"Here he comes," the driver informed his partner. "These Bureau guys are right on time." Oakland Police Department's Sergeant Ronald Long detested stake-outs. He and Officer Jeff Pecower had spent numerous days and nights sitting in unmarked cars just like this one. As members of the anti-drug task force, keeping an eye on a perp was, after all, a dull but fruitful piece of business. Tonight was unusual. The perp was supposed to be an FBI target. The third man visiting the stakeout was their first sign of the Bureau's interest. Long and Pecower had known they would be visited by an "interested party," as the detailing officer had put it. Long rolled his window down as the Interested Party reached the side of the car.

"Bruce Galloway, Special Operations," he whispered extending a hand toward.

"Sergeant Long. Officer Pecower. Nothing to report. All is quiet." Long did not see a shield, nor did the Interested Party show one. Galloway, dressed in black, carried a standard briefcase. He looked like the typical, timeworn operative that came and went on special jobs for FBI case work. "What can we do for you, sir?"

Galloway looked into the car, searching with his eyes for nothing in particular, searching out of habit for signs of anything wrong. "I'm here to check the car you are covering. Continue on as you were."

Galloway moved away from the stakeout, down the street to the left of the OPD officers, moving for all the world to see as if he were leaving on an early commute. As he made his way to the passenger door of the gray Subaru he crouched, opened his case and pulled out a flat, black door jimmy.

Long and Pecower watched him disinterestedly, making nervous comments about how difficult FBI agents could be to work with. Galloway popped the Subaru open, returned the jimmy to the case. Then Galloway and his case disappeared into the rear seat of the small hatchback. Less than ten minutes later he and his case emerged. He closed the door, looked up and moved back toward the stakeout vehicle.

When Galloway reached Long and Pecower, he squatted by the window. He pulled a folded piece of paper from his breast pocket and handed it to Long. "Use these words in your report. Follow procedure. I did not visit you. Keep a close watch until the suspect leaves. Her car is clean except for a stinking roach in her glove box, but we do expect some action in the late morning." With that he stood, turned and walked back the way he'd come to disappear around the corner.

The OPD officers whispered small talk to each other, drinking coffee from a thermos, until shortly after dawn when they took turns walking alone to a nearby fast-food restaurant to empty their bladders and to fill the thermos. As the commuters rose in the growing light to dress, to eat and, eventually, to make their way to their cars for the drive to work, Long relocated the stakeout to a more advantageous position with a better view of the Subaru. The new location also offered more visual cover for the Chevrolet from anyone looking out of the house across the street from the suspect's vehicle. The stakeout the prior evening had seen the perp enter this house, apparently for the night. No movement in the home had been noticed since the lights went out about 1:00 a.m. Now it was about 11 a.m., and another car was approaching the Subaru, pulling up and parking directly behind.

Both Winwood and the male driver of the new car were clearly visible to both officers. Winwood bounced from the car, nervously tried the doors to the Subaru, gestured wildly about finding them locked, returned to his car, took his guitar from the rear and crossed the street towards the house. The driver locked up and followed Winwood up the walkway to the front door, entering behind him.

Long made note of the make, model and license number of the new car. He described the males who exited the car, noting that forty minutes after entering, Winwood, the other guy, another female and a small woman in her early thirties left the house. They carried packs, guitar cases and a violin case. The group of four people moved across the street to the cars. Winwood moved gear from the new car to the rear of the Subaru while his friends packed the various cases into the rear seat area.

The small woman started the car. Her passenger rolled down his window as they drove toward and then past the stakeout. Long started his car and followed the Subaru while Pecower radioed their movements to the back-up unit that would pick up the Subaru as it made its way into the nearby feeder road heading toward the freeway.

BLACK MARIAH

Robert awoke on the office couch to the sound of trucks ripping through the industrial area where Northcoast Citizens located the organizing office it shared with several other groups. A long L-shaped room filled with desks and layout tables, it was the nerve center for the electoral and signature gathering campaigns for Humboldt County's radicals.

Once a month for seven years Robert and Hannah had laid out the *Activist* here, often finishing so late that they would just curl up on the only couch and let the sun waken them in the morning.

Today Robert was there alone. Hannah was meeting in San Francisco with the rich backers of the Forest Forever initiative that would be on the November ballot in California. Robert stayed in Humboldt to direct the activities of the campaign for Clean Air, Clean Water and Clean Government that Humboldt County measures A, B and C represented.

Robert's first waking thoughts were about how many days were left until the election. "It's the 24th. That leaves twelve days to election day June 5th." Robert's scratchy morning voice cracked as he rolled off onto his hands and knees, a stunt that turned into a comic search for his socks, then his shoes and finally enough change for a cup of lousy coffee from the truckers' cafe across the street.

"Actually, I don't believe they make the coffee by boiling lice. It's not that simple. The lice are lightly roasted first which gives the result that charming brown color," he had explained to the person behind him in line that morning, which only befuddled the poor woman who said something about it being too early for small talk.

Robert turned to the morning paper, hoping nothing of interest appeared. His pre-coffee brain was too flooded with enigmas of the past week. He didn't catch the democratic candidate for congress attacking Vera and Isaac as too radical, with their ideas for Redwood Summer which in his mind would only cause violence. The candidate had survived the Jonestown massacre and was running for office only a year after being released from federal prison on charges stemming from the murder of a congressman in Guiana.

Instead, as Robert sipped the evil brew at the picnic bench outside the cafe, his thoughts turned to the past news about the bomb in Cloverdale, the fake bomb in Eureka and the computerized death threats numerous people had received.

"So many mysteries," he had said to Hannah on the phone last night. "After weeks on end of manufactured news a bomb goes off on the morning of the day the Secretary of State is due to report that the Forest Forever initiative qualified for the November election. But there is no news about it at all—just a small two-sentence article buried in a regional newspaper. This Cloverdale bomb is a partial dud. It blows up nothing, just sits there to be found on LP's mill loading dock with a sign saying 'LP Screws Mill Workers.'

"I do not get it. *The Times*, WeCARE, Campbell, have been publishing and bemoaning the so-called EF! bomb manual—which of course someone made up to slander us. Fake manual yields fake news. On the day the Forest Forever initiative qualifies, *The Times* runs an article about how Vera and Isaac are terrorists, according to what they now must admit are fake fliers spread by some industry Astroturf group. Then complete silence for almost two weeks when this damn Cloverdale bomb thing is just hanging there to use against us. Maybe one of the goons messed up and didn't call in to say we did it. Maybe they were embarrassed to make anything out of it. And, of course, there was no news about the death threats. After all, we could be sending them to ourselves. Right?"

Hannah had harrumphed at the longish speech, saying something to the effect that Robert only saw bad even in something as good as not being falsely attacked every time there was a chance. "Things are looking up, Robert. We've got our ace in the hole, rather, on the ballot, even if a couple of rich capitalists helped us get it there. We will win. Even the industry is playing it out that way. The Forests Forever campaign has money and a staff. We will work hard, but we will win. Isn't that good enough for you?"

Robert had no answer. It was the mystery that was annoying him. Coffee swilled, paper read, he wandered back to the office to find the "ABC" campaign staff gathering for phone banking. Rounds of good morning and back to work.

Lunch came, and Robert was alone in the office except for the Central American Action group led by Felicia Oldfather. This was their regular Thursday meeting to talk about death squads and refugees. He lurched for the phone on its first ring. "Northcoast Citizens."

"Robert, its Andy. We're putting *Econews* to bed tonight. The radio reported that Isaac and Vera were bombed. Vera's hurt bad. Can you confirm this for me?"

"Wait." Blood was pounding at Robert's temples. "I thought you said Vera and Isaac were bombed."

"That's what I said. That's what the radio news is saying. Happened in Oakland. Do you know anything?"

"I'll get back to you." Robert hung up the phone, then dialed the Mendocino Environmental Center for news.

Betty answered. "Yes, Robert, it is true. Vera's bad. They were in her car headed to Santa Cruz when it went off. Sorry, I didn't call you right away. We're all devastated."

Robert hung up after mumbled goodbyes. "Andy, it's true," he was saying into the phone moments later. By then the Central America activists were bunched around his desk. He looked up at them and said again, "It's true. They were bombed. Vera might not live."

Felicia, never at a loss for the ironic, said, "They'll blame them for it."

"What?" someone asked.

"Don't be surprised if they are blamed for bombing themselves," she repeated.

"This isn't El Salvador, for god's sake," Robert blurted.

"Oh, yeah, I forgot," Felicia snapped back. "I don't think you have been paying enough attention, Robert. And, for the record, I hope I am wrong. But I doubt it."

That night the Northcoast Environmental Center was abuzz with activity. Andy was busy typing a story into the computer when Robert came by to see if anyone besides himself wanted to get blind drunk and wake up from this nightmare. Andy rose from his desk to get Robert a beer and a joint before escorting him to the TV monitor and tapes from the early news reports on CNN.

"They have been playing this all afternoon on the local stations. You remember when the ammo train ran over Brian Wilson at Concord? This clip will stay with us for as long as that one has." Andy punched the buttons as he talked and up came an image that at first was hard to interpret.

"My god, it's Vera," was all Robert could say before he had to catch his breath. There was no sound. Andy saved that for Robert's second viewing.

THE COPS

With Pecower and Long following, the Subaru turned left onto the feeder road. As it was heading downhill under a rail over-crossing, the car exploded, throwing glass into the street with a loud whump. Lurching to the side of the road, the car came to a halt. Grey smoke filled the air, spreading the smell of burning chemicals. Nearby stores emptied of customers and clerks. Passers-by gathered near the Subaru, while various shouts of shock and pain rang out in the silence that followed the last echo of the explosion.

Long reached for his radio unit and informed his lead officer that the car had exploded on Broadway near Huntington. Within five minutes, a fire department emergency vehicle arrived on the scene. An Oakland Police Department cruiser in the area was there five minutes later. Long and Pecower moved off to return to the office to fill out their report. As they drove, they speculated about the explosion. "They must have had a bomb in one of those guitar cases." Their conclusion would be important to the later investigation, but they knew that their role in the stakeout would remain classified and secret from the public.

THE NEWS

The news traveled fast through the activist community, but Robert had already fled the Environmental Center before it had reached Arcata. He had gone "underground," as he was fond of describing his favorite place to play pool. He stayed very late, until he could not care about much of anything. Then, staggered back to the office and passed out fully clothed on the couch.

It was in the early morning before he learned that Isaac and Vera had been arrested for the bomb. "Police Arrest Bomb Victims—it was their bomb say FBI." Robert sat silently at the local bagel shop, deep into his own thoughts. He kept his journal updated during his first cup of coffee, while in between scribbles he either ignored or eavesdropped on the caffeine-powered discussions going on around him.

"I think they did it."

"You believe the FBI?"

"Yes, I do, and I can tell you why. First, Dave Foreman; second, Isaac on *60 Minutes;* third, the Earth First! bomb manual; fourth, Isaac's songs about spiking; fifth EF!'s use of violent imagery; sixth...."

As the last speaker's voice trailed off into memory, Robert picked up the thread: "Sixth, the Cloverdale Bomb; seventh the Earth Night Action; and eighth, if they didn't do it to themselves they were asking for it. Only problem is, none of that is evidence."

Having burst his own bubble of anonymity, he rose and headed for the streets before any of the students, professors or whoever could get his attention. *Where did that come from?* he asked himself. Then it dawned on him. *We are under siege.*

As Robert reached the sidewalk, he glanced around for a clock, then his memory flashed a picture of Hannah and he remembered she was arriving on the overnight bus from the City.

"The bus," he said, as he turned towards the Greyhound station to see Hannah burdened with her pack and briefcase heading towards him.

"Hannah! Am I glad to see you."

"I want coffee. Get me coffee, now." Hannah gestured towards the nearest doorway and they went into the poorly lit but nearly empty bar. "Let's hide in here and talk. I've got to get this off my chest."

"Two coffees, Jimmy, and make mine Irish," he demanded. "Dearie, we are all in for a landslide of horror, and this bomb is the first stone down the hill."

"I spent most of yesterday on the steps of the hospital. People were stunned. Isaac's in jail and Vera is in surgery." Hannah sat at a lunch table with her head near the table top, leaning as far forward as she could. Robert hunched forward on his elbows, cupping his hands around his ears to hear her even if she whispered.

"People here believe the cops, and many are afraid that there are more bombs to come. I wouldn't be surprised to see our ABC campaign staff dwindle to a few, if any, volunteers. This may have been one of the most devastating single events imaginable. The Contra assassination manuals called this type of act 'disarticulation.' I hate to put this into the worst light possible, but we could be murdered in our sleep tomorrow and people would say that we asked for it." Robert had begun to shake his head in dismay. Hannah reached forward in a gesture of tenderness, putting her hand on his forearm.

"Well, then, life has given us lemons today. What can we make of them? I must campaign for Forest Forever. We must put out a few more issues of the *Activist* and you have the ABC campaign to run. What else is there to do?" Hannah's voice had reached the level and tone that mixed completely with the refrigerator hum in the bar and the whooshing sound of cars passing by outside. Only Robert could hear her.

"This is war or the promise of war," said Robert. "We either join the war or make some peace. Let's declare peace. It won't stop all of the pain we will feel, but it may stop some fool from doing something even more stupid. I don't know what that is yet. Let's talk to the church people and mainstreamers who might want to make peace now."

"Listen, Robert, I spent an hour last night with the Forest Forever staff—Leo McElroy and Gail Lucas. They are afraid of the effect this will have on the initiative. Leo says Isaac and Vera are not on our side because they will not support the campaign we need to run to win. Gail and the Sierra Club denounced the call for Redwood Summer because they knew that tying Forest Forever into Earth First! would ruin the initiatives chances. Now they are saying that bomb may as well have been in the ballot box."

Hannah was right about the landslide. For the next seven days she would work to hold the dwindling campaign together, to no avail. Robert was right about demanding peace. Ministers and elected officials came forward in a large demonstration of sensibleness and changed the over-charged rhetoric into a county-wide pledge that the summer would not be a bummer. That may have helped prevent some violence, but it did not stop the landslide.

On the Thursday before the election, Robert's daily trip to the post office brought the usual selection of campaign literature. Today there was a hit piece against ABC and it was a bombshell. Robert jammed it into his pack, thinking, "later for this shit." As he strode from the building, he ran head on into Wesley Chesbro, one of the elected officials who had gone to bat for ABC.

"Robert, I didn't tell you this, but..." Wesley's head rotated slowly to check for other ears. "Sheriff Satterwitte showed the board a photo in a confidential briefing on the bombing. He showed us a picture of Vera with an Uzi in her hands. The Sheriff didn't know where it came from, but you can be sure the timber goons have it. Maybe the newspapers will hold off printing it until after the election. Things do not look bright, what with this morning's hit piece. I wish Isaac and Vera had been on the other side, instead of our side."

"No, you're wrong Wes. Hard as it may be, we must stick with our friends. They are all we've got."

"I appreciate your loyalty. Next week, let's talk about this again, if you want. Gotta get back to work. WeCARE is asking the county to oppose Forests Forever at today's meeting. I don't think there is anyone speaking in favor of Forests Forever anymore. Guess it doesn't matter. The other four supervisors would need lobotomies to vote against the industry, even if they wanted to nuke Humboldt Bay.

THE LORD'S AVENGER

MAY 24, 1990

I built with these Hands the bomb that I placed in the car of Vera Greene. I come forward now emboldened by the Spirit of the Lord to spread the Message spoken by the bomb so that All will hear it and take it into their hearts. This woman is possessed of the Devil. No natural Woman created of our Lord spews Forth the Lies, Calumnies and Poisons that she does with such Evil Power. The Lord cleared my Vision and revealed this unto me outside the Baby-Killing Clinic when Vera Greene smote with Satan's words the humble and Faithful servants of the Lord who had come there to make witness against Abortion. I saw Satan's flames shoot forth from her mouth her eyes and ears proving forever that this was no Godly Woman no Ruth full of obedience to procreate and multiply the children of Adam throughout the world as is God's Divine Will.

Let the woman learn in silence with all subjection. But I suffer not a woman to teach, nor to usurp authority over the man, but to be in silence.   *Timothy 2:11*

She and her blasphemous host try to abort the children of Adam and erase us from the Face of the Earth which was Created by God to be our Home so that we will fill it with our Numbers in His Name. She spoke Satan's Words yet the Lord did not strike her Down. Darkness fell upon my Spirit. My prayers sought guidance so I would know if the Lord was calling me to Wield His Sword.

I could hear no Answer but Satan marched on and caused great Uproar over the land. This Woman Possessed of the Devil set herself on the Honest man of toil who does God's work to bring forth the bounty that He has given us to Take. All the forests that grow and all the wild creatures within them are a gift to Man that he shall use freely with God's Blessing to build the Kingdom of God on Earth. They shall be never ending because God will provide.

All of it is God's Gift for us to Take and use so that we can build our Civilization in the Image of the Creator. The devil is sorely displeased by our Godly Dominion and he sends his demons to sow Confusion and Doubt in our numbers. This possessed demon Vera Greene to spread her Poison to tell the Multitude that trees were not God's Gift to Man but the Trees were themselves gods and it was a Sin to cut them. My Spirit ached as her Paganism festered before mine Eyes. I felt the Power of the Lord stir within my Heart and I knew I had been Chosen to strike down this Demon.

I was His Avenger. The demon must be struck down. The Light filled me and my Faith was impregnable. Great joy Filled me as I set to work.

The righteous shall rejoice when he seeth the vengeance: he shall wash his feet in the blood of the wicked.   Psalms 58:10

I put the bomb in her car. And the Bomb was Hidden and the hour hand Moved and the bomb was Armed and administered Divine Justice. But it did not kill! I had wanted that she should be cut Down quickly like a diseased horse that must be put down but the Lord Willed that she should Live on in Pain

suffering the vengeance of eternal fire   Jude 7

So that others would Cringe with Fear and Horror at the Terrible Scourge of the Lord. Now all who would come to the forests and worship trees like gilded Idols have been Warned. They have seen the Fate that awaits them.

To me belongeth vengeance.   *Deuteronomy 32:35*

To those who share the demon's pagan faith I warn you to Return to the Lord.

But if you Heed not this Warning and go into the forests to do Satan's Bidding surely you will Suffer the Punishment of demon Vera Greene.

I HAVE SPOKEN. I AM THE LORD'S AVENGER.

TWO WEEKS LATER

SOMETIME DURING THE 1980S

T he following words
1 EVOLUTION

2 REVELATION

3 REVOLUTION

had been scratched into the tabletop in the kitchen of the Woodrose Café in Garberville. Robert Devine noticed it for the first time in June 1990.

Robert and Harris Collins often met at this kitchen table with the roar of the noisy food preparation making it unlikely for anyone to overhear.

Harris looked seriously hung over and closer to Robert's age than he was. "Are we looking at something old or something new?"

"Both." Robert grinned with realization and cleverness.

Harris was not amused. "You hired me—or should I say, enlisted me in your army of eyes and I must say that I don't mind being unpaid, I work as hard as if you did pay me. I know you work for free, in modern terms, but I also noticed you had a beer yesterday, and in some circles that means you have the money to pay the bartender."

Robert must have lost his poker face. Harris was taken aback.

"Robert, I am sorry. I had to vent a little. Lawyers measure themselves with their bank accounts. My office rent is due and this Lord's Avenger letter has me so absorbed I have not seen a paying client in two weeks."

"Harris, you're a funny guy. Over the last ten years you have been in the center of the action—just where you wanted to be. We have both gotten what we bargained for. I got a lawyer. You caught a buzz or the buzz caught you."

"I know, and you know I appreciate what you're saying. It's just that to be even a little-known fixture of this movement means I am included in the 'and others' in every threat we've received. Now with Vera in the hospital, Isaac shunned and the election lost, we are rewarded with this letter that abuses all of us, and especially those who know or admire Vera." Harris not only sounded defeated, but his lightly graying hair seemed to pull his head down into his chest.

"My friend," Robert said, "whoever sent that letter knew things at a time when only one person, or a group of people acting as one, could have known. The revelation is wrapped in the ideology of an offshoot of the Pentecostals—an unpleasant amalgam of fear and hatred for other humans, and the very creation they claim was given to them as a gift. They call themselves Dominionists. That we are sharing life on earth with such people is frightening to many. To have to face this threat is first to know that such a threat exists, and then with little fanfare, attempt to confront it."

Robert was on a roll. "Let's put this threat firmly in the hands of the CIA, the timber industry public relations firms, Republican campaign organizations and whatever black bag groups thrive on protecting their masters with violence, whether in the US or in the defense of blood-thirsty dictators—like General Rios Montt, who lives not far from here, waiting for an indictment on crimes against humanity while he attends church services in a Pentecostal Dominionist church known to be controlled by the CIA. Maybe we are facing more than a threat; we may be facing the equivalent of the CIA's death squads right here in Humboldt County."

Harris seemed enlivened by Robert's rant. Pushing his fingers through his hair, he looked hard at Robert, then said with a sigh, "And there you have it. Is that it? Did we know we were arousing these people? I don't know about you, but I, acting as a citizen attorney general as provided for in law, was using the courts to enforce laws passed through the state and federal legislative systems and signed by the chief executives as provided for in our constitutions. For this I get the Lord's Avenger?"

"Yes." Robert had thought about saying something flippant, but feeling the weight of the moment he went on, "No help here, Harris. There is no way to go back. However, we do have a choice of how to go forward. Over the last two weeks the vacuum created around us has been impressive. The county campaigns crumbled after the bomb. People removed our lawn signs. Volunteers left. In Garberville, Isaac was treated to a total blackout. People crossed the street to avoid him. Waitresses refused to serve him. It was so bad that I saw him crossing the street one day as I was walking away from the office. He looked so forlorn. I stopped in the middle of the street and hugged him.

Harris sat in silence, slowing shaking his head from side to side. "It hardly matters any more. I guess we know who did this then. And I guess we chose this enemy…"

"Not enemy. Wrong word. It's more like we are forced to dance. It's the nature of life, and right now we have a very bad dance partner. It's like trying to learn the steps, but we can't hear the music."

"Okay. We chose that partner. Now what?"

"Good question. The Dominionists and people like the Lord's Avenger who follow the path of 'Engaging the Enemy' premise their behavior on a belief that Satan and his demons are in the world—literally—and as Christians they are to engage in spiritual warfare with them. That is who the Lord's Avenger may well be….If that person—or persons—are fairly characterizing themselves."

"So we attack them?"

"No."

"Okay. Then we make fun of them and isolate them?"

"No."

"We don't want to start a religious war?"

"Too late. I was thinking about starting a religious peace, and how we might use this moment to bring that about."

Harris sat shaking his head from side to side. "Wasn't that what Jesus tried. Look what they did to him."

"Not funny, Harris."

ONE YEAR LATER

Dear Hannah,

How's law school? Bet you're doing fine. Thanks for the request to bare my soul a little.

It has been hard for me to talk about it. Now it seems distant. There was a bomb. It hurt my friends. They are being blamed. A cycle of violence that had begun before my birth has my friends swept to the edges of history.

I have never been able to tell of my own fears about who did it. I have never been able to admit that I too saw suspects everywhere. I trust no one but me and thee and I am not sure about thee.

I saw it happen, not there exactly, few were, two friends, the FBI, the bomber, bystanders who would learn from the news in the coming days about how my friends were terrorists and that if they did not do this to themselves, they none the less deserved to be bombed. "Violence begets violence," they said. Over and over again my friend I can't believe I'm on the eve of destruction."

The bomb? Someone put it into their car—her car. Who? Where? When? Look at it. Can you hear me plead and cry to you to look at it? Who did this? Who?

So sorry to show you my sorrow, show you my anger. I scream into the wind here on this beach and the wind only answers with voices of all for all to hear: The wind and the flow of all sounds carried forever —a most beautiful thought.

Vera will never recover her wholeness. Damaged now, crippled, deformed not just in her physical being but in fact eternally warped by the name of her assailant and the words he dared to write. Damn him. Damn him and the god he said he acted in vengeance for, damn him for his angry actions.

Sorry again, it rises and falls and as it eats at me it takes me places I do not want to go.

Isaac and I returned from Mexico in December. He is in such a state of sorrow and confusion. So much so that mine is a whisper to his roar, in comparison I'm calm.

The TV images. Was there blood? Yes. Was anyone screaming? Yes. Was anyone helping? Yes. They lived. They both lived but one was bleeding in places the camera could not show and both would be injured in ways we could not see in the seconds of film they showed every hour on CNN, twice a day on the rest of the networks, but we taped it and I watched it and watched it until the frames are in my memory. And the tears cannot wash away the pain I shared in the hatred I felt for the one or the ones who did this to them: Who did this to us.

This is coming to an end. Something new will take its place.

Be brave.

Robert

ISAAC

The earth spun on. The Sun circled the sky, wind blew and rain fell. The seasons changed as ever before—though different now in that sometimes subtle, sometimes drastic way climate change had come to be.

Nothing very drastic was visible on the Northcoast. The sea rise took some agricultural areas out of production. Cliff edge dwellings had been slipping into the Pacific at a steadily increasing rate. But the forests had remained healthy so far. The theory that a temperature rise would endanger the ancient coastal redwood forests was always under study. So far so good. Downside being no one knew what was ahead in the way of temperature rise.

The CEH Institute had spent about $5,000,000 over the last five years to monitor the effects of the climate change on the species in the Headwaters area. Periodically, a journalist would revive the story of how Headwaters was formed and interview scientists to see how it was faring. Once in a while one of them would catch up with Isaac in New York.

He was not surprised to see a flash for a live talk with a Global Time writer. He was surprised to find out who it was. "My God, Raina Barns, I haven't seen you since Vera..."

"Since my mother's funeral, though I did catch you last year on the twenty-fifth anniversary of the takeover. Some kind of religious holiday, I guess. So how are you, Isaac?" Raina spared no time and kept on going. "Got a job as a writer for GT and Headwaters is my assignment today. Got a minute?"

"Uh..."

"A group of biologists at CEH have concluded that the southern most groves have stopped growing and the northern grove may be next. Had you heard that?"

"Raina, I am in shock from realizing how many years have passed since we last talked. You look great." And, *if the monitor image of her was not enhanced, she did look just like her mom right down to the manner of speech.*

"Look, Raina, I have a studio meeting in five minutes. Call me again will you?"

"Yes, but for two minutes tell me what you think of the CEH report." She would not be pushed aside by Isaac no matter who he thought he was.

"Okay. I choose to see that the forest is healthy. I refuse to comment on reports that the forest is a patient—nevermind a sick patient. Raina, that damn CEH is just trying to squeeze a little bigger tax advantage out of this crying wolf routine they pull every so often."

"That's it! That's all I get from you? No way Isaac, pay attention. A task force has been set up to try to come up with a plan to maintain the species until After."

"You believe in the After? Please help me. Why not see this for what it is. For a century we played and now we are going to pay. Mother is in charge and we have nothing to say about it. For all the crap that guy gave me, Robert said something right once. He told me that I was too negative and my imagery violent. He told me to imagine Eden all around me. So I do or I couldn't live in this unnatural city. Let Mother take care of her own. Nothing CEH does will save anything. Coho are gone. On and on. So I have chosen to see Eden all around me."

"That's denial Isaac." Even in the digitalized world of virtual presence he could feel the wind of her shouted words rustle his hair.

"Yes, Raina, it is. I am sad to say that is all I have left." He turned away from the screen then back to face Raina and her holographic image across the worktable between them. "Got to go. Really call again." He waved as he pushed the terminate button with a smile and a nod.

Isaac rose slowly thinking about the young and how annoying they could be these days. "Shit, don't they respect us for what we did? Why the hell am I to blame, of all people? Shit."

"Isaac." Journey put her hand across his shoulders. She had entered the room causing Isaac to end his call. She knew he wasn't talking to her but to some god Isaac preferred to have heard his frustrations of the moment. "Come on dear. You are off to the studio then to Austin and Denver. So get your tail in gear."

He stood up into her embrace with an air of surrender to her orders. He knew instinctively she knew what was best. "You and Mother are so bossy these days."

They walked together towards the elevator. She reread his itinerary to him while he let his mind wander to Vera Greene Grove on the ridge-top near Ferndale. She was scattered there on the edge of a meadow surrounding a ten-acre ancient fir and redwood grove. She can see Headwaters from there. She'd do what could be done to keep it safe, he hoped.

ANCIENT HISTORY

The trail down was made by deer and bears.

It was the only way down to the beach without using climbing gear or just throwing yourself off. It was possible to safely descend the fifty vertical feet from the edge to the pool formed by the small creek. Robert had been following the creek until it leapt off the cliff, hitting the seawall halfway down and showering freshwater over the rocks in a fanning pattern like a canopy. His imagination burst with visions of the world of rainbows he was about to enter.

As he reached the base of the cliff, crawling backwards and downwards from foothold to fingerhold, he found sand to step onto rather than the wet rocks. *Leave it to the deer to find the good way down.* When he was through counting his blessings, he turned to look out through the umbrella of water spray that shielded him from a clear view of the outer world. The sun's rays did not have a clear path through the shroud of water. The fractured, multi-colored light left him squinting to see his way forward. *Nice!* Already wet from his descent through the spray he did not hesitate to step past the umbrella to enter the direct mid-afternoon sunshine.

From beach level he saw more of the cove than he could from above. The creek outlet to the Pacific was clogged with sand, and the creek disappeared into a low dune after forming a twenty-foot wide pool against the cliff. Looking back up the bluff, Robert saw a problem: Scrambling down was easier than climbing out. And it could be days before he would leave. If he could find shell fish at the creek mouth, he would stay. If not, it would be kelp for dinner and a shorter stay. Water was no problem.

Beyond the creek to the north and south the ninety-foot-long cliff grew higher and more precipitous, with points of sheer rock extending out into the ocean so far that there never was a tide that would allow passage in either direction. The cove was completely closed. The areas at the base of the rock outcroppings were small copses of coastal redwoods.

At the edge of the shadows to the north was a series of small hills no higher than his shoulders. "Shell mounds," he said. Speaking out loud to no one was a habit that bothered others. Hannah thought he was talking to himself alright, but to his other self. One was smart and knew things, the other embarrassingly silly and ill-informed.

"I knew that," he said, then chuckled at his joke at himself.

His stomach rumbled and he turned to find the source of the shellfish harvests. As he surveyed the cove, it occurred to him that a visit by bears could be a problem since the exit was such a slow climb. He had seen bears bound up sheer cliffs ten feet up at a time. *Maybe they all can't do that.*

Turning from his food search he entered the woods to his south, looking for a place to spend the night. "Three hours of light left," he told himself. His rule was to find defensive positions first. Retreat and halt was a useful and honorable tactic if one knew where to retreat to. The southern wood was near the stream-fed pond so he wasn't surprised to find the bears' bed there.

Heading north he scanned the redwoods on the bluffs above, hunched against the onshore wind. The bluffs formed a solid barrier with no path up or around except the way he had come down.

Then he saw the fire pit—a ring of rocks so old the rocks were imbedded in a pad of soil a century old. The ring was in the middle of a little clearing about fifteen feet across. He looked up. In the redwoods were sleeping platforms high enough that the bears would go elsewhere for prey.

He climbed to the sturdiest platform and inspected the rawhide straps that held the main beams in place. A few repairs and a bed made of scavenged resources emerged. He used his knife to cut plants for a soft spot for his hips and shoulders.

Next the fire.

The knife he carried in a sheath was part of a belt that laced through his oiled buckskin pants. His shirt, also buckskin, was long-sleeved with cords for weatherproofing. His shoes were sandals. The long braids he had put his hair in for cleanliness hung down his back. There was a pouch in his belt for the flint, another for fire starter. Around his neck was his medicine pouch.

He had nothing else with him.

Almost no one came to this place. It could easily have been ten years or fifty years or one hundred since the last visitor. There were no recent signs of people, but there were signs of the ancients: the beds, the pit, the mounds. He had found the cove while sea canoeing the coast. The sea was rough the day he saw it, and he only got a glimpse, but he found it overland today.

The Lost Cove he called it. The cove had not been on the maps he had seen. One could find the stream on the topo maps: a very short no-name creek that flowed through some redwoods and into the Pacific Ocean. It had met his expectations.

There were good supplies of shellfish and firewood. In an hour he had both a fire and a full belly. He tossed the empty shells on the nearest mound.

In the last hour before the dark of a new moon, he laid out the firewood he would need just as his old friend Ken Littlefish had taught him to do. Littlefish was a Road Man and a Fire Man. He carried medicine from place to place along the coastal regions, helping people on the Red Road. He also kept the fire during the Grandfather ceremonies.

Robert knew Ken from the old days with AIM, but as these memories arose he set them aside in favor of the chores before him. He took the pouch from his neck, sat at the base of the falls in his best yoga position and slowly consumed some of the peyote he had brought with him. A little piece, a little water, a little more peyote. Half-eaten he put the remainder away, rose and headed for the perch he had refurbished. He took off his buckskin shirt before sitting with his back to the redwood's trunk.

"I will dream and then sleep. Dream first," he thought. He stirred the fire for the flame which, as the night passed he would stoke enough to keep his attention centered while his thoughts flowed with Grandfather.

They came to him.

Just two at first. Then more and more until eighteen people sat in the circle. They chanted the chant to the ancestors and another to Grandfather. Robert kept the fire as the warrior songs were sung. He passed his pouch around the circle after having a little bit more and a little water. The pouch passed around all night.

As the sun rose, the little grove remained in the shadow of the bluffs. Robert released the circle. Grandfather was gone for the day and Robert awoke in his perch with no trace of bears anywhere.

He had "sat up" on his own before. He had been on the Trinity River with the same purpose. Grandfather, dreams and then stay, meditate, find a new vision for the future.

That night on the Trinity, he had experienced the river spirit rise up and out across the small island he was camped on. *Did we talk about relations and the hoop?* The next day he saw the river differently. He knew that like the Nile that brought life to the delta, the Trinity was a community and the life of the planet pulsed through it. If there was anything alive in or near the river, it owed its life to the salmon and steelhead who gave their bodies to fertilize soil for the trees that grew up over the stream, the redwoods and firs, the oaks and madrones that shaded the water from the heat of the mountains so the fish could procreate and the trees could grow and the people could eat. The shellfish he ate last night were fed by the stream that flowed from the forest above. Whenever people came to this spot, food was here.

"Like magic."

He had never met the seventeen who joined his circle, but he knew they had come to meet him. He had brought the medicine like a good Road Man and kept their fire as he had been taught.

...a multitude of conspiracies contend in the night.
Clandestinism is not the usage of a handful of rogues, it is
a formalized practice of an entire class in which a thousand
hands spontaneously join. Conspiracy is the normal
continuation of normal politics by normal means.
—Carl Oglesby, *The Yankee and Cowboy War*

The events in *Black Mariah* are based on the real events. I began the book before the bombing and it was largely completed by five years after the bombing. All the players are as identified except for the activists. Robert Devine is based on my life but isn't me. Vera, Isaac, Hannah are based on more than a single person. This is fiction in the micro and history in the macro.

There was a bombing in the book. This website is a forum for finding who are the likely suspects in the real-life bombing.

Start with the FBI.

In *Black Mariah*, two people are arrested for the car bombing of Vera and Isaac: Vera and Isaac. In 1990 the real victims, Judi Bari and Darryl Cherney, were also arrested and charged. Their homes were searched. Nails were drawn from the walls in a search for evidence. Entire theories were invented by the FBI to make the evidence prove their case, that the bombing victims weren't victims at all, but were in possession of and transporting an explosive device.

In fact, it was none other than Special Agent "Boyle," the Eureka bomb school instructor, who was in charge of the Oakland crime scene. "Boyle" stated that the position of the bomb was behind the front seat and declared that two bags of nails were taped to the bomb to provide shrapnel. Officers on the scene quoted "Boyle" as saying, "I've been looking at bomb scenes for 20 years, and I'm looking at this one, and I'm telling you you can rely on it. This bomb was visible to the people who loaded the back seat of this car."

It took three years and a court order for the victims to gain access to the FBI's evidence and crime scene photos that clearly indicated that the bomb was not behind the front seat, but hidden beneath it. Analysis by Supervisory Special Agent David R. Williams, the FBI's chief bomb expert, also proved that the bomb was armed with a motion sensor and a timer and that it had not exploded accidentally. When the victims announced a press conference to release the photos and the expert analysis, the FBI agent in charge of the case, Richard W. Held, retired.

So, why the cover-up? Who was the FBI protecting?

My guess is that the author of the The Lord's Avenger letter was the bomber and Special Agent Richard W. Held, in charge of the San Francisco FBI Office from 1985–1993, discouraged his team from following that lead. (More on The Lord's Avenger later.)

Let's take a look at Richard W. Held for a moment. His career began in Los Angeles in 1968 where he was the lead agent in matters involving "black extremists." One year later, the L.A. Black Panther Party leader Elmer Gerard Pratt, aka Geronimo, was arrested for murder. The key witness was FBI informant Julius Butler and Held was his control agent. Geronimo spent twenty-five years in jail before a judge overturned the conviction based on "prosecutorial misconduct."

Held's next important field assignment was the Pine Ridge Reservation, the "framing" of Leonard Peltier and the cover-up of FBI operations.

Held began his upper-level FBI career in 1979 in Puerto Rico as Special Agent-in-Charge of the San Juan office. The Puerto Rican Independence movement was in full swing and Held oversaw the counterintelligence program that created files on 74,000 activists, plus conducted raids on offices, destruction of private property and arrests.

Throughout Held's professional career, his oversight consistently operated within the FBI's Counter Intelligence Program (COINTELPRO)[1],

---

1   COINTELPRO or Counter Intelligence Program is a nation-wide effort of the FBI and the large urban police departments to infiltrate groups

the purpose of which was "protecting national security, preventing violence, and maintaining the existing social and political order."[2] According to FBI records, 85% of COINTELPRO targets were groups and individuals considered subversive. These included Doctor Martin Luther King, Jr., nearly every group protesting the war in Vietnam, many organizations involved with women's rights, The National Lawyer's Guild, the American Indian Movement and the Southern Christian Leadership Conference.

When Held left Puerto Rico in 1985, his next posting was San Francisco. Coincidentally, in the year prior to the car bombing, an extensive counterintelligence campaign was waged against Earth First!, with over thirty death threats delivered to members in the spring of 1990 and significant quantities of fake Earth First! communications advocating violence and sabotage released to communities and the press. Given Held's history, one could say, if it looks like a duck and quacks like a duck, then it must be COINTELPRO.

COINTELPRO actions in San Fransisco explain the withholding of evidence as a propaganda move to paint the bombing and Earth First! as black dogs of domestic terrorism, but it doesn't explain The Lord's Avenger letter.[3] The letter clearly sucks the life out of COINTELPRO's attempting to overthrow the government but was used to infiltrate and destroy any group that worked counter to corporate goals. It was revealed to the public in the 1970s. The FBI has infiltrated organizations such as the American Indian Movement, the United Farm Workers, as well as communist organizations. When the Soviet Union dissolved it turned its focus to environmental groups. Groups that advocated peace in Central America during the 70s and 80s received the same treatment.

2   "Final Report of the Select Committee to Study Governmental Operations With Respect to Intelligence Activities, Book III, Supplementary Detailed Staff Reports on Intelligence Activities and the Rights of Americans"; Final Report, S. Rep. No. 94-755; 1976.

3   Earth First! is not an organization. It is a statement used by many to express their common goal. People began using EF! In the early 80's and in Humboldt County it began with the effort to save a coastal redwoods grove that overlooked the Pacific Ocean above the Sinkyone Wilderness. By 1985 the radical nature of its "members" actions were commonly known. By the time of the bomb some of its members were called terrorists.

domestic terrorism story and places the blame on a psychotic, Bible-obsessed, seemingly lone wolf. Let's take a look at this letter.

After the bombing, the first event was the arrest of the victims. The second was The Lord's Avenger's letter claiming responsibility for and providing detailed descriptions of the car bomb and the Louisiana-Pacific's Cloverdale Mill bomb. The letter was mailed in the North Bay region while the bombing victims were still in custody and the contents indicate that it was written in its entirety after the bombing or edited for the results of the bombing. It was mailed four days after the bomb according to the date stamp on the envelope.

> *I put the bomb in her car. And the Bomb was Hidden and the hour hand Moved and the bomb was Armed and administered Divine Justice. But it did not kill! I had wanted that she should be cut Down quickly like a diseased horse that must be put down but the Lord Willed that she should Live on in Pain*

Now, twenty-four years after the bombing, The Lord's Avenger is still a mysterious felon. Putting a bomb into a car intending to kill or maim is a federal and state crime. Why hasn't any law enforcement agency made any public effort to identify the author of the letter bearing that name, although DNA was found on the letter and stored.[4]

Let's look more closely at The Lord's Avenger. From the Bible quotations, he obviously sees himself as a religious fanatic of the Christian variety.

> *I was His Avenger. The demon must be struck down. The Light filled me and my Faith was impregnable. Great joy Filled me as I set to work.*

> *The righteous shall rejoice when he seeth the vengeance: he shall wash his feet in the blood of the wicked. Psalms 58:10*

---

4   "Who's Bombing Her Now?" by Bruce Anderson; Mendocino County Today; AVA News Service; 2 January 2013. http://theava.com/archives/19384

The Lord's Avenger is also, demonstrably, a militant fundamentalist of the worst variety.

I built with these Hands the bomb that I placed in the car of Judi Bari. I come forward now emboldened by the Spirit of the Lord to spread the Message spoken by the bomb so that All will hear it and take it into their hearts. This woman is possessed of the Devil. No natural Woman created of our Lord spews Forth the Lies, Calumnies and Poisons that she does with such Evil Power. The Lord cleared my Vision and revealed this unto me outside the Baby-Killing Clinic when Judi Bari smote with Satan's words the humble and Faithful servants of the Lord who had come there to make witness against Abortion.

His god is a god of vengeance, who is also a lazy god. When the lazy god does not strike vengeance as required by the actions of Bari, The Lord's Avenger must act on behalf of god. That is his claim.

My Spirit ached as her Paganism festered before mine Eyes. I felt the Power of the Lord stir within my Heart and I knew I had been Chosen to strike down this Demon.

There have been other similar crimes by other militant fundamentalists, the largest number involving racism. But beginning around the time of The Lord's Avenger bombing, militant fundamentalists began to burn abortion clinics and kill abortion doctors. When captured, they used a "defense of necessity" similar to The Lord's Avenger's lazy god defense. The Lord's Avenger is very specifically interested in Judi's actions at the 1988 abortion rally held in Willits. In the first paragraph of the letter, he writes:

The Lord cleared my Vision and revealed this unto me outside the Baby-Killing Clinic when Judi Bari smote with Satan's words the humble and Faithful servants of the Lord who had come there to make witness against Abortion.

The late 1980s was a special time in anti-abortion history. Operation Rescue West, a conservative Christian group, was formed in California by individuals who also supported the lazy god defense. A key slogan used by the group was, "If you believe abortion is murder, act like it's murder."[5] While Operation Rescue initially used non-violent sit-in tactics, it is believed to be a feeder organization to the Army of God, which is most definitely interested in violence to stop what they claim is violence. The group is associated with murders of abortion providers and is also handy with the lazy god defense:

We the undersigned, declare the justice of taking all Godly action necessary, including the use of force, to defend innocent human life (born and unborn).[6]

The language used by both The Lord's Avenger and the Army of God have what is called Dominionist tendencies. Dominionism is a Christian nationalism theory that states Christians are entitled to earthly dominion and should seek leadership positions to ensure that God-given mandate.

And God blessed [Adam and Eve], and God said unto them, "Be fruitful, and multiply, and replenish the earth, and subdue it: and have dominion over the fish of the sea, and over the fowl of the air, and over every living thing that moveth upon the earth."

In Eureka the Gospel Outreach Church (also known as the Lighthouse Ranch) was one organization close to the scene spreading Dominion Theology. Ex-President of Guatemala and convicted mass murderer

---

5   *Abortion: Between Freedom and Necessity* by Janet Hadley; Temple University Press; 1996.

6   THE SECOND DEFENSIVE ACTION STATEMENT; http://www.armyofgod.com/defense2.html.

General Efraín Ríos Montt was a Lighthouse Ranch member, resident and lay pastor.

In 1990 those who tried to find the author of The Lord's Avenger letter were told that his political theology and biblical quotes did not fit easily into organized religion. What was missed at the time were the Dominionists. In the following passage, The Lord's Avenger stakes his Dominionist claim to use the earth as his bible mandates. It was the statement of a terrorist.

All of it is God's Gift for us to Take and use so that we can build our Civilization in the Image of the Creator. The devil is sorely displeased by our Godly Dominion and he sends his demons to sow Confusion and Doubt in our numbers. This possessed demon Judi Bari to spread her Poison to tell the Multitude that trees were not God's Gift to Man but the Trees were themselves gods and it was a Sin to cut them. My Spirit ached as her Paganism festered before mine Eyes. I felt the Power of the Lord stir within my Heart and I knew I had been Chosen to strike down this Demon …Now all who would come to the forests and worship trees like gilded Idols have been Warned. They have seen the Fate that awaits them.

The timber corporations were not to be left out of this violent stew. In 1988, the first conference of the Wise Use movement was held in Reno, Nevada. The movement's ideology includes decidedly Dominionist language, that human use of the environment is "stewardship of the land, the water and the air" for the benefit of human beings.[7] Ron Arnold, founder of the movement, claims that environmentalists act "to reduce or eliminate industrial civilization and human population in varying degrees" and that environmentalism, as a movement, is "the excess

---

7   *A Wolf in the Garden : The Land Rights Movement and the New Environmental Debate*, edited by Philip D. Brick and R. McGreggor Cawley; Rowman & Littlefield Publishers, Inc.; 1996.

   "Overcoming Ideology" by Ron Arnold; http://www.cdfe.org/center-projects/wise-use/

baggage of anti-technology, of anti-civilization, of anti-humanity, and of institutionalized lust for political power."[8] Wise Use is an amalgam of different groups, including loggers, miners, farmers, off-road vehicle users and resource extraction industries like Amoco, British Petroleum, Chevron, Exxon/Mobile, the American Farm Bureau, Dupont, Yamaha, General Electric, General Motors, National Cattlemen's Association, the National Rifle Association and the timber firms Georgia Pacific, Louisiana-Pacific and Pacific Lumber. Their mandate was clear: to destroy the environmentalist movement by infiltration and destruction from within, for "Failure to reform environmentalism from within will invite regulation from without..."[9]

In 1987, when a representative from Pacific Lumber met with the public relations firm Hill & Knowlton (now Hill+Knowlton Strategies), Wise Use was an integral part of the strategy to combat the Redwood Summer movement.[10] Hill & Knowlton already had an impressive backlist of dirty tricks PR, including the 1953 campaign by Big Tobacco to prove that cigarette smoking did not lead to lung cancer. Faking Earth First! flyers were right up their alley.[11] The combination of grass roots lumber worker groups and infiltration allowed the firm to create a ready-to-use narrative that includes both Dominionist and anti-communist themes. They made their opponents out to be anti-god and anti-American. Framing they called it. Ironically they managed to frame Judi. Bari and Cherney sued the FBI and the Oakland PD for collaborating in this framing. The case was settled out of court, after a trial, for $4.4 million, although Bari had passed by then of breast cancer.

When *Black Mariah* ends, the public relations corporations defeated a state-wide initiative to limit over-logging and watershed destruction. They did so using the bombing as proof that the proponents were

---

8   "Overcoming Ideology" by Ron Arnold; http://www.cdfe.org/center-projects/wise-use/

9   Ibid.

10   http://www.sourcewatch.org/images/e/e4/Fake_EF_US_memo.pdf

11   Hill & Knowlton are now a paid consultant in the PR campaign to influence decisions on the process of gas extraction known as fracking.

terrorists. They also defeated three local Humboldt County initiatives using a mailing with a photo of Vera's car on the side of the road after the bomb had ripped it apart. The bombing was very useful to the Wise Use movement. It was months after the election before the victims were freed as suspects.

So, what have we got? There's the FBI agenda and their cover-up; Operation Rescue, Gospel Outreach Church and Dominionist rhetoric; there's the timber industry working with the saboteurs of Wise Use and Hill & Knowlton; there's even the possibility that Vera's ex-husband was responsible.[12]

And, there's The Lord's Avenger, who not only described in detail the two bombs, but had a vendetta against Judi for her pro-choice politics, her environmentalism and her uppity femaleness.

It looks like a perfect storm of multiple characters bent on the destruction of what Judi Bari stood for. But someone put that bomb in the car, someone is responsible.

Domestic terrorism, as it is called, is the violence powerful corporations weild to destroy the aspirations of any competitor or detractor. The Northcoast of California is not the first place domestic terrorism was used to defeat environmentalists. Nor was this the first time opponents of extractive corporations were abused. Victims of tobacco, pesticides, nuclear dumping, deforestation and landslides, oil patch madness or any other endeavor of the capitalist corporate world are all treated similarly. There are always Lord's Avengers and they are everywhere corporations need them to be.

Law enforcement could have found The Lord's Avenger if they wished to do so. The timber corporations could have condemned the bombing, if they wished to do so. Who knows? Maybe *Black Mariah* will serve the purpose of exposing The Lord's Avenger. A solution to this crime might

---

12   "The Bari Bombing: Pen Names, Pyrotechnics, and Paranoia in the Timber Wars" by Don Foster; Anderson Valley Advertiser; http://www.theava.com/bari/foster.html

"Who's Bombing Her Now?" by Bruce Anderson; Mendocino County Today; AVA News Service; 2 January 2013. http://theava.com/archives/19384

help Vera, Isaac, Candy, John and Robert's friends and community live in peace.

History is the memory of humanity. There is the notion that the Lord's Avenger, the author of the letter, still lives, and that other people know who he is. The memory of humanity is the memory of all of us together. *Black Mariah* is my contribution to this memory. Each of us may have something to offer in the effort. If you are one, go to findthelordsavenger. com.

I would like to thank the many people who contributed to *Black Mariah*. A great number of them are family and friends, plus some neighbors from Humboldt and Mendocino Counties. I especially want to thank editor Heather Shaw, whose patience exceeded mine.

Bob Martel
October 4, 2014

Made in the USA
Charleston, SC
05 February 2015